droll

tales

To Arthur Smyles, my dad

droll tales

☞ *Iris Smyles*

Turtle Point Press
Brooklyn, New York

Requests for permission to make copies of any part of the work should be sent to:
Turtle Point Press, 208 Java Street, Fifth Floor, Brooklyn, New York 11222
info@turtlepointpress.com

The following stories were published previously in a different form: "Shelves" in *The Baffler,* "The Autobiography of Gertrude Stein" in *Vol. 1 Brooklyn,* "Philip and Penelope in a Variety of Tenses" in *Hotel,* "A Fortune of Cookies" in *The New Yorker,* "Aboard the Shehrazad" in *The Capricious Critic,* and "Exquisite Bachelor" in *Splice Today.*

Library of Congress Cataloging-in-Publication Data
Names: Smyles, Iris, author.
Title: Droll tales / Iris Smyles.
Identifiers: LCCN 2022003490 (print) | LCCN 2022003491 (ebook) | ISBN
   9781933527611 (paperback) | ISBN 9781933527680 (ebook)
Subjects: LCGFT: Short stories. | Humorous fiction.
Classification: LCC PS3619.M95 D76 2022   (print) | LCC PS3619.M95 (ebook)
   | DDC 813/.6—dc23/eng/20220202
LC record available at https://lccn.loc.gov/2022003490
LC ebook record available at https://lccn.loc.gov/2022003491

Cover design by Keenan Design
Interior design by Misha Beletsky

Paperback ISBN: 978-1-933527-61-1
Ebook ISBN: 978-1-933527-68-0

Printed in the United States of America

First Edition

contents

glossary of terms not found in this book

Soufflettic: to move like a soufflé.

Lord Creamy: a local noble.

Scottsdale, Arizona: a village in Italy.

Qui: three fifths of silence.

Vanderpump Rules: a midevil irrigation system.

Midevil: of or referring to the Meddle Ages.

Upevil: a violent or sudden change or disruption.

Frog Dance: a dance performed by frogs in which frogs imitate other frogs in a mocking manner.

The Meddle Ages: a time in Europe after the fall of the Roman Empire and before the Renaissance when everyone was getting involved in other people's business.

Wedding Ring: invented by J.R.R. Tolkien in his book *The Lord of the Rings*, it is one of three rings that make the wearer invisible to everyone but Sauron.

Three-Cheese Ravioli: a slang term used to mean marriage counseling.

Frozen Three-Cheese Ravioli: a postponed marriage counseling session when one or the other spouse can't make it.

Spoonerism: an ardent belief in spoons.

Gravelax: a cold dish made from the bodies of exhumed salmon. Also, a diet pill marketed to the terminally ill whose goal is a narrower coffin.

Upheaval: the northernmost territory of the Kingdom of Evil.

Gargoyle: a female statue of Christian faith affixed to the side of a building.

Cotton Balls: the testicles of an elderly king, sometimes harvested and used to remove eye makeup or disinfect cuts.

Flying Dutchman: a man from the Netherlands arriving by plane (often encountered in an internet chat room).

Deus Ex Machina: when one's ex turns up at a party hosted by a mutual friend and one is not surprised but also still surprised.

Error: a period of time.

Mistake: a failure to take or a taking of the wrong thing. Also, (slang) a drag queen who behaves selfishly.

Bette Middler: a precursor to Better Middlers.

Middler: an early modern tool used for opening soda bottles and stuck windows.

'Pataphysics: the science of imaginary solutions. Also, exercise regimen incorporating Pilates, yoga, rope climb, and rabid squirrels: popular in the late aughts.

Metaphysics: a branch of science in which you sign up for exercise classes and don't go.

Apostrophe: any event occurring after a rophe.

Iota: singular nominative of ota.

Ota: catch phrase popularized by Buckwheat in TV's *The Little Rascals*.

Myopic: possessive of opic.

Opic: a motion picture about the life of a rock legend.

Biopic: two motion pictures about the life of a rock legend, occurring twice monthly or twice weekly.

Biweekly: to pass without strength an object or person.

Feud: the substance of breakfast, lunch, or dinner, and sometimes snacks.

Repast: a do-over.

Disambiguation: the severing of two or more simultaneous marriage contracts.

Rage: contraction of *re* and *age*, meaning to review the past with anger as a guiding principle.

Coliseum: (slang) derived from the expression I-call-it-as-I-see-um, uttered frequently by Roman Emperors after sentencing a gladiator to death.

Fact: (verb) contraction of *fake* and *act* meaning to act fakely. (noun) A false statement.

Matter: someone who is more like Matt than Matt is.

Sand: the sadness of conjunctions that were supposed to last forever, resulting in beaches.

Meaning (derivation of mean): the unpleasant sentiment behind what is actually stated. See: The meaning of life. Life has no meaning. You mean everything to me. Why are you being so mean, I thought you loved me.

For ever (née forever): A consequence of divorce.

Eaternity: an idea in Greek mythology that the afterlife is a 24-hour diner located on the second floor of the Mid-Manhattan Mall.

Lemon Merengue: to move like a whipped desert.

author's note

A woman begins to walk home—it's only a block away—but before she can get there she must get halfway there. And before she can get halfway there, she must get halfway to the half mark (a quarter of the way there). Before walking a quarter of the way there, she must walk halfway to the quarter mark (one-eighth of the way); and before one-eighth, one-sixteenth; and so on, completing half of each resultant half before being able to complete the whole. If each half continues to be divided in half, the halves will become infinitely smaller, and she will get infinitely closer. Thus, traveling an infinite number of finite distances, her journey will take an infinite period of time to be completed. The woman will never arrive.

medusa's garden

1   I grew up in the suburbs. It doesn't matter which one. And studied ballet. I suppose there was a time before I studied ballet, but I don't remember that. What I remember is how my mother, father, and two older brothers would come to my recitals and watch me twirl and turn and leap. Ballet slippers, then pointe shoes, and then a male partner to raise me even higher, above him, for a moment suspended, going nowhere.

"Pull up! Reach!" our ballet master used to say. "I want you to defy gravity," he'd call out over the music, "to leap, knowing you must come down, but to leap anyway! Refuse fate, my little cursed ones, that is the ballet, to make a great show of your refusal, while being broken on the back of it."

When I was seventeen, I landed wrong and injured my ankle. I recovered but was never the same. You learn to dance through the pain though, and then the pain becomes its own pleasure, the joy and suffering inextricable. Blisters bursting in pink shoes, toes bleeding into each pirouette, beauty like a flower blooming on the heap of your destruction. Every ballerina is a collection of injuries, and we are proud of them. In the dressing room, we'd bandage our feet, showing off to one another our well-earned wounds.

Albert says that's what smoking is like. "Why do you smoke?" I asked him once, after I discovered him puffing secretly next to a payphone. I'd never seen him with a cigarette before. Furtive blue curls disappeared into the air above him, as he leaned against the booth in his abstracted way.

"Because it will ruin me."

When I was eighteen, the company didn't promote me. I auditioned for other companies after that, in San Antonio, in Nebraska, and then all over the world. For a year I traveled, auditioning for all the major and minor ballets. I'd never traveled before and found I liked flying even more than I liked leaping, which could only get you so high.

After the start of my travels, when my partner was lifting me I felt still too close to the ground and thought dreamily of the stewardesses on the flight over to this or that audition, their effortless altitude, so much higher than I could ever pull up, so much higher than I could ever jump, so much higher than my partner could ever raise me. I thought dreamily of the women staying up there for hours, suspended in the sky, gracefully distributing nuts.

Eventually I was offered a position in the Milwaukee Ballet chorus, but I turned it down. Over a payphone at the airport I told my parents, my brothers—they'd gathered round the speaker to hear my news—that I'd been rejected. They wouldn't have understood if I told them the truth, that after all that training, all that traveling, I'd quit. Instead, I let them console me. After I hung up, I walked over to the airport check-in desk where I was due for my flight home and asked for an application.

Passing the nuts, telling people to lower their tray tables, performing that gentle dance in which I point out the emergency exits and model application of the life jacket and oxygen mask.... What did I learn up there in that high artificial air? You always put the oxygen mask on yourself first, even before a small child or lover. What good are you to anyone else if you're dead goes the logic.

I did not have a small child or a lover, had never had anyone besides my parents and brothers with whom to concern myself; I'd flown to all my auditions alone. And I began to wonder if there would ever be in my life someone on whom I'd be tempted to put the oxygen mask first. When I think about love I think about that. About doing something unreasonable.

I never knew what to do with myself after we landed. I'd go for long walks through the cities, munching on the nuts I'd pocketed from the airline. I'd visit museums, monuments, wander park lanes, and photograph the statues frozen in mid-gesture, while all around them the world blurred. A man sitting at the foot of one statue, turning over a map. A couple flirting before another, oblivious to the stone gaze set upon them. Friends playing Frisbee nearby, hitting a statue in the teeth.

I photographed a granite woman nude to the waist, her dress about to fall, in Plaça de Catalunya. She looked like she was about to swim in the nearby fountain but never would. I photographed a granite man steps away in the same park, walking, blowing a flute. At the Piazza della Signoria in Florence, I photographed Michelangelo's *David*. His stone curls, his deep-set brow, his gaze—just to the side—which I read is in the direction of Rome. And then lower, I photographed his penis, restful against his testicles. I wondered then about Goliath's penis, Goliath's testicles. There was no respective statue. In Lisbon, I photographed a marble man and two women sitting under a fountain. The water rained over them as they sat perfectly still: him looking at her, whose head was turned in shyness, and the other woman, looking at them both.

I walked a lot, stopping now and then to take pictures, staring at statues the way you can't at people, examining their faces and the thoughts they concealed, waiting for them to start—statues are always about to do something—whatever they were about to start.

And when I got hungry, I'd stop into some tourist trap and lunch alone.

I was walking down Las Ramblas on a layover in Barcelona one spring, going nowhere, which is my favorite place to go, and after a time, the restaurants that line the boulevard dwindled so that eventually it was just the open boulevard, a broad stone path crowded with tourists, shaded by tall leafy trees, flanked here and there by a statue, now one next to me, that blinked.

A small crowd was gathered round a giant American penny with a copper man stuck still in its center. There was a hat a little ways in front of him and when a child approached and dropped in two euros, the statue blinked, came alive, and said to the crowd, "Heads or tails?"

The child, startled, answered, "Tails." And at this, the penny began to turn, flipping through the air a few times, before landing with the head of the coin facing us. The audience applauded and the copper man said, "Two out of three?"

Someone else threw a coin into the hat. "Heads!" a woman yelled. And the penny spun again. More applause.

I watched a while as the crowd grew and thinned and replaced itself with new onlookers. Mostly he remained still until activated by someone's loose change. There must be some kind of rod through the middle of the coin, I figured, around which he rotated. Some of the living statues use rods, Albert told me later. There is a levitating guru in Piccadilly for example, with a rod hidden in his sleeve. He sits Indian style, three or four feet off the ground, holding a staff.

Las Ramblas has lots of these performers, so too London's Covent Garden, Florence, or any city where tourists converge. A green Statue of Liberty, a bronze Abraham Lincoln, Michelangelo's *David* (his penis censored by loincloth), Nikia with wings, Garibaldi drawing his sword, a pewter no-name chimney sweep...

Not all of the living statues are modeled on famous figures. Many, like the chimney sweep, are anonymous. Though the famous are often anonymous too. In public parks the world over, forgotten generals and poets loiter in perpetuity. And while there are many Lincolns and Napoleons standing still on Barcelona's Las Ramblas, there are just as many "types." A no-name bronze cowboy, for example. Is he a cowboy that no one remembers, or a people that everyone does?

One no-name looks like he's falling but never hits the ground. He's suspended horizontally, a look of surprise stuck on his face. It's done with some rods in his pants, Albert says, so that he's suspended there, forever falling, the better to evoke a sense of the present, what happens between the things we remember happened: beginning to fall—having fallen.

Most of the falling men wear top hats. Most of the no-names wear antiquated clothes to visually set themselves apart from the onlookers that pass. To set themselves apart from the present, which they're imitating, they set their present in the past. If they wore baseball caps and jeans, I mean, if they looked like everyone else, no one would notice them paused in a moment, no less leave a tip.

I sat down at a nearby café and watched the Living Penny over a Diet Coke. More couples and groups of friends and families approached him with questions. "The Sagrada Família next, or shopping in the Gothic Quarter?" a woman's voice asked at a table near my own. "Let's flip for it," her companion answered cheerfully, before they paid their bill and walked over.

At the end of the day I walked over, too, and threw my own coin into the now full hat. The statue blinked his unblinking eyes before turning them toward me. "Heads or tails?" the copper penny asked. I thought for a moment about everything I'd been thinking about. "Heads," I said at last. And then the penny spun and spun and spun, until it landed facing me. And like that, it was decided.

2 Once, I was Bernini's Medusa.

In most depictions, Medusa is rendered vanquished, a head severed by Perseus. He holds her by her limp snakes and her jaw is slack. A glance at Medusa would turn you to stone it was said, so when Perseus sought her head he approached her using his shield as mirror, the way hairdressers ask you to hold one at the end of a cut, so you can see how they trimmed the back. "How's that?" the hairdresser asks, showing you your limp snakes resting against your shoulders. Ironically or not ironically, Bernini sculpted his Medusa from stone. I have long curly hair and when I was little, waking up early for ballet practice, my father would say, "Brush your snakes!" before I'd collect them into a tight bun.

For my Medusa, I set up an oblong box as a pedestal and around my neck layered silver necklaces, painting the whole pedestal silver too. And then above that, my snakes curled wild, mid slither, stuck still framing my stone face. Bernini's is my favorite Medusa because of her eyebrows, because of her gaze cast just left, like she's not looking at anyone but thinking of someone, looking at him in her imagination. She looks lonely and pained, not because she's dead, for that would mean the end of pain, but because her face is frozen as it was before she died, as it was in life. It must be awful to have everyone turning from you, or else if they do return your glance, to have yours met only with stony expressions.

I figured Medusa wouldn't be that difficult to pull off since I could conceal most of my body in the pedestal and so had only to worry about the composition of my face, my not blinking. Within the first hour a few people stopped and put coins in my hat. I don't know if it was a compliment or a criticism that they all felt so comfortable staring at me, not worried at all that they might become stones themselves. Was Medusa's house filled with statuary, I wondered then? Standing still for so many hours, your mind goes to all sorts of places.

Was it Medusa who invented the sculpture garden? Her yard must have been full of men who'd noticed her first in their periphery, who'd turned, about to say something, but then froze before they could utter a word. Like the way Dante froze when, overcome with nerves, he saw Beatrice in the street. Like the way poets describe love at first sight. Did Medusa love any of them back, I wonder? Was there one statue in her garden over whom she wept?

They say Medusa was beautiful once, that she'd turned many heads, including that of Poseidon, who then raped her in Athena's temple. Athena, learning of the desecration, blamed the young Medusa and punished her by transforming her beautiful curls into snakes, making it so that any head she turned thereafter would also turn to stone.

The hardest part that first day was not blinking. The body blinks to keep the eyes moist, so when you force yourself not to blink for half an hour they become dry and start to tear on their own. After an hour, the tears were coming hard, transforming me into a kind of fountain.

I've always found it strange that fountains should depict water pouring from the mouth, if not water issuing from the penis of a small boy. What does it mean, this perpetual vomiting, this perpetual pissing? And then, if you're going to sculpt a boy urinating in perpetuity, why not make another with perpetual diarrhea? Why are some things considered beautiful and others vulgar, even hideous? Why aren't there any fountains of women squatting?

If I were a sculptor, I'd make a fountain of Ophelia bleeding from the wrists inside the pool into which she'd fallen, her life pouring out of her forever, dying always but never being dead. But I am not a sculptor, I am a sculpture. And that first day I was Medusa, stone-faced and weeping.

You get better at the not blinking. I couldn't perform Medusa Crying today. The continuous weeping was a happy accident of my inexperience. I was Medusa Crying all week until the airline called me in for a flight to Madrid.

In Madrid, I visited the Prado. Once I started statuing, I used all my work trips for research. Wherever I'd land, I'd visit museums and parks as I had before, but now with an eye out for my next piece.

Once, I was Gustave Courbet's "The Origin of the World"—a painting of a woman lying down, her legs splayed, her vagina, covered by hair, open. In London's Covent Garden, I painted my genitals in oil, cast a white sheet loosely over the top of my body for verisimilitude, and set up a gilded frame showcasing my lower half. When a coin was thrown into my hat, I crossed and then uncrossed my legs in acknowledgment. Living statues only move for tips.

I wasn't there five minutes before a policeman rushed over. I covered up as asked and then explained to him about my art. The policeman was understanding and let me off with only a warning. Then he asked me to dinner.

I met him later that night at a noisy Italian restaurant he called, "London's best-kept secret," though it didn't seem that anyone had been keeping it; it was rather crowded.

"Where are you from?" he asked over the din.

"The suburbs."

Then he leaned across the table, looked right into my eyes, the small candle flame lighting him from beneath, and said, "I want to know everything about you." Then he told me all about himself.

After dinner, he insisted on walking me home. I told him I'd rather walk alone, but he told me he was a gentleman and therefore could not allow that. So I led him to the Ritz hotel and outside the revolving door he kissed me. He put one hand on the small of my back, touched his lips to mine, and then opened his eyes. I blinked. He blinked. Then I walked back to my actual hotel.

"The Origin of the World" was Courbet's most scandalous painting. It was banned upon completion, just as I was. "I love it, but nudity is controversial," the policeman had said, twirling his pasta.

Today, Courbet's painting is displayed prominently in Paris's Musée D'Orsay and no one is offended. There is no controversy, though the painting's no different than it was when it was first unveiled. As long as it's part of the past, I guess, people aren't offended. It's the present that makes everyone uncomfortable. Nudity is only its reminder, stirring some feeling that reminds us we are alive, which is, Albert says, a controversial state. The past is over and the future hasn't started, but moments are interminable and every one of us is trapped in them. The present being a jail, it's only natural, I suppose, to want to look beyond its bars. Eternity is too troubling, so most people avert their eyes; they look toward the future or else away toward the past. Because if you look at the present, it might turn you to stone.

I saw a model of Rodin's *Iris*, a sculpture I don't like, at the Metropolitan Museum in New York. *Iris* is a small bronze figure with her legs spread wide, her hand holding one of her feet, outstretched. But no one calls it vulgar. Iris was an ancient Greek messenger goddess that traveled along the rainbow delivering messages between gods before the post office was invented. What message did Rodin imagine her conveying in this piece, I wondered, as I looked into her vagina through the glass vitrine? From whom to whom was this message being carried? Maybe Iris wasn't the subject of the piece, but just the name of the model who sat for it.

Stone nudes litter the parks, and their vaginas and penises do not shock because they were sculpted long ago, and their subjects are long dead, and through their deaths their vulgarity has been transmuted into beauty. Inside the museum, standing before Courbet's painting, people stare freely. While my body, no matter how still I stood that day, no matter how expert the patina I'd painted onto it, no matter how much history my brush-stroked genitals evoked, made everyone look away.

"It is that way," Albert says, "because statues are monuments to the past, while we, the living statues, are monuments to the present. But the past was once present too, and that's what we are saying when we stand still for a very long time. You and I," Albert told me, "we are memories before they are remembered."

3　In each city, the stewardesses would go off to the bars with the men they'd met in the first class cabin, or if they hadn't met anyone in the first class cabin, they'd go off together to meet the men in the town. Me, I'd go off alone to the hardware store to buy paint and supplies, and then to my hotel room to work on my next piece.

I think it's important not to be just one thing. You've got to be a new one thing every day or at least every week or every other week or month or year. Picasso had many periods after all, not all of them blue. And Rodin didn't keep making the same thing over and over, though he did make many *Kisses*. You almost can't walk into a museum without seeing one of his *Kisses*.

The original *The Kiss* was made to ornament a larger bronze work entitled *The Gates of Hell*, borrowed from Dante. The lovers he depicted were Francesca da Rimini and Paolo Malatesta, the younger brother of Francesca's husband who killed them both upon discovering their affair in thirteenth century Italy. In his *Inferno*, Dante meets the couple in the second circle of hell, where together they are being cast about in a tempest along with Cleopatra and Helen of Troy and various other "lustfuls," as punishment for their sin of getting carried away.

Separating it from *The Gates of Hell* and enlarging it, Rodin originally called the piece *Francesca da Rimini*. It was the critics who applied the more general appellation *The Kiss. The Kiss*, too, caused controversy where it was displayed. Today its provenance is largely forgotten, and the statue is regarded by most not as a warning against love, but as a symbol of its splendor. It's a favorite postcard image among college students making the Grand Tour.

Rodin produced three in marble and a handful in plaster, terra-cotta, and bronze. Of the marble editions, one ended up in the stables of an eccentric American art collector who, commissioning the copy, insisted in the contract that "the genitals of the man must be complete." After the collector's death, his *Kiss* ended up at the Tate Modern, next to the WC, which is suggestive of love's phases, perhaps one of the five stages of grief that is said to follow in love's wake. I read that in one of the inflight magazines.

Another was made for a museum in Copenhagen, and still another—produced by someone else after Rodin's death—sits in the Rodin Museum in Philadelphia. According to French Law, of the 319 *Kisses*, only the first twelve constitute originals. The French supposedly invented the French kiss, but looking at Rodin's statue it's hard to imagine that Paolo and Francesco would not have used tongue.

Once, I was Lady Justice.

Once, I was a colorful Picasso looking at herself in the mirror.

Once, I was Venus coming toward you on the half shell.

Once, I was Cleopatra holding the aspic that would kill her.

Once, I was Ophelia drowning. I drowned every day for a week.

Once, I was an American tourist. Fanny pack, shorts, and sneakers, all stuck still in bronze, not knowing my pose until I found an American tourist in the throngs that same day. I'd waited on my plinth, not knowing what I was waiting for until I spotted her in the crowd, examining a map. And so I examined my own bronze map. What do people look for in art, after all, but an echo of themselves, some feeling of recognition and with that consolation?

Albert says we process empathy through the mirroring of facial expressions. That we do it unconsciously when we speak with others. We don't know it, but we tense our faces the same way that theirs are tensed, tracing the symptoms back to their cause, the physical back to its emotional source, and that's how we can understand another person's inner life. Though you can never truly understand another person's inner life, Albert says. "We are all strangers, especially to ourselves, which is why empathy matters. We need others to show us who we are."

"People who've had Botox show a diminished capacity for empathy," I responded, noting a study I'd read in one of the inflight magazines, "because they are unable to move their faces."

"Wrinkles are impressions left by our experience—the faces you made, the feelings you had. It's awful to erase them," Albert answered.

I agree with Albert about almost everything, but Albert's a man and I think he misses some of the point about being a woman. Wrinkles on a man are prized because his experience is seen as a kind of wealth. But calling a woman "experienced" has always been pejorative. Unlike a man's, a woman's wrinkles suggest poverty, how much of her innocence has been lost, how much of her time has already been spent. Men gain experience, women lose their virginity. I didn't make up the language, I just learned to speak it.

This is why men love younger women, I think. Their seamless faces are a blank canvas onto which they can make their mark. Such untroubled surfaces are perfect to mirror a man's feelings back. Men are sculptors and, like Rodin, they're looking for a really good stone to sink their chisels into. So I don't blame older women for wanting to erase from their faces all the people that have looked at them, all the people who've marked them. I don't think it's time they want to erase at all, but maybe just some of the people who took it from them. Or maybe they just don't want to look poor.

It's a sad thing to be a woman, I sometimes think, standing on my plinth, nearly naked and covered in silver paint. To hold onto the riches of youth, you've got to give up all that made you old, the whole map of how you got here. Your history for a face-lift.

"Why can't she grow old gracefully?" I've heard men and young unmarked women say. But who wants to lose? And what if you don't have to? What if your face could be an Etch A Sketch, and all you had to do was shake your head yes. All you had to do was see a doctor who'd shake it for you, and then you could start all over again. And then someone might look at you and see only a perfect reflection of themselves, and love you for it. I don't know what I'll do when I get old.

"Loss is inevitable; your choice is not whether you will lose, but *what* you will lose." That's what Albert says.

Me, right now, I long for wrinkles, for experience, for life, for my face to show me who I am, who I one day will have been. But when I'm older, who knows? Maybe I'll want a clean face with which to start all over again. Maybe I'll hate all the lines and all the truths they betray about me. Maybe I'll hate everything I've done and all the things done to me and hate my face for the proof it offers. Maybe I'll hate myself.

For a few months, I improvised this way, mimicking onlookers in the crowd. In silver, bronze, or granite, I'd spot someone and freeze in their form, trying to feel what they felt. It's a thin line between homage and parody though, between empathy and ridicule. One young woman slapped me. She was crying. I'd sought to comfort her. So I cried in exactly the same way she was crying and then she slapped me. It's not an easy life, ours. You get slapped and worse. Albert's been kicked, pissed on, and sometimes they throw lit cigarettes at you and don't even leave a tip.

I don't begrudge the girl who slapped me, though it hurt. Considering the incident later, I recalled how as a kid my brother teased me. How I retaliated by calling him stupid. How he retaliated by calling me stupid in my own voice while making my own face back at me. The madder I got, the madder he got, which made me still more mad. That he wouldn't respond, but kept showing me back to myself was intolerable.

After I got slapped, I began reacting instead or mimicking. Looking out into the crowds, instead of imitating, I'd freeze in answer to a look. I'd freeze in laughter or pity, whatever someone's look asked of me.

Albert says the person looking creates what he sees. That the observer shapes the object observed. An object unobserved is like an event that hasn't happened, he says. Like Schrödinger's Cat, alive and dead at the same time until someone looks in the box containing it, until the box is opened.

Albert follows all the latest developments in the physics of the very large and very small, in cosmology and quanta both, because, he says, physics has a lot to tell us about love. "Eventually all the galaxies will smash into their partner galaxies and form a larger one, and the universe will keep expanding, and eventually all these new monster galaxies will be so far from one another it will be as if they are each alone in the vast eternal dark, none of them even knowing of the others. But first the sun will swallow the Earth. That thing there, up in the sky, that gives us life and vitamin D, which is essential for both emotional well-being and strong bones, will steal our lives, too. And no tablet taken with meal will be enough."

Once, I was Schrödinger's Cat. Albert and I have a lot in common, in that regard, though he would never be the cat, but more likely Schrödinger—that's his style. What I did was make a large-scale diorama with cyanide poison inside, and on the lid I'd painted, "Schrödinger's Box. Open." Then, when a person opened it, I'd choose life or death. I'd either jump around and lick my paws or lie there very still, as if I'd been dead for a long time already.

Playing dead, you get to thinking about all sorts of things. Remembering moments, making up others, you get to thinking too about whether there's any real difference between the time before you were born and the time after you die, between memory and imagination. If there is such a thing as infinity, Albert says, then imagination is just front-facing memory. In an infinite world, everything will happen eventually and so imagination is simply recalling what hasn't yet. Who have I been, who will I be, I wondered, lying there, poisoned.

When I was thirteen, two of my classmates began kissing on a bus to a bar mitzvah party. They kissed for a very long time, their mouths opening and closing over each other's, mapping in their motion the infinity symbol. They were the first in our class to kiss and I think they were performing for us, because the whole way there, a whole half hour, they never paused. Once, I was a statue of myself that day, looking out the dark window of that bus, pretending not to notice them.

Once, I was a statue of myself later that year, as I pretended not to hear my schoolmates' jeers. I had no friends except for my next-door neighbor Christine, owing to my rigorous ballet schedule. Though maybe without ballet it would have been the same, just without ballet.

"I don't like her," Nicole had said on the school bus home. "I don't know anyone who does. Do you?" she asked Jared, before putting the same question to all the kids one by one. I remained silent, looking at the back of the seat in front of me, pretending to be very interested in the graffiti, pretending I didn't hear any of what was being said. At last Nicole asked my next-door neighbor and best friend—we wore two halves of a gold heart. She'd presented it to me one day, like a proposal. The heart said, "Best Friends Forever."

"Do you?" she asked Christine. I don't remember exactly what Christine said. What I remember is the long walk home from the bus stop after. The silence. She hadn't said yes.

Why was Picasso blue? Why was I that day on my plinth? Maybe I was lonely, though I didn't think I was lonely at the time. You can't know you're lonely if you've only ever been lonely, and I didn't know I had been lonely until after I met Albert.

Once, I was a blue statue of myself on the bus, as I pretended not to hear anyone.

Once, I was a statue of my best friend after we got off at the same bus stop, when she turned to me and said, just before we reached our houses, "Wanna come over?" But that one was hard to do, because I hadn't been looking at her while she spoke but at the trees framing the road, the pavement holding us up. I didn't want her to see me seeing her seeing me seeing her.

Once, I was a painting in storage, blocked from exposure in brown paper. This didn't fetch much in the way of tips, but we don't do it for the money. Only the Romanians do it for the money. The difference between us and the Romanians is that we want money only so that we can keep doing it. It's an artist's life that few understand. Albert understands.

Once, I was a statue with pins on its head put there by the city, so the pigeons couldn't land on it and destroy its majesty. I wasn't worried about them landing on me and destroying my majesty, but I wanted to depict the fear of desecration and how acting on that fear is itself a desecration. Because the pins ruin the statues. The generals in their crowns of shit are much more beautiful, I think. Proud, dignified, durable.

Once, I was Seneca in Cordoba.

Once, I was La fornarina, Raphael's mistress and model.

Once, for the whole month after my father died, I was my father in gold, the way he looked waving goodbye at the airport before I left home for the last time. Once, I stood just like him, my arm raised mid-wave. And when tourists tipped me I said, "Goodbye."

Once, I was a rough, uncut stone. The sculpture before it is sculpted. The thing waiting to be revealed through subtraction. I was potential. The art before it is art. I was raw material, the starting point for the artist who would look at me and pick up his chisel and turn me into something new by chipping away at what had been. I was a would-be statue and you, looking and dropping a coin into my hat, were the artist who might make me. Did you see something in me? Would I always be a boulder, or perhaps a *Kiss*?

4 Staring stiff from the rock that day, I saw a man stooping to leave a tip in my hat, but then instead of leaving money, he picked up the hat and ran off. With difficulty, I started after him, my legs encumbered by my costume, until at last I gave up on my feet and, like a boulder dislodged from a mountainside, down Las Ramblas, I rolled.

The crowd parted for us: The man, running, got farther away. Me, on my side now, growing dizzy as I picked up speed. Then, cutting in from the side, a green Statue of Liberty began running too. She jumped on his back. He tried to throw her off, but her coppery weight was too much for him. The two fell to the ground.

When I caught up, he'd already gone, leaving Lady Liberty alone on the stone floor, panting. I offered my hand to help her up. Instead of her hand, she gave me my hat back, full of money.

"Debbie," she said, raising herself up.

"Thank you, Debbie."

"We must to stick together," she said with a wink. Then, dusting herself off before the crowd of onlookers, we began walking back the way we'd come, silent but for our heavy breathing, my feet, sticking out small beneath the boulder, shuffling along beside hers concealed by her copper robe. Back at my plinth, I left off the question mark. "May I take you to lunch."

We collected our things. It was five p.m., still early enough to make tips but the day seemed over on account of the altercation. I offered to take Debbie wherever she liked. "The Ritz?" I suggested, though I'd never been inside. She pointed at a McDonald's. "There. They have good hamburger," she said in an accent I could not identify.

"Take table," she commanded, as we walked in. "They know me here," she said, striding ahead toward the register. I found a table in the front next to the window and sat down on a revolving seat that was screwed into the floor. She returned with a Big Mac for herself and a Happy Meal for me. "It comes with toy," she smiled, laying the box on the table before me.

We ate in silence, and when we finished she said, "Where are you from?"

"The suburbs."

I unwrapped my toy, an Ewok, and set it down just to my right, so that we were both facing Debbie.

Debbie removed her green crown and matching green bathing cap and shook out her hair, blond and brittle, the strands tough and tired.

"You will come to the guild tonight," she said. "You will meet Albert. You are alone here?"

I nodded.

"Now we go," she said, crumpling the paper from her Big Mac. "Take your Ewok."

We walked down Las Ramblas to where it opens by the harbor, me half stone, Debbie half copper. From there, we walked farther into the expanding dark, the sky glowing deep blue with a sliver of moon, like a smile, looking down on us. "See the moon?" Debbie asked.

I nodded.

"It hates us."

She led me down some steps into a clearing next to the water, where a group of more than a dozen was gathered round a can of fire.

I heard voices as we approached and made out a few rogue words: "The Romanians . . . War is coming . . ."

"We are here," Debbie said, approaching the group, approaching specifically a stoical gray-haired man who was seated as the others were, in a folding beach chair. She looked around until someone brought her a seat. "For you," she said to me, motioning toward the chair.

I sat down.

"This is Albert," she said, plopping down onto the gray-haired man's lap. He pulled her legs over his lap, looked me over, and then back at the fire. He addressed the group:

"We are the Guild of the Living Statues, descendants of the tableaux vivant, keepers of the tradition and protectors of each other," Albert announced. Then to me, "Tell everyone who you are."

"I'm from the suburbs."

"When living statues meet other living statues," Albert interrupted, "we don't ask or tell who we were before we began statuing, or who we are when we are not statuing, or who we'll be if we stop, though it's not a secret. We say instead who we are when we are still. Who we were first and who we were later."

Albert patted Debbie's backside lightly, and she rose, then took a seat on the floor next to him. He began:

"Once, I was an exile of the gods and a wanderer. Volcano food, I was eaten whole but for a sandal....

"Once, I was put to death for believing heavenly bodies were not gods but hot rocks stuck in the sky....

"Once, I took a lamp into the day, searching the streets for an honest man.... Once, I held my breath until I died....

"Once, I was Nero, nephew of Seneca, whom I had killed....

"Once, I was Empedocles....

"...Anaxemter....

"...Diogenes....

"...Cleanthes....

"...Antipeter of Taris....

"Albert's into the stoics," Debbie whispered to me.

"...Chrysippus....

"...Panaetius....

"...Posidonius..."

Albert went on, the fire lighting him against the deepening dark.

*　　*　　*

The next day, Debbie found me on my plinth. "Come. We go to the McDonald. Albert does not like the McDonald, so I must to go alone. But now I have you."

Debbie took the last bite of her Big Mac. "You like?" she asked, as I finished my burger and held up the Darth Vader toy that had come with my Happy Meal.

I nodded.

"Albert is very serious. He loves Tolstoy and does not believe in Happy Meals. "'All Happy Meals resemble one another, each unhappy meal is unhappy in its own way.' This is what he says." She shrugged. "He is enacting the history of Western philosophy on the plinth. He is very serious. When I met him five years ago, he was Cleanthes. I don't know philosophy, but he explains me."

"What were you when you met?"

She motioned to the Statue of Liberty costume she had on. "I don't have this mania to change all the time. Why to change all the time? For me, it is job. I hate to job, but we all must job."

"I have to work tomorrow," I answered, and explained about my upcoming flight to Lisbon.

When I returned the following week, I walked down to the water and found the group where I'd left them.

"Too many people are standing still," said a voice as I approached. Then the words, "Plinth war . . ." "Blood on the pavement . . ."

Joining the circle, I sat on the floor next to Debbie.

"It was the Romanians," Debbie whispered to me, motioning to Albert's bandaged head. "There was a brawl. They want to take our spots, but we've held these spots for years."

More voices came from the circle:

"Strength in numbers . . ."

"We need to band together . . ."

The war with the Romanians bound the guild tighter, and we began posing in groups, the better to defend our territory and ourselves.

We staged large elaborate hunting tableaux, Portuguese battle scenes, Mexican mural paintings, a black-and-white photo taken at Coney Island in 1924. . . .

It was during this collaborative period that my education truly began. I was taught how to lower my heart rate to make my breathing less visible, how not to blink, and the long noble history of our art, beginning with the tableaux vivant often staged in medieval pageants and coronations, later taken up by P. T. Barnum, and extending all the way to us. But the multiperson collaborations, however beautiful and however prudent, meant that we were each earning less, too. And then, not negligibly, before the collaborative, we had each created our own works, had managed our own selves, whereas now we were being managed by Albert. I didn't mind, for I was still learning, but I could appreciate the restlessness growing among the older guild members who began to talk of throwing Albert over.

"I've had enough of his philosophy," said Carmine, who, before the consolidation, posed alone as a falling cowboy. He claimed, frequently, that he'd been the first to fall. By that time Albert had us enacting Rafael's fresco "The School of Athens." Albert was Aristotle holding his ethics. Debbie and I were the stone statues holding up the stage on which the many philosophers, the other guild members, stood.

We'd been performing "The School of Athens" for three weeks when Carmine finally said this aloud, first in an irritated whisper and then in full voice to the collective as we surrounded the fire.

"There is no need for mutiny," Albert said, approaching the circle, silencing Carmine after only a few words. "I leave for Nice tomorrow, and you can do as you wish." Albert turned and retreated to his tent with Debbie following close behind.

Later that night, Debbie found me, one of the last still surrounding the dying fire. "You will come with us. It is arranged. I told Albert you are my little baby. How can I leave my little baby?"

I nodded and held the flats of my hands open toward the quiet flame.

I found Albert waiting outside McDonald's in the morning.

"Debbie's inside using the bathroom," he said, barely looking at me.

I looked at him not looking at me and then leaned up against the wall beside him.

Across the street, one of the Romanians was dressed as the alien from the movie *Alien*. A young boy posed beside the alien, as his mother took a photo, and a small crowd gathered to watch. The alien kept changing his pose to look as if he were about to attack the boy.

"Stupidity is a virus," Albert said. "They wear Halloween costumes now and the people love it."

"Hello, little baby," said Debbie, bursting from the door. She pinched my cheek, and the three of us walked on.

At the airport, I went by myself to Terminal 3 and turned in my uniform and letter of resignation, then met Albert and Debbie outside our departure gate.

☛ 5 Nice in winter bloomed with the scent of oranges. Albert quoted Smollett as a bus drove us from the airport along a dusty road flanking the turquoise coast. "Smollett hated everything but Nice, and it was he who popularized it as a winter resort for the sickly and English. I hate Smollett, but he was right about Nice," Albert went on.

"Matisse won a canoeing trophy," I interjected, having read that in one of the inflight magazines. "When he lived here, he was an avid canoer."

The bus turned up a side street and began climbing into Cimiez before depositing us some distance from our hotel. The air was still and warm, the light, brilliant. After the growl of the bus died away, there was only the sound of cicadas, a lone bird, and dust. We walked with our bags, Debbie complaining of the heat, Albert and I listening to the dust.

Albert negotiated our rooms.

"Little baby," said Debbie, before we parted, her arms draped around Albert's neck as she looked at me. "Albert," she said, turning her face up to his. He was looking off in the direction of the concierge who'd gone to fetch extra towels. "What is it?" he asked.

"Let's all go out for dinner tonight, on the promenade with the tourists, to celebrate our arrival. Come at seven p.m.," she said then to me. "Meet here at seven p.m., and we will walk down to the town and explore."

"Thank you," I said, as she kissed Albert on the cheek and then turned his face to kiss him on the mouth.

My room had two large beds, both of them lumpy, and a juliet balcony with blue doors overlooking the courtyard—a few tables hemmed in by fruit trees and plantings. Out in the distance, just above the trees, were two layers of blue: the ocean, then the sky.

I wondered what to do with myself. I examined the sticky brochures left on the dresser. I examined the digital clock on the nightstand between the beds: 4:05 p.m. It was too late to go to the Matisse museum up the road. What did Matisse do when he first arrived? I sat on one of the beds, then lay on it, then, looking up at the slow ceiling fan making its rounds above me, shut my eyes.

"You remember life in moments. How someone looked when they said a thing," Albert says. "Nothing lasts but these moments, like photographs. The cast of someone's eyes when you thought they weren't listening . . . Life is a flipbook." I remember the look of the slow ceiling fan before I fell asleep that afternoon, like a clock that had been sped up, telling not one time but all of them.

Against the Côte d'Azur, we were Matisse's "The Dance." We had constructed two life-size dolls from stockings stuffed with laundry to make up the missing fourth and fifth dancers in our circle and wore body stockings to cover our nudity with a costume of nudity. We were five dancers ecstatically paused. We danced for three weeks, before we moved inland to Masséna Square. There, we were Schopenhauer's Parable of the Porcupines.

"Seeking respite from the cold, the porcupines rush toward each other to share their warmth, only to find that with closeness comes pain, as they are pricked by each other's quills, and so rush away again to escape the pain, only to rush back after to escape the cold. After a time," Albert explained over dinner, as the sun dipped below the horizon and the blue water lapped at the pebbly beach where we sat with our picnic of salami and apples, "the porcupines remain at a middle distance from one another, which offers partial warmth and partial relief. Though their comfort is incomplete, there is less risk of getting pricked, and this middle distance, Schopenhauer explains, is society."

"I don't mind a prick," Debbie answered, before quaffing her wine and giving Albert a long kiss. She lay down on her back to seize the sky.

The quills we stretched from wire hangers, attaching them to pillows, which we'd sewn onto the backs of our body suits. In a fearful bundle we huddled together, motionless. And when we got tips we ran from one another, before returning and resuming our pose. A few meters away a pewter cowboy was falling before a more appreciative crowd. Debbie, in the evening, despaired of our meager earnings.

"He's a hack," Albert said, when Debbie mentioned the cowboy. "Let him fall at last and break his head."

"Even artists must eat, Albert. If we keep this up we will be eating from the dumpsters," answered Debbie.

They argued every night until Albert introduced a new idea: John William Waterhouse's "Echo and Narcissus."

"What is this now?" asked Debbie, impatiently.

"Narcissus falls in love with his reflection in a pool of water, while Echo, who can do nothing but repeat the words of others, falls in love with Narcissus, as he looks lovingly at himself. Love has trapped them both. You know the painting?"

Debbie rolled her eyes.

"I can paint the backdrop," I volunteered. "I can stencil the still pond among the trees. I will use one of the hotel sheets."

"And I will build the frame," said Albert.

"And I will go swimming," said Debbie, regarding tomorrow's plan. "I need a day off."

Once again we posed against the blue sea and sky, dotted with couples aloft, parasailing for 50 euro a trip. Waterhouse's painting leaned against the promenade railing, inside of which lay Albert (Narcissus) supine, with a reddish cloth draped over his buttocks. Albert mesmerized by his reflection, as he gazes into a pool in which I lay looking up, mirroring him. And Debbie (Echo), longing for him silently beside a near tree, looking at him looking at himself.

A tip in the hat, the sound of change exciting our movements: Narcissus disturbs the water, reaches down into his reflection hoping to grasp his beloved's face, before I turn my head and replace his reflection with a rippled panel of opaque pond. "Where did you go, my love?" Narcissus asks his face, now gone, and then Echo echoing forlornly, "Where did you go, my love?"

"Who will recognize such a painting? Abe Lincoln! Liberty Statue! Darth Vader! This is what people recognize. This is what makes the people stop and take to picture and give to money!" Debbie said after two slow days.

"Go ahead and be Darth Vader, Debbie."

"What about you, Little Baby? You agree with me or Albert?"

"It is a dilemma."

"You see!" said Debbie. "She doesn't want to say the truth."

"No one is stopping you from being Darth Vader."

"You are stopping me!" she said, unwrapping a toothpick and applying it to her gaps. She looked out at the dusky sky. "You are stopping me," she mellowed. "No one is saying it is not beautiful, but beauty will not fill our bellies."

A few days later, Debbie took me to McDonald's, bought me a Happy Meal, and explained she would be leaving for a week. "In Amsterdam they have the Living Statue Competition and there is prize money. Even if you do not win the main prize, there are many tourists and much money and all the guild will be there. Albert will stay here. You can stay here or come with me as you wish. I leave tomorrow and will return Monday. Take your Yoda," she said standing, regarding my Happy Meal toy.

Debbie was gone before breakfast the next morning. I walked down into the courtyard where Albert sat as usual, reading yesterday's paper. The sound of insects and birds, of my metal folding chair as I pulled it over the gravel up to our breakfast table, was amplified by Debbie's absence. Albert turned the page and, finding me there behind his paper, said, "Debbie has gone. She'll be back next week."

"Yes," I said.

He looked back at the paper, then put it down. "And what will you do with yourself?"

"I don't know," I said, picking at a hangnail. "Maybe visit one of the museums. The Beaux Arts."

He brought the newspaper back to his face. I picked an orange from the bowl between us and began peeling it with my fingers.

"Why do you read yesterday's newspaper when there is a new one at that table over there?"

"I don't care for the news. I am interested in history. Why don't you drink coffee?" he returned from behind his newspaper.

I shrugged.

"I'll come with you to the museum."

A bumblebee bumbled over a planter beside our table. I ate my orange.

"It was built in 1878, in the former home of the Ukrainian Princess, Elisabeth Vasilievna Kotschoubey," said Albert, reading from the museum guide. His voice, low, echoed in the mostly empty corridor. Our shoes sounded against the marble floor as we made our way into the first room. "Walk beside me, please. It makes me feel like I've enslaved you the way you always trail behind."

I don't remember what I saw. I'd never been to a museum with another person before and found it difficult to concentrate on what I was looking at, distracted as I was by what Albert was looking at. I tried to imitate myself alone, walking over to a separate painting and looking for a while as if lost in my own experience, and then after a suitable time, or if Albert lagged behind, I'd wander into the next room, or else lag behind myself, as if enraptured again and unaware.

I mapped our meandering routes around and across the rooms as we passed each other, fell back, turned round and crossed. This is what I remember, not the paintings or the statuary, but the two of us as if viewed from above, our paths threading the hours until taken all together, time and our movement through it had its own shape, became a sculpture in itself. I turned the thing around in my mind, trying to see it from all sides. Albert was speaking:

"You could be her."

We were looking at a white marble bust of a woman, veiled.

He turned and looked at me. I faced him. He was taller than me by a head and he tilted his back farther, lowering his eyes to meet mine. His face reminded me of a palm laid open before a fortune-teller, but I understood none of its lines. A furrow appeared between his eyes.

"Your ugliness," he said, "moves me." He took in his hand one of my curls, pulled it straight, then let it drop against my chest. "You're like a monster."

Medusa's Garden 27

He smiled and, for the first time, I saw his teeth, yellow and small, with a gap between the first two. He had a boy's smile, like the statue of a boy brushed by weather and moss, pissing into a wishing well far from the estate's main house.

"Are you angry?" he asked, still smiling.

I studied his hair, which was brown and gray like the Atlantic and formed waves that broke against the sides of his face. He had freckles. Beating the sea with chains, I thought, the phrase appearing from nowhere. It's something the Greeks used to say as an expression of futility. Because you can't change the ocean, you can't change water. Only land erodes. You have to be solid to erode.

He turned and began walking. "This isn't an original," I said, regarding Rodin's *The Kiss*, which bisected the staircase. "Of the 319 *Kisses*, only twelve constitute originals." I looked at the man's large hand grasping the woman's bare hip, her smaller arm curling around his neck, their lips not yet touching. "I read that in one of the inflight magazines."

He went outside while I used the ladies room. When I came out I didn't see him, so I walked a while alone toward our hotel. That's when I came upon him by the payphone, smoking.

"I didn't know you smoke."

"I don't," he said. "Don't tell Debbie."

"But Debbie smokes. I don't think she would mind."

"It is my secret. The only thing a person can truly own is a secret."

"I can keep a secret."

"Who says I want to share it with you?"

"Why do you smoke?" I asked.

"What will you do today?" he said, putting the newspaper down in the courtyard the next morning. I put down my orange.

"The Matisse museum."

"I will come."

We didn't speak as we climbed the mountain where the museum stood. Albert squinted and breathed and now and then paused to put his hands on his hips. I paused and put my hands on my hips. Then we continued.

"What will you do today?" Albert said, putting the newspaper down in the courtyard where I'd laid half my orange.

"I will swim."

"I will come."

We took the hotel towels to the pebbly beach, to the stretch unoccupied by the beachfront hotel beds. I fell asleep under the sun, my shirt over my face. When I woke an hour or minute later, I pulled the shirt from my eyes and saw Albert sitting up next to me, smoking. The smoke mingled with the clouds passing over me, passing over Albert's face, like a bluff overlooking the water. Then he stubbed it out in the pebbles, stood up, and walked down to the tide line. He walked in up to his knees and, standing there with his hands on his hips, looked out.

I felt hot from baking and followed a moment later. I can't swim, but waded in to where Albert stood. Then I bent down low so that I was submerged up to my chin, and swam around him, using my hands on the seafloor to move me. Albert watched as I circled him.

"Are you hungry?" he asked.

"No."

"Let's have lunch then."

We went to the beachfront hotel where F. Scott Fitzgerald stayed. It said so on the inside flap of the menu, above the appetizers.

"Monster," he said, "shall we share the mussels?"

When the mussels arrived, Albert showed me how to eat them with a tiny fork. Then he said, "There are no opera competitions, nor painting competitions, nor writing competitions. There are, but only for amateurs. Artists do not compete. Artists do not do it for the money or for the glory, but because they must. What a hideous job this would be were it a job," he said. "The Amsterdam competition is a circus."

When we left, he took my hand. His was large but fit mine well. It felt like when you find a nice tree to sit beneath and rest your back against, a tree that just happens to fit perfectly the curve of your spine. It felt comforting, I mean. Impersonal, like good fortune.

"Your hand is like a pebble or a worry bead." He put it in his pocket and counted my fingers with his.

At the hotel, he walked me back to my room and followed me in. Afternoon light spilled in from the balcony window, partially covered by old drapes, like a dress that has fallen off one shoulder. The slim light washed the room in golden dusk, making it look like a room in a summerhouse that's been closed for the winter season.

He sat on the bed. "Stand over there." He motioned toward the balcony, at the corner adjacent, where the light lay hard on the carpet in a flat streak.

I went there and faced him.

"Take off your clothes."

When at last I was naked, I stood contrapposto.

He said, "Tell me who you are."

"Once, I was Bernini's *Medusa*. In most depictions, Medusa is rendered vanquished, a head severed by Perseus. He holds her by her limp snakes and her jaw is slack…"

He rose from the bed and moved toward me as I spoke. With his hand, he traced the outline of my body, the curve of my waist, the declivities where a sculptor had chipped some of me away. He touched my hair as if curious of the medium.

"Once, I was Courbet's 'The Origin of the World.'"

"Show me."

I went to the bed, lay down, and opened my legs.

"I see," he said.

He came over to the bed, knelt down next to it, took my ankles in his hands, and turned my lower body toward him.

He kissed me between my legs, then pushed one of his fingers inside before moving it slowly in and out. Then he sat next to me on the bed and put his finger all the way inside so that he was holding me firmly.

"You are the whole world," he said, his eyes zigzagging across my face, my body, and then my face again, "and I have you in my hand."

He released me, then stood up, unbuttoned his shirt, then his pants, removing everything until he was naked. His body, like his face, was freckled and lined, like a secondhand statue of Poseidon at an estate sale. His muscles shone under his loose skin, as if the skin itself were a shroud. His penis was larger than David's. And instead of lying idly against him, stood out.

He lay on top of me and pressed himself inside, slowly, as if he were forging a path, as if he were building a road through me. Where was he going? Where did I lead? When he was all the way inside, he hovered over me, his face over my face, his hair crashing over his features, covered in so many lines. He smiled and looked at me and held me perfectly still. How long did we look into each other's eyes? What did I see in his?

Ocean, stars, violence, galaxies colliding and drifting off, everything and nothing, until he moved again slightly, as if we were music ascending to the next octave, and after a time, another octave, then another, touching something, saying something, meaning nothing and everything and there in the beginning and there in the end, and terror and happiness and my bleeding toes and fate and my refusal and the emergency exits on either side of the airplane cabin and futility and eternity or none of it, and every color, and every sound, and something darker and deeper that I knew intimately and not at all and in his eyes my eyes until we ceased and became nothing together.

"I saw a *David* in Lisbon. He'd draped a cloth around his waist to cover his genitals. You could be David. You have his hair and brow and seem always to be looking elsewhere. David looks toward Rome. But the loincloth is a corruption. When you are David, you must make a black bar, like they place over the private parts in street signs advertising strippers. You must be David, vandalized by censors. David, Renaissance stripper," I said, looking up at the fan.

"My arm is falling asleep," Albert said, prompting me to lift my head so he could take his arm back. "I am no longer young. I would have to be David in his waning years, King and philanderer, deadbeat dad of Absalom and Solomon, possessor of all his hair."

"How old are you?"

"Fifty-two. I could be David looking toward Texas. I was born in Texas." We both looked toward the fan, as if it were a screen on which his description now played. "I lived there until I was forty-three. I went to Rice University. I met my wife as an undergraduate; she was a year ahead and didn't want to date me because of it. She was concerned with marrying, was vocal about it in her odd rebellious way. All the girls then were talking of men and fish and how they didn't require bicycles, though many of them rode. But she, she was radically old fashioned and around her, it was easy to fall into a complimentary mode, to become a gentleman caller offering a corsage, to shine your shoes and iron your shirt in anticipation of a date. She radicalized me.

"My age ruled me out as a prospect, she informed me, and anyway she didn't like my hair. 'It's rude,' she said about it, noting its length, the way it fell against my ears as it does now. 'Then we will be friends,' I assented. We shared lunches and teas and dinners and walks. She gave me her time, provided I understood I could not keep it. She introduced me to her boyfriends when we ran into them on the quad. She called them 'her suitors.'

"She loved one, Christopher, and at last he proposed. She told me on a Thursday afternoon during one of our walks across campus. I was walking her to astronomy. It was the spring of her senior year. The semester was almost over and she'd been troubling over Mars. His timing had been perfect. She explained in great detail how, under a tall tree he'd gotten down on one knee, how handsome he looked when he held out the ring, how it was everything she wanted and how she said no.

"I remember the sky was a perfect blue that day, the light so democratic the way it touched everything equally, the light on her face, the way it got caught in one of her tears, illuminating its interior like a small hidden room, before it rolled the rest of the way down her cheek and disappeared. I think of that. In my memory, I go back to that moment. I close up on that tear and I try to see what's inside of it. I think we were.

"Then she kissed me for the first time and then I was looking at her hands, trembling in mine, as I promised to love her forever if she'd marry me."

He turned and found my eyes, sideways on the pillow, directly in front of his. He held my gaze for a moment and then raised his higher, looking at my hair, which he began picking up in isolated strands, saying, "Hisss, hisss, hissssss..."

The next night, he held me on top of him. He took me by my hips and raised me up high, so that I was like a bird flying over him, suspended for a moment, going nowhere.

Then he lowered me onto his cock. And after, when we were lying side by side, watching the ceiling fan for what it played, he said, "In Texas I was a heart surgeon." Then he turned to me and looked into my eyes as if into a crystal ball. But instead of the future, he began reading the past:

"We married, and I finished medical school and found work at a local hospital. Every day during surgery I was required to stop and restart the heart of one of my patients, and after a time, I found I envied them their pause. There is no such thing yet as elective heart surgery. But imagine being able to stop time—the heart is a clock after all. Standing still is the next best thing."

The next night he rolled off to the side and said, "I had two sons. I think of them, all of us at the dinner table in the early evening after they'd finished their homework, before my wife put them to bed. But that's another tableau. The kids grew up, the wife grew old, and the father disappeared. None of us exist anymore."

Albert stood up and, naked, walked over to the desk where he'd set a bottle of red wine when we'd walked in. Watching him uncork it I thought, I've never seen a statue like this. I studied the hair on his legs and thought about the leg hair that statues lack.

"Hair continues to grow after you die. If you dug up a grave, all the men who'd been straitlaced in life, visiting the barber once a week to keep things neat, would look like The Beatles, except their faces will have rotted. I read that in one of the inflight magazines. I wonder if the leg hair grows, too. If the women who take care to shave every day, in death are bohemian."

Albert poured the wine into a clear plastic cup and drank the whole thing. Then he refilled it. Then he took another plastic cup from the wrapper and filled that one too. He brought both of them over to the bed and handed one to me. I took a sip but didn't like it and put the full cup down on the nightstand.

"My wife could not stand still," he said. "She was always going here or there or making dinner or eating dinner or cleaning up after dinner or coming home or going out. And when we had sex, still, she could not stop moving. I wanted to remain inside of her, inside the moment, but she'd say 'faster' or 'harder,' always 'er.' To 'err' is human they say. But perhaps they mean 'er.' Perhaps that is man's fundamental mistake, to change by degree." He swallowed some more.

"But maybe I don't want to be human," he said, searching my eyes. "Maybe I want to make a different mistake. Maybe I want to be an alligator or a cheesecake. Maybe I want to be a stone." He stood up and refilled his cup and drank it all at once. "We should get back to work tomorrow. Do you know who you'll be yet?"

"Rasputin."

6 The next morning I did not meet Albert in the garden but went out early alone to walk first along the Promenade des Anglais, and then among the antique stalls lined up for Sunday's flea market. I bought a pair of binoculars from World War II that I thought I'd give my dad were he still alive, and a pear. Then I went to the hardware store and some other places to gather materials for my next piece.

I'd decided to be Vladimir Zolotukhin's sculpture of Grigori Rasputin in Tyumen where, last year, I had a brief layover. The sculpture shows Rasputin standing beside an empty chair. The statue stands out front of the hospital where he underwent treatment after being stabbed in the stomach in 1914. Following his recovery, he stayed on, working as an orderly. In the statue, his beard is long, as is his coat, and his hand, with which it was said he was able to heal or seduce, rests on the back of the empty chair.

When I stood in Masséna Square, bronzed and bearded in my long coat, tourists now and then sat in the empty chair, as if I were offering them a seat. They smiled, then their friends and family pressed the buttons on their cameras.

Debbie was the last to sit in my chair. It was a little after six p.m., judging by my shadow. She plopped down and said, "Hello, little baby. Did you miss me?"

Together we walked along the promenade to where Albert was waiting to have dinner. Me in my bronze beard, she in a tank top and her new long flowery skirt she told me she'd bought from a gypsy. I carried my chair in front of me until we arrived at the Ruhl Plage and found Albert reading last week's paper.

"Little Baby has become the Dutch Sinterklaas and you, Albert, how have you spent the week?" she asked, plopping down on his lap, so that the newspaper crumpled against him. I put my chair down and sat next to it.

"She is Rasputin," Albert corrected her.

I put my elbows on the table and held my bronze beard in my bronze hands.

"You can't eat like that," Albert said to me. "Go back to the hotel and change. We'll stay here."

The sun was setting as I left them, as Albert was speaking of his latest piece: "Empedocles, the pre-Socratic, believed the world was divided into two opposing forces, love and strife. He was regarded variously as a physicist, a magician, a theologian, a healer, a politician, a living god, and a fraud—like me...."

The sky deepened in color, as I walked back to the hotel beneath it.

By the time I'd washed everything off, the world beyond my window was black. The only light left in the room came from the bathroom from which I'd emerged. I heard voices in the courtyard and opened the balcony doors to find them, Albert and Debbie, under a great moon, the two of them framed by orange trees, arguing, as if in a play, facing me three quarters of the way, like actors before an audience. The moon, their spotlight, lit only them. The trees, stage left and stage right, were still. Albert had his arms folded while Debbie moved hers in sweeping circles as she spoke.

I stood naked in contraposto, watching them, when at last one of Debbie's arms swung in my direction. Following it with her eyes, she saw me.

"Albert's my boyfriend," she yelled toward me and then to him. Albert and I stood still. When we did not answer, Debbie looked at me, motionless, and then at him, unmoving. "One day, Albert, they'll dig a hole in your honor," she said. Then she stepped back a few paces, so that she no longer had to turn her head back and forth between us. She stepped upstage and calmly addressed us together:

"Once, I was not Bathsheba, nor Liberty Statue. I was not Porcupine nor Matisse Dancer. I was not Athenian. I am Debbie. I have always only been Debbie. I was born in Bulgaria and sent to school in Switzerland, then returned home to take over my father's law practice. I had older brother to work at post office. He was mad, but only on weekends and holidays. The rest of the time, he delivered the mail. He died in a fire after falling asleep with a lit cigarette. My mother and father died shortly after, of heartbreak and lit cigarettes. I did not like my suits. I did not like my hair. I did not like the desk where I sat or the window I looked from.

"I sold the firm and moved to Greece, where I found work as a card dealer in Casino Patras and after five years, met my husband at the tables. He would come in after one a.m. every Tuesday. He drove taxi and drove us home every night. Our little baby was born dead. After, we flew to Paris for vacations. One day I went for walk and did not return. In Paris, I met Albert under a tree pretending to be Cleanthes. I said to him, 'I am Debbie.' I am Debbie. I have always been Debbie. I will always be Debbie," she said.

Then she walked inside and I did not see her again.

☞ *7* We go from town to town together, and Albert teaches me to myself. At night, after the still day, he'll stand me in the corner of our hotel room, run his hands along my waist and over my hips, marveling at my smooth skin, how life-like it is, and then marvel at what's missing.

"Once, I was a great stone," I recite for him as he takes off my clothes, as if he were a sculptor creating me through subtraction. I am his statue, his invention, and Albert loves his work.

Whether what's missing is missing because of what I've lost, because of what's been taken, or because of what I haven't yet got depends on your view of time. Are all stones cut from larger ones? Was the world once complete and perfectly meaningless before breaking up into all of these individual pieces? Were we, Albert and I, once whole? And Debbie, and the guild, and the tourists, and everyone and everything else? Was there something complete before all this beauty and ugliness?

The big bang, the universe beginning from a single point, and everything spreading out after and changing, some pieces coming together, others flying apart, meteors meeting and becoming planets, gases coalescing into stars before they explode too, and all the pieces go running from one another again like Schopenhauer's porcupines.

Albert caresses my waist, chiseling memories, dust and fragments on the hotel floor, swept up and thrown away.

We go from town to town together, and Albert teaches me to myself. And after the still day we lie together. He looks into my eyes, and I ask him:

"How do I feel about you?"

"You love me."

"What am I?"

"You are my mirror."

"What am I for?"

"You are for me."

"What do I want?"

"To be still."

"What do you want?"

"Never to die."

"How do you feel now?"

"Like a stone."

"How does a stone feel?"

"Like me."

"Am I a stone?" I ask.

"Come here, monster. Come here . . ." he says, crushing me in his hard arms.

When the moments pass, where do they go? Albert runs his hand along my perimeter, appreciating what's not there by touching what is. My body is a silhouette of all that I am not. And my story, the story of how I got here, is also the story of how I didn't.

"You are water, Albert. You are time."

8 Once, in Covent Garden, I thought I saw Debbie among the Romanians.

It was September, overcast, 2:45 p.m., though the gray light made it seem it could be any time. The sun itself was invisible, leaving the shadows disordered. The statues that day cast confused silhouettes, all in different directions, as if each, lit separately by its own sun, existed in its own world.

There was an Alien working the corner outside McDonald's where I'd gone alone for lunch. She was standing next to her plinth instead of on it and had just removed her mask to address a Darth Vader who'd removed his. They turned and walked away before I could see her whole face.

Albert does not mention her, but once, some months after that, we were in Prague having dinner, when a troupe of fire dancers began performing in front of the restaurant where we sat. One was juggling torches, while two others, flanking him, were spinning balls of fire attached to chains. The diners applauded as the figures disappeared into the shadow of their work. The fire, spinning faster and faster, created circles of light, like the periphery of a clock, like my ceiling fan in Nice, and when the flames came close to one of the dancer's faces I thought, for a moment, I saw Debbie.

"Another circus," Albert said, turning his back on the dancers and picking up his tiny fork.

I know Albert and I won't last forever, maybe only another month, maybe only another day. He reminds me of this always. "The moment is all there is," he says, but he doesn't need to. Was it Albert I saw that day spinning in the penny, I sometimes wonder as Albert settles over me, pausing? Was it Albert who welcomed me to my new life?

"Everything is temporary," Albert likes to say, after the litany of troubles that come with the life we've chosen: the thrombosis, the peeing dogs, the pigeons, the Romanians. I look up at him, imagining an oxygen mask, the plane hitting turbulence, the masks descending from the overhead, my reaching toward him, before the plane itself blows apart.

When I say I will always love him, he reminds me that he's only my first love. "There will be others," he says. He says I will leave him, but nobody has ever left Albert. He says always that I'll grow up and leave him, but I know what he really means is that he will leave me. I'm his mirror after all and one day, I know, he'll look into my eyes and watch himself go.

Once, Albert and I were Rodin's 320th *Kiss*. We stood under the leaves on Las Ramblas perfectly still, breathing each other's air, his large hand grasping my hip, my small arm draped over his neck, our lips about to be joined, our eyes closed, blocking everything but the moment, and then blocking the moment, too. Behind my eyes, I imagine us in a museum one hundred years from now, in the Tate Modern next to the lavatory, or in the Grand Hallway of Nice's Beaux Arts, or in the shadow of someone's neglected garden.

Rodin's lovers are going to hell. That's the story that comes after *The Kiss*. But for now, before, Paolo and Francesca are lost in their ecstasy, free within a moment they are also trapped in. For now, they are eternal. What comes after eternity is another matter.

Once, we were the thousandth copy of Rodin's *Kiss*, the millionth copy, one of the billions the world will keep making. I don't believe in hell, though if it's anything like Dante's description, I don't think I'll mind it. Flying around in an endless gale, never landing, suspended for eternity, alone in the wind.

Name _Sylvia Clark_   Date _November 23, 1977_

Teacher _Mr. Barnett_   Class _5-b_

Instructions: Diagram the following sentences.

1. I guess I knew Nancy would be at the party.

2. She was there with her new boyfriend, Ted.

3. Ted is not very bright.

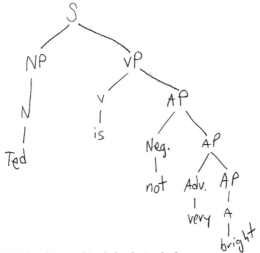

4. Ted and I were friends, but he is a bad person.

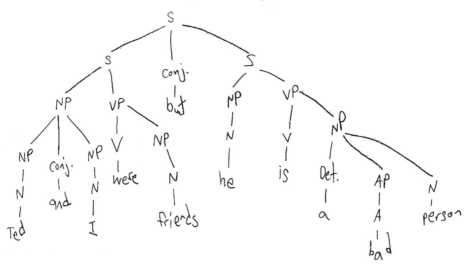

5. Nancy looked beautiful and was laughing a lot.

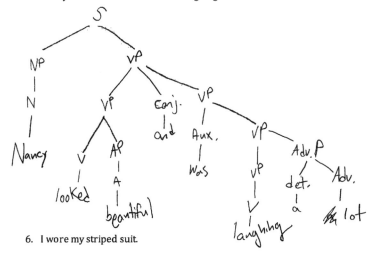

6. I wore my striped suit.

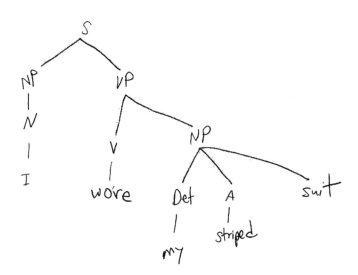

7. Everyone looked nice except for Ted.

8. Our hosts made lasagna.

9. Everyone laughed politely at a joke that was not funny.

10. Nancy made eye contact with me.

11. After dinner, Nancy went to the bathroom.

12. I followed Nancy to ask her a question.

13. When I got to the bathroom, Nancy was kissing Jeff.

14. Jeff is not her boyfriend!

15. I wondered if I should tell Ted, the way Bryan told me last year.

16. When your heart breaks, it does not make a sound.

17. The silence of heartbreak is deafening.

18. The silence may echo for months or years. You can't hear anything else.

19. For a long time, I blamed Ted.

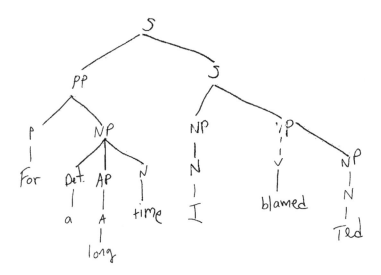

20. But now I know Ted and I are the same.

21. I hate you, Nancy!

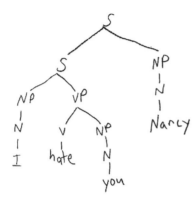

22. I thought I loved you, but I know now it was only an idea that I loved, a

shadow-puppet of your making; I loved a shadow.

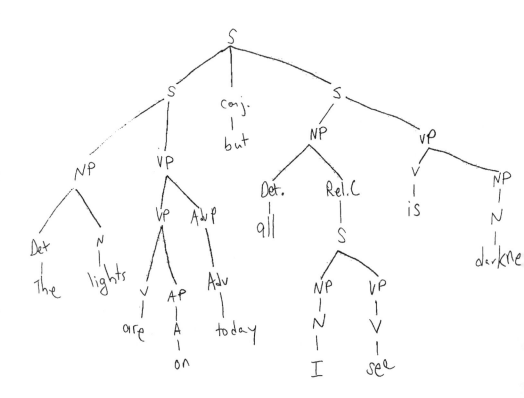

23. The lights are on today, but all I see is darkness.

the two jacobs, with an introduction by a third

I had a magnetic backgammon set when I was a kid. It was made for traveling. The pieces would stick to the board so that should you be in motion, the pieces would stay in place. I ended up playing more with the magnetism than the actual game, as backgammon opportunities rarely presented themselves, certainly not in the back of our small family's rental car on the long drives through Europe we made during school breaks.

Ruined castles, café au lait, and how many oil paintings of women beheading men or some other such violence? "Well, look at that, Jacob? Isn't *that* interesting?" Mom would ask and I'd nod, not wanting to disappoint her. It certainly was interesting, but what kind of child wants to be interested all the time? Not me. Not then. Adults forget that novelty is not actually novel for kids, since everything to them is already relentlessly new. To recognize something, to see something repeated, now that would have been special. I suppose that's why I liked watching TV. Reruns of shows I'd already seen were my favorite, whether I had liked them the first time or not. There was comfort. There was reprieve. Exhausted from wonder, there was the restful boredom I longed for.

In Europe we stood before priceless antiquities, so much less appealing than the clearly priced toys advertised between TV shows. I liked knowing what something cost. I liked the idea, too, of possessing it, as if the thing's value would then be transferred to me. Sure, the paintings of various mythic atrocities were interesting, but if you couldn't take them home and hang them above your sofa or store them in the playroom closet, what was the point?

I learned backgammon from a kid I met in Santorini one summer—his parents owned the restaurant downstairs of our hotel where my parents and I every day took our lunch. After, while Mom and Dad napped, I'd sneak down and play with Theodoris, who didn't speak any English but communicated just as well through the movement of his pieces. That's one of the things I like about the game—it provides a common language, much simpler and more true than any spoken one. There's your moves, your opponent's moves, and then the dice—fate, luck, circumstance, whatever you want to call it, the things that happen outside of your control, the double sixes or snake eyes. I never liked chess because it excludes all variables and is therefore false, artificial. It leaves no room for chance. No room for weather.

Theodoris and I played together every afternoon for three weeks. I don't remember who won the last round. I don't think we said goodbye, which is just as well, as we'd never said hello. He just pointed at the board he'd pulled down from a high shelf, and then at me who was standing there with my hands in my pockets, and began setting up the pieces. I must have been upset when we left, because my parents bought me this magnetic set in Athens before we boarded the plane home.

Backgammon was not popular in our Long Island town, so even if I were lucky enough to find a second player, I'd first have to teach my opponent the game's rules, which both of us found taxing. Following these brief lessons, we'd get through maybe half a game before my playmate would begin insisting that it was boring (novel, in other words), and could we not instead play *Super Mario Brothers*, which, of course, I didn't have.

In the wake of these failures, we'd walk over to Charlie's house down the block. Charlie had all the newest stuff, and *Super Mario Brothers,* of course, when it first came out.

I never saved the princess. I got very close, but in the end that makes no difference. You can't almost win anything after all; that's just another way to describe losing. I had made it to the castle, had passed the swinging chain of fire, and was sweating within the dragon's lair. The princess was just beyond, waiting for me to triumph, when the dragon got me.

Most kids kept playing at that point, obsessively restarting the game over until they won. It was the winter of our fourth grade's discontent, I remember, when my classmates all began showing up to school bleary-eyed and exhausted, having pulled all-nighters at their respective Nintendos. Every member of our class saved the princess that year; it was a rite of passage that I observed but did not make.

"My parents wouldn't buy me a Nintendo, Doctor," I imagine saying one day in therapy, having reached middle age and with that having decided to pay weekly for a cure to all my metaphors, "so I convinced myself that I didn't want one." My mother, on whose shoulders I shall rest the blame for all my course-defining defects, gave the same reply she gave to all of my requests growing up. When I'd ask for whatever new G.I. Joe I saw the neighbors playing with, she'd answer simply, "You don't want that, Jacob."

Devil woman! I have never been very strong willed and so, wanting to be on the winning side, I adopted hers and moved on. Of course I didn't want that. When I am past middle age and still have found no cure for myself, perhaps upon retirement from whatever profession I decide to enter, I will buy all of the splendid toys I wanted but never acquired. Can time be gotten back? Will the princess be dead by the time I arrive? Will the dragon limp to greet me when it is my turn on that far-off day and, instead of shooting fire for me to jump over or duck under, invite me in, for he is tired and has been lonely these last years waiting for me?

"My birth was the first of my misfortunes," wrote Rousseau in his long and irritating memoir. It is among mine, similarly, to have been born to parents with "taste."

"Doctor, instead of taking me to play laser tag or jump in a pool full of brilliantly hued balls at the local Mouse Center, they took me abroad to see the colorless dusty ruins of Olympia where, they explained, 'the games' had originated."

"You repeat yourself, Jacob," the doctor will not say then. For this, I will pay him.

"Doctor, instead of setting me free among the wondrous board games I saw advertised on TV—those deliciously crude and hungry hippos, that uproarious festival in which children compete at surgery, the seductive and dangerous Peppermint Forest of Candy Land—my parents decided I was to be more the 'gaming' sort."

Following my summer with Theodoris, they furnished an entire playroom in the basement with a set of alabaster craps, a Scrabble board of cruelest ivory, dominoes made of bone, a pool table of the finest felt and African blackwood, antique mahjong tiles, and a chess set with heavy Roman pawns bronzed with their swords drawn. In summer, I wore short safari suits. In winter, I was Cary Grant on a veranda, my wool trousers pleated and high-waisted, matching my sport jacket with complementary cravat. On my tenth birthday, I was presented with a silver yo-yo from Tiffany and a deck of gold-tipped cards for solitaire.

"At sleepover parties, doctor, the other boys would take turns trading super jump kick moves they had picked up in their rounds of the game at home, while I had nothing to trade. Feckless in my smoking jacket, yo-yoing in place, one by one I'd watch them attain the castle." Eventually, after the princess had been saved and everyone had gone to sleep, I'd stay awake alone before popping in the *Tetris* cartridge. This game I liked, this game I knew instinctively. Colorful shapes fell from the top of the screen, and I'd order them into complementary declivities at the screen's floor, before the completed row dissolved with a satisfying sound. Tetris was invented by an only child I am sure; even the two-player version, with its dual walled-off boards, is essentially two players playing alone.

Despite my lack of friends, my parents furnished the playroom almost exclusively with two-player games, whose rules, obviously, I had to redesign to make suitable for one. Thus my backgammon set became my Box-o-Magnets. If I faced them one way, they would fly toward one another and line up exactly edge to edge. But faced another way, like side to like side, they'd fly apart. Owing to this, I could put one chip on the board and chase it with its twin all over the board without the two ever touching, as just the nearness of the one set the other in motion.

There were two Jacobs and for both this was a problem.

How many of us recoil when a stranger says at a party, "You remind me so much of my friend Raul"? Or when a friend tells you that your exact replica, your evil, good, or middling twin, was spotted earlier that day dashing around a corner on the other side of town, or earlier that summer on the Paris Métro, or the winter prior pissing on a side street in Bangkok, or in the booth next to yours singing karaoke just before you arrived? Or perhaps you were the one saying this to someone else when you were astonished to have met a girl, just like a girl you used to know, who somehow didn't also know you, who had no recollection of breaking your heart. Why shall the twain never meet? Why do magnets fly apart?

For all four years of college, the two Jacobs had belonged to the same set of friends, each trying the whole time to chase the other out, but instead, inadvertently, locking each other in orbit. Like Jacob moons to a phantom Jacob planet—a theoretical Jacob whom both of them circled—the motion and position of one Jacob was often determined by the other's. If one of them were to somehow move out of the ellipse, the other would fly off into space—a Jacob loose, at large in the cosmos. Instead, running from each other along their reliable circle of friends, it was the Jacobs' shared antipathy that paradoxically kept them close.

The Jacobs moved seasonally, so that when one friend saw one Jacob, another friend would be seeing the other. Occasionally one Jacob might appear to move in retrograde, and as a result very rare, they might eclipse each other at a party. But mostly they were propelled through time and space, across acquaintances and friends, separately but correlatively.

It was a Tuesday in March. In places where the sun reached one felt warm, as if it were spring, but walking under a shadow, one was quickly reminded of the still-present winter.

Jacob, son of Howard and Judith Stein of Manhattan, had just finished lunch with his friend at a diner on 23rd and Third, one block north and two blocks west of his apartment. Jacob offered to walk Iris home.

At a Walk/Don't Walk on 35th Street, where the West Side Highway cuts the city from the Hudson, Jacob said: "I had told them to call me from the video store, and Mike said, 'Sure Jake, fine Jake, talk to you later Jake,' so naturally I assumed that meant he would call me from the video store. Am I crazy?"

Jacob had been making a point in all of his conversations since college to refer to himself as Jake, but his friends still called him Jacob. Though he did not mention it to his friends, it had become a point of lengthy discussion between him and his therapist. They determined together that his friends' resistance to his preferred nomenclature showed that they were, in fact, unwilling to give him a break and, further (he had inserted this into the diagnosis), that they felt threatened by his virility, by a certain untapped power they suspected he possessed. His friend Mike, for example, when he'd call would say rather casually, "Hello, Jacob," though he was obviously baiting him. Jacob was furious but, intent on being the bigger man, said nothing.

Jacob continued: "An hour and a half later, I still haven't heard from them, so I call Mike up again, and guess what he tells me? He's like, 'We're leaving the video store now, and we rented *Nashville*,' which I've already seen, which he knows, though so have they, about half a dozen times. So I'm like, 'Great, I saw that already and I don't want to see it again.' Then Mike's like, 'Why? It's awesome?' And I'm like, 'You know how I feel about Altman.' And then he's all, 'Look, Jake,'" (he'd said Jacob) "'If you don't want to watch it, that's fine.' And I was like, 'Look, yourself! You said you were gonna call from the video store! I expressly asked you to call so this wouldn't happen, and now it's happened,' and he's like, 'Well, I forgot, I guess,' and I'm like, 'Bullshit, you forgot, and at least you could have gotten a Coen brothers film. Now the whole night's ruined. You ruined my night. Thanks a lot. It's ruined.' Then he goes, 'Whatever, Altman is better than the Coen brothers anyway,' and I'm like, 'I'm not having this argument with you again,' and he goes, 'So are you coming over?' and I go, 'No. They're showing *Beverly Hills Cop* on TBS. I'll just watch that.' And he just goes, 'Suit yourself,' meaning he accepts no blame for the night's debacle."

"So you watched *Beverly Hills Cop* again?" Iris asked, as they approached the Intrepid.

"Twice," Jacob fumed. "They had it on Instant Replay. You know how they chintz you now and show the same thing twice in a row on TBS?"

"I didn't know they were doing that."

"It's terrible. I had started watching it fifteen minutes in, so after it finished I figured I'd watch the first fifteen I'd missed, but then one thing led to another and I watched the whole thing again and then a Steven Seagal picture. I got no sleep. I'm exhausted. How was your weekend?"

"Fair to miserable. Everywhere I turn I see Felix's bare ass. He's basically living with us now. And they're loud, too, pardon the expression."

"What expression?"

"I was going to say 'fucking loud,' but then got hold of myself. They stay up all night and I can't sleep from the noise, pardon the expression—I was going to say 'goddamn,' but got hold of myself— so I've resorted to drinking huge quantities of whiskey until I pass out. It's awful. I'm constantly drunk or else hungover, and I'm not even having fun.

"And the mornings are even worse than the evenings. Every day begins with Felix bare-assed in the kitchenette, blasting the stereo as he makes eggs and plays air guitar, pardon the expression. So naturally I end up getting high with him and May, you know, in an 'if you can't beat 'em join 'em' kind of way, which kills my day. How am I supposed to finish my novel under these conditions?"

"How's that going by the way?"

"I'm taking a break from it to work on other things. Been getting really into literature in translation actually. Just finished Chekhov's 'The Lady with the Dog.' It's fascinating work, translation. It gives you a much deeper insight into the social and cultural underpinnings of the original text. Like, how do you translate a mood? You can't be literal about it; you have almost to reconceive of the piece entirely. I'm translating Mallarmé now. Eventually, I'll have translated all of the French Symbolists into Pig Latin. That's the goal. Then I guess I'll try and find an agent. But the point is, they never leave. They keep saying they're going to leave, but then they never do. They say, "Oh, we're gonna leave right after 'the game,' which, so far as I can tell, is always on and has never not been on. So I sit there, watching football with them, right? Figuring it'll be over any minute, right? While May screams at the TV, as if she even knows what's happening, pardon the expression. And then Felix has to console her, 'cause she gets all worked up over their team. He's all, 'Calm down, sweetie,' and then he starts farting to cheer her up, which makes May get weirdly lovey-dovey until they're making out again next to me on the couch. And then May's like, 'Felix, no! Iris is here! You're making her uncomfortable. Suddenly my comfort matters. And I'm like, 'No, it's fine.' So that was Saturday."

"Why don't you move out?"

"She's the one with the boyfriend! She should move out!"

"Yeah," Jacob said, pressed over the railing, squinting absently at the dark water below, "but is she going to?"

"That's not the point."

* * *

In Clinton Park, they took up two swings out of a set of four facing east toward the highway and beyond that, the city itself. On the far end, one swing was occupied by a freckled boy who, once they got on, jumped from the highest point and landed low in a crouching position, before running to his mother, who was already yelling at him.

They swung in silence for a few minutes before Jacob said, "I'm thinking of going into analysis full time."

"Don't you already?"

"No, I go to therapy three times a week for forty minutes, but if I committed to analysis, I would go every day for a full hour. I just feel like I've got a lot of work to do, you know? And I never felt ready to commit to it before. I was so busy with college. But now might be the right time."

"Or you could get a job."

"Yeah, no," he considered, "I have too many issues that need to be sorted before I can start my career, otherwise it just won't work. How's the bookstore?"

"The store detective is on to me. I'll be reading something in the stacks, you know, just before I shelve it, and look up to find his eyes looming above the shelf. It's so violating, like when a tall person walks into a public restroom and you see their head over the partition. It's really annoying, too, because then I have to stop reading and pretend I'm shelving until he leaves. I can't get through a single paragraph; I end up rereading the same thing over and over again, which only slows my shelving, so it's not like he's helping any."

"I thought the store detective was for shoplifters."

"Exactly. I don't know what his problem is. Otherwise, it's not bad. I do enjoy dressing like a librarian."

"Is there a dress code?"

"No."

* * *

At 57th Street, seeing how the day showed no signs of ending, they decided to continue into Central Park.

"Binkies—now with more bacon! 'Cause if you like Twinkies and you like bacon, you'll love Binkies! You take the two most amoral foods and combine them. It'd be huge," she said. "I bet they had them in Rome, you know, toward the end."

"Jake's Crack and Steak House. 'Cause if you like crack and you like steak, you'll love Jake's Crack and Steak House."

"You'd have to make sure your customers order the crack after the steak, though, otherwise they won't be hungry."

"But seriously," she asked at the duck pond, "where *do* the ducks go in the winter?"

"Is Orange Julius the full name of the inventor of the drink, or is it just Julius, and orange pertains to the flavor? There's no Pink Julius or any other kind of Julius . . ." Jacob paused to think, then shook his head. "Yeah. It's baffling."

"What's weird is the way you never see them advertised but they are nevertheless in permanent stock," he went on, navigating the ramble.

"They don't have to advertise. Twinkies are an institution, a fact more than a food. I wonder if they're in the dictionary."

"I'll check when I get home." Jacob kicked at an old leaf that had attached itself to his shoe. "Who eats them is what I wannna know. I don't know anyone who actually eats them!"

"I used to eat them. My mom bought them in bulk. I think had we been god-fearing people, she wouldn't have. My mom really gets me sometimes. How can you go around buying Twinkies? If I were a social worker and found Twinkies in a household, I'd yank the kid right out of there."

"Maybe your mom bought them as a sort of moral test?"

"Well, I failed then. I ate a lot of them. They're delicious."

"We should have a Twinkie and booze party and keep careful count of who eats them and how many. That would be a really interesting experiment." Jacob regarded a squirrel as it regarded him.

"So then Jake says, 'I can't hang out, 'cause I busted my thumb sliding down a banister last night.'"

Jacob puffed. "What the hell is that?"

"He said he was at a party and one thing led to another."

"Who of our age has a banister?"

"Have you ever hung out with him when he's drunk?"

"I try not to hang out with him at all. His bourgeois platitudes unnerve me. Actually, that's not true, I just wanted to work 'bourgeois platitudes' into conversation."

"I'm that way with 'urban malaise.'"

"I can't stand his whole Woody Allen shtick. He's from Atlanta and has a mild disposition. It's ridiculous. Plus, the whole Jake thing: 'Hi, I'm Jake. Call me Jake.' It's so actorly."

"Anyway, he speaks highly of you."

"He's just trying to be the bigger man, which is also irritating. I'm the bigger man. Me. I am."

"So he'll be drinking, right, not showing any signs of drunkenness except that he gets more quiet than usual, and then, out of nowhere, he begins apologizing, in a whisper, for his 'loquaciousness.' That's how he says it. By the way, you'll like this: I asked him if he kept vocab. flashcards in his nightstand in place of the bible to read before going to sleep every night, and he just looked at me."

"He was probably wondering how you knew."

"So he'll be all reserved and big wordy, pardon the expression. God, I can't speak anymore. I think I'm getting stupid from overexposure to May and Felix. Anyway, the next thing I know, he's scaling the nearest wall. We actually got kicked out of a club for this. The bouncer didn't even allow him to come all the way down;

they just plucked him off the wall and deposited him outside. He was wearing flip-flops and one fell off and I had to go back in and get it. After that we rearranged the letters on a bulletin board outside of a church. I don't remember doing it, but he said it was hilarious.

"What'd you make it say?"

"I forget."

"And then another time, a bunch of us were walking along Sixth, between A and B, right? And out of nowhere, Jake gets up on the hood of a parked car and starts leaping from hood to hood all the way to the end of the block. When we caught up to him, he was just standing there with his hands in his pockets, and he goes, 'Sorry about that,' and that's it."

Jacob shrugged.

"You should make a movie where you just go on walks with different people and talk to them about their resentments. You can call it, *I Hate That*. I'm gonna get a knish." —Iris

"Here, give me a piece." —Jacob

"Gross," she said, finishing the knish and squinting across the baseball field. "Why did I eat that?"

"It's important to eat certain foods periodically, if only to remind oneself that one doesn't ever want to eat them again."

"Remember that guy, what's his name?" Iris asked. "The one with the hair? You know who I'm talking about? He was, like, always just there? No, seriously, you know who I'm talking about. He was like this guy who was just, like, always there freshman year. I run into him all the time now. I always run into people I have no desire to see, but the ones I do want to see, I never see, or if I do, I'm hungover and there's dried vomit in my hair."

"If I see someone I recognize, I automatically cross the street."

* * *

Iris regarded the small new leaves on a particular tree. The wind blew. "Simone de Beauvoir talked about male brothels. There was a specific example she cited in San Francisco, but she said that, ultimately, male prostitution would not satisfy the feminine destiny. I love that she wrote an entire book about feminism solely to justify her unhealthy relationship to Sartre."

"Is that really why?" Jacob asked.

"I should stop reading it. It's depressing how much I identify with her description of all the non-liberated types."

"I feel the same way about masturbation in *Portnoy's Complaint*," said Jacob, who, inhaling deeply, noted to himself that fall was in the air, though winter was not yet over and summer had not yet begun.

"That's another thing. Why are men's novels so chock-full of cock? Especially the literary ones. Meanwhile, there are zero vaginas in the Edith Wharton universe. Female writers never write about vaginas, but for some reason—is that the reason?—their work is taken less seriously. Meanwhile, cocks abound. And to critical acclaim!"

"That's what you should call your novel," Jacob said, regarding a statue flanking the Central Park promenade that was also regarding him.

"What's what I should call my novel?"

"*Cocks Abound to Critical Acclaim.*"

"Yeah," Iris said thoughtfully. "But wait. So I'm watching this French film the other day. Typical French fare—older married woman, adolescent boy, and a touch of incest 'cause I think she was his aunt or something. Anyway, the main character is a violin student in love with the middle-aged wife of his instructor. So he goes one time to sit in longing outside of their log cabin in the middle of winter or whatever, and there is this voice-over describing his quiet passion, and it's all very romantic and then the next subtitle reads, 'It was cold where I sat on the log, and my testicles shriveled when a frigid wind blew.' I mean, is that really necessary?"

"That's what's called 'significant detail,'" said Jacob. "From that detail alone, I can guess the temperature, pressure, and nearness of an approaching cold front. Call me a misogynist, but I'm not sure vaginas are as weather sensitive. Not to change the subject, but you know Henry James scalded his balls? I read that in his letters."

"What are you gonna do now?" Iris asked, looking up the street at a flashing Walk sign.

"I don't know. I'm supposed to have dinner with my parents tonight, so I'll probably just go home, stare at the wall for an hour, then iron my pants. You?"

"Go home, I guess. Ugh. They always leave the door unlocked when they're having sex. It's like they want me to walk in on them. It's like May's so psyched to finally not be a virgin she's got to parade it around. They probably implanted some kind of tracking device while I was passed out from the whiskey, so they could always know when I'm about to walk in the door. I can see her being like, 'Quick, she's coming! Unlock the door and get that hairy ass unsheathed!' They're driving me crazy, Jacob. I mean, you know how I feel about swearing."

"My therapist has actually been encouraging me to swear more."

"Call me soon," she said, putting her hand out for a shake.

"Come on, Ms. Smyles. You can manage a hug."

"It's just that, I know you're trying to cop feels," she said, standing stiffly in Jacob's arms.

The wind rose as they stood near the entrance to the subway. He whispered in her ear. "My balls feel like compacted acorns."

"Gross."

"I'm sure it works better in voice-over."

Jacob, son of Alice and Samuel Beller of Atlanta, traced the spine of the girl with her eyes closed. Half covered by a white sheet, she lay next to him while he looked out the window above her. A warm March light cast in on them from the south.

He had met her the previous night in a bar on the Lower East Side that many of the local college students frequented, that he'd frequented when he was in college, too. She was twenty, still in school, studying painting at Cooper Union, and from New Hampshire. It was her second year, and she lived in a dormitory provided by the college.

She'd been impressed when she arrived at Jacob's apartment after midnight because she didn't have to be signed in by any dormitory guard, and because once upstairs she could pour a glass of water from the kitchen sink without any concern over dining hall hours.

Earlier that night she had been impressed by his easy attitude, his knowingness. For her, ordering a drink at a bar was not yet routine, but when Jake ordered, his manner of speaking to the bartender, the way he placed the amaretto sour in her hand and then sipped his own Bushmills on the rocks, made her feel worldly, as if her meeting a man and having a drink with him at a bar, "a highball," he'd called it, were indeed a casual thing.

For her, nothing was ever casual. In high school she'd been shy and spent most of her time in the art room. She had never been "cool" or easy going, was nothing like Lauren Bacall or any other of the old movie stars she admired in the films she borrowed from the library, until she met Jacob, who'd made her feel somehow totally in control of the situation, though it was he who had begun speaking to her, he who'd purchased the drinks, he who had asked the questions, and he who took her home. He had a way, despite these facts, of making her feel as if it were all her doing, as if she were seducing him, and like this, he'd seduced her.

She'd had sex with only one person before, her high school boyfriend of four years who now attended The University of Pittsburgh and didn't know what his major should be, with whom she had broken up during the summer following freshman year. She had been waiting patiently since then to meet the right guy. And though she had said confidently, next to the sink, "Listen, Jake. I'm not going to have sex with you tonight, we'll just hang out a while;" the way he reacted, "We can do whatever we want," disarmed her.

It was his use of the word *we*—boys who had tried with her before never said *we*. This dialogue was common enough, but always the boys had said, "We can do whatever *you* want." The *we* Jacob used made it feel completely different, made it sound as if they were deciding together, responsibly, like adults, what the best course of action would be. The *we* had released her from thinking that it was her responsibility to stop, that it was expected of him to try to go further, that she had to be on her guard because in the game of love he was her opponent rather than her ally.

Jacob's "whatever we want" changed everything. If they had sex that night, it would not be because she suffered a defeat, it would not be him conquering her, it would not be because he was a man and was therefore supposed to follow through if allowed, but because he and she had decided together, because *they* wanted to, because they were on the same side, because he liked her and she liked him.

Not that she thought of all these things or even any of them while he was taking off her bra, but just that his "we" invited her to attend to a question that had never before occurred to her: What did she want? Always, before that, it had been a matter of what she didn't. Until then, sex had been a matter of *noes* and shades of *no*. Even her past yes had been made through no's absence. But with this new question they began kissing, he began unbuttoning her shirt, and so she began asking this man between her still denim-clad legs, "Do you have a condom?"

Which somehow she managed expertly to slide on before guiding him into her above and astride him. Though she had never in her previous romances taken control, here she was now grabbing the bedpost to keep it from slamming against the wall, bringing him to climax between her thighs, here she was in command of both of them.

He had a way with his hands, cautiously touching her face afterward, her cheek, her hair, as if she were made of porcelain and he didn't want to leave fingerprints. He kissed the side of her face, her closed eyelids, her forehead, and her chin in a similar way, a way that was somehow both intimate and anonymous, as if she were a rare, delicate thing picked up off the shelf to be carefully considered. She had never been so closely observed, and through his careful observation, she felt as if she were meeting herself for the first time, that he was introducing her to someone special, whom she liked.

Through a variety of experiences, the effective caress is distilled. Though people insist or like to insist that each caress given, each movement of the tongue, each gaze is unique to each pairing, in truth these gestures are often an echo of previous ones. So when the girl with her eyes closed whose spine was being traced felt an unlikely combination of intimacy and anonymity, it was because Jacob, having had many mornings like this one, was grasping the situation as much as he was grasping her. He traced the unique contour of her spine, as he had traced many spines before.

Jacob gathered her round the waist and exhaled into the nape of her neck.

When Jacob's girlfriends would think back to these nights, though—recalling the way his hand had outlined their bodies, the way he had made so careful a study of them—and expect, therefore, the phone to ring at any minute, it was because they had confused an acknowledgment of their special curve of the back for a testament, meditation, and promise of love.

Her name was Heidi, and they did it again in the morning before going out for breakfast.

He asked her where she wanted to go, and when she didn't answer he took her there anyway. He was careful to maintain her feeling of control over the situation, which had, in the few moments of dressing, descending the stairs, and emerging onto the bright street, abruptly flagged.

She stood on the sidewalk awkwardly now, not knowing exactly how one acted in such situations, if he really wanted to see more of her and so had asked her to breakfast, or if he had wanted only a way out, a way to get her out of his apartment politely, and so had traded on breakfast as the best means of escape. She was about to make her excuses, too, to get out of there fast, and thus avoid his wanting to avoid her, when he emerged from the doorway a moment later, looked at her as he skipped down the stoop, and touched her face gently before kissing her sure on the mouth.

He grabbed her by the waist and pulled her toward him. "God, you're beautiful," he said, looking at her squint in the sun. And she, trying to hold back a smile and offer instead the gentle irony that had so charmed him the night before, said, "I bet you say that to all the gods."

He took her hand and they began walking west. "So where would you like to go?" was his response.

She considered herself smart and knew he had likely behaved this same way with many girls before; it was exactly this air of experience that had hurt her feelings and attracted her to him both, as if by seducing him last night, she were actually winning him back, as if she'd already lost him to the past, as if their first meeting were the commencement of that loss.

But if she saw through him, if she showed him what she saw

and overtly acknowledged that she was one of many in a long line, would that make her special in that line? Could she win? If he had, in fact, seduced her into seducing him by putting on his well-rehearsed show, could she become after the curtain fell—after the sun rose—the critic reviewing it? Could she tell him now how it was or wasn't convincing?

They took a booth at the 7A diner, a place she had never been. She usually took her meals in the college dining hall. They each remarked on what a beautiful day it was, for beautiful days are always remarkable even if they're all the same. Slipping into her seat, she tried not to show her excitement at all of the hiply disheveled diners surrounding them. It was a very New York scene, she thought, and felt suddenly as she had only very rarely in the last two years, that she was truly living in Manhattan, that she was at last a grownup.

Most of the time she felt just outside of it all, as if she were always approaching the city from the bridge, always about to arrive but never getting there, and she liked him even more.

His expression across from her, as he read the menu with a wrinkled forehead under messy curls, seemed exactly to encapsulate New York's worried and chaotic charm. Its neurotic dignity was how she thought of it. Here, thoughts, like buildings, sprang up in odd juxtaposition, creating tensions that exhilarated, annoyed, and provoked. The way the trash piled up on the sidewalk, for example, to her, looked beautiful. In her hometown, trash, evidence of life as it was being lived, was never seen but removed quickly and cleanly. But New York City was full of waste, of things being used and discarded, creating temporary monuments of garbage. It was romantic. It was cruel. Jacob looked up while a collection of silverware sounded in the kitchen. "Do you know what you're going to have?"

"I like the way you pronounce every word fully. It's very refreshing," she said smiling at him, "your stiffness of speech. The casual is so overrated, don't you think?"

"Thank you, Heidi," he said, pronouncing each consonant pointedly. The waitress, in a worn black T-shirt with the neck cut out and a tattoo of a red heart encircling the word REGRET on the inside of her forearm, appeared beside their table. She had a shock of yellow hair pinned back haphazardly, and a pale, very striking Icelandic face. She was beautiful and didn't seem to care. Heidi watched Jacob to see if he noticed her beauty, her not caring, the whole effect of it. Jacob smiled and said something, which made the waitress laugh, who then answered, "No, the tattoo has nothing to do with you."

Heidi, distracted, hadn't heard the first part, so when they both laughed she didn't know what was funny and offered instead a polite closed-mouth smile. After they ordered, Jacob leaned across the table. "Would you mind if I sat next to you?"

Next to her, he opened her hand under the table and traced the lines on her palm.

He looked at her face as she looked straight ahead, not being sure where to look.

She let the busboy refill her coffee one more time than she actually wanted because she was starting to become nervous again. Breakfast was ending and they would be saying goodbye and she realized he still hadn't asked for her number.

He paid for their breakfast without any fanfare, which she liked because the boys she knew in college never offered to pay, or if they did they were awkward about it, made it seem too big of a deal, which made her so uncomfortable she often insisted on treating them instead, if only to allay their discomfort, which resulted in a battle over the check which, when she won, humiliated them both. The effusive thanks that followed only made things worse and prompted her once, upon leaving a restaurant, to open the door for her date and say gallantly, "After you!" He did not kiss her goodnight but waved as if he were spotting her across the room, though they were standing within two feet of each other. "I'll call you," she'd said, waving back.

Outside, Jacob and Heidi walked north without saying a word. Then Jacob said, "So what are your plans today?"

"I have a class at five but, I don't know if I'm going to go." She was going to go, but now... "You?"

"It's such a great day. Would you like to go for a walk?

"Sure."

"Is it too far for you if we go by the East River?"

"No. Yeah. No. That would be fine."

They crossed Fifth Street and continued east in the shade. The stubborn winter air was still very present and only tempered in the areas where the sunlight touched it. "Are you cold?" he asked. "Do you want my sweater?"

"No," she said, with folded arms. "I'm fine."

Two blocks later she put his sweater on over her own.

They walked north along the East River and failed to find the entrance to the promenade, which had been gated off for construction.

"It's nice being near the water. I always forget that Manhattan is an island," she said looking at the side of his face.

"Me too," he said, looking through the fence, having spoken and heard her remark many times before.

"It's such a great day," she said again.

Jacob took her hand, which she had made available some time ago by letting it hang discreetly at her side.

23rd Street, under the sun

JACOB: Have you been to the Central Park Zoo?

HEIDI: No. I haven't explored much of the city yet. Most of my friends just hang out around the area.

JACOB: You have to see the sea lions. You have a certain sea-lion quality.

HEIDI: I get that a lot.

JACOB: Let's go right now. Let's go right now, what do you think?

HEIDI: Sure.

(*He pulls her hand taut in their new direction.*)

HEIDI (*crossing FDR Drive*): Do you think I should incorporate more slang into my vernacular?

JACOB (*raising his voice over the traffic*): What?

HEIDI (*raising her voice*): Do you think I should incorporate more slang into my vernacular?

JACOB: I think you should speak Latin.

She didn't have a MetroCard, so he swiped her through the subway turnstile and then reached back for her hand. On the platform they sat next to each other on a bench, continuing to hold hands even though they'd gotten soggy from being clasped for so long. Remembering a *Cosmo* article that said "clammy hands" means "bad in bed," she worried he might think she had sweaty palms, but then figured, clasped together, maybe one couldn't tell whose hand was the clammy one. Anyway, he didn't seem to notice. Or was he thinking about that too?

At the zoo entrance he insisted on paying her admission while she feigned frustration over his unnecessary chivalry. He said, "A princess never pays," and she said, "If I'm a princess, what are you?" and he said, "Your suitor, your knight, your jester, your cantaloupe."

"Cantaloupe?"

"Your sweet, melon-shaped refusal. But I will win you," he said, finding her eyes.

Jacob made up a story about each species exhibited, and Heidi responded with a teasing sarcasm, of which she hadn't before known herself capable. They moved through three hours this way, their language becoming more strange and more their own.

"I'm going to start smoking today," she announced, as a bored polar bear rolled off into the water. "I require a vice."

In the Giraffe House, Jacob asked if it was a problem that he was slightly shorter than her.

"Of course," she answered. "You should ride an elephant to make up for it. You'd look good on an elephant. Though I'm not sure where you'd keep it in New York."

"I have an alcove," said Jacob.

"Or, if you're open to plastic surgery, you could have your toes removed and reattached to the top of your head. That would give you at least another inch." When he moved close to kiss her, she stopped him and said, "I will allow you to kiss me now."

"Are you going back downtown?" Jacob said at the entrance to the 4, 5, and 6.

She nodded. "You?"

"I think I might meet up with some friends."

"Oh." She looked down. "I guess this is goodbye then. By the way, I preferred the naked mole rats to the sea lions. Their habitat reminds me more of dormitory life."

"Heidi," he said, looking squarely at her. "I've spent the whole day with you, and still you've somehow managed to avoid giving me your phone number."

"Well, Jake," she pronounced his name carefully, "you never asked."

"I'm terrified of rejection."

"Do you have a pen?"

"I'll program it into my cell, wait." He reached into his bookbag and removed a large phone. "Okay, go."

"555-631-2405."

"Is that your real number?"

"It's my father's. You'll have to ask the king's permission before you're allowed to take out the princess," she said, smiling nervously. "That's just the way we do it in the kingdom of New Hampshire."

"I was actually about to ask you for his number. Do you think he'll like me?"

She looked at him sideways. "No. This is probably it for us."

"We'll have to meet clandestinely then. Like, at the mall."

"By the Orange Julius. We can wear disguises."

"We can go disguised as each other."

"I will have to make myself shorter."

"Come here," he said.

Heidi looked at him and feigned reluctance before coming closer, before he kissed her, before she closed her eyes.

"I guess I better get back," she said after. "Stir-fry in the dining hall tonight."

"You shouldn't miss that," he said, kissing her again.

"Yes, well," she said, separating. "Oh, your sweater, wait!"

"That's okay, you can borrow it."

Was the city filled with his abandoned sweaters?

"No, it's okay. I'll be fine on the way home. Thanks though."

"Please keep it."

"I'll just give it to you now. It's not a big deal," she said, making it a big deal.

"Heidi," he said looking into her eyes, "We're going to see each other again."

"I know," she said, taking it off. "Here." She handed it to him. "I better go," she said, looking at his mouth and then his shoes.

Jacob placed his hands on both her shoulders and leaned in to kiss her goodbye. Heidi waited for him to kiss her goodbye, unable to move or kiss back. He came close to her face, which remained level, close to her mouth, which remained in place, and then at the last moment he moved just to the left, so that his mouth landed between her cheek and lips. He looked at her again with his hands in his pockets. Heidi opened her mouth but nothing came out.

"I'll call you tomorrow," he said reassuringly, as her eyes zigzagged across him a few times, before she turned and waved and disappeared down the subway steps.

Jacob stood for a moment and looked around, then removed his jacket to replace his sweater. He pulled his phone from his bookbag and dialed.

"It's Jake. What are you up to?"

Mike worked as an assistant at a boutique literary agency in Manhattan. He spent a lot of time reading manuscripts from the slush pile, none of them good according to Mike, and conversations with him often turned toward what he referred to as "the excremental cannon." Jacob considered himself a writer, though he didn't do much actual writing.

Still, he was not *not* a writer—he had taken a poetry workshop back in college, where he had also written an experimental play titled, "Hide the Matzo!" It was called "bizarre" in the school newspaper. Not even he was sure what it was about.

Since then, he had dabbled in a lot of things: oil painting, pantomime, sculpture, Fibonacci numbers, Zulu history, French architecture, documentary filmmaking, astrology, fencing, interior design, Belgian cooking, international relations, archaeology, Rollerblading, linguistics, saxophone, astronomy, salsa, criminal justice, feminism, aquatic therapy, community garden preservation, comparative religions, anesthesiology, penguin sex, water sports, veganism, communism, libertarianism, anarchism, Spain, clothing design, event planning, psychology, and boat building. And while fascinated by each, after an interval, he either lost interest or forgot he was interested.

Auxiliary careers aside, the dynamic struck between Mike and Jacob was very self-consciously that of Mike's Edmund Wilson to Jacob's F. Scott Fitzgerald. Jacob was romantic and weak willed, like Fitzgerald, while Mike was severe and highly critical, so they intimated to each other. To both of their delights, Mike would spend a lot of time ruminating on and castigating Jacob's many flaws. Jacob, in turn, would listen dutifully, for the most part agree with Mike, become occasionally angry and then, after being told that his unreasonable temper and inability to be honest with himself was a major obstacle to his growth, acquiesce, and for the most part enjoy the whole thing.

Jacob was terribly self-involved—one of Mike's recurring observations—so, good or bad, any analysis of his character was attention he relished. Even when Mike's remarks sent him spiraling into an unpleasant depressive display, he thrilled to the wound, though he would not admit this, for it allowed him to roll up inside himself and ponder for a few minutes, maybe even a few hours, all the layers of sorrow and shame that made up his mental disfigurement.

Jacob's frequent expressions of self-deprecation were not so much a confession of insecurity or low self-esteem as they were a celebration of his uniquely flawed mosaic-like character. To put himself down was also to exalt. Polishing his "personal failings" until they sparkled, he liked to show them off, the attractiveness of their sheen proven by the number of women who had already been glamoured by them.

Though Jacob never advertised his sexual conquests, but rather covered them up with more self-deprecation, Mike was acutely aware of his success in this department and more than a little jealous of his friend's mutually agreed upon unworthiness. It had been openly noted many times that Mike had the superior mind, was physically more substantial—he was six feet, two inches to Jacob's five feet, seven and a half—had a job, was in a band, had ambition, discipline, and yet, for reasons inexplicable to Mike, women always fell for Jacob, leaving Mike to go home early Saturday nights and strum his guitar alone before returning to his poetry manuscript.

"Probably go back to Brooklyn, watch *Nashville* again; Matt has it out from Blockbuster," Mike told Jacob over the phone.

Often in college, due in part to dormitory life, pairs develop, dynamic duos, and in the case of Mike and Matt, un-dynamic duos. Mike and Matt, since their meeting in college three years ago, had forged a bond of brilliant dullness. Boredom was the thing they shared more than anything. They were not bored in a disdainful or interesting French sort of way, nor did they view boredom as a thing to be remedied. Moreover, boredom was their habitat, their climate, and métier. Seeing themselves as those still waters that run deep, they cultivated their bland exteriors as a means to suggest the wild invisible torrents coursing beneath them.

Matt, who was fond of quoting, put it—"'As the artist matures, the personality falls away.' —Freud."

Matt worked as a bank teller at the Chase on 57th Street, and in his free time cultivated a T. S. Eliot–like persona minus the affected speech patterns. Chipping away at literature in loud quietude, he lived on the outskirts of his favorite books and was concerned primarily with criticism and footnotes. This passion, along with his passion for discretion, manifested in occasional surface ripples—a quote emerging now and then from his otherwise extended silences.

And though he viewed himself as an artist, as an intellectual, and as an aesthete whose purpose was more than mere survival, his art was vague. Rather, he did not actually, nor did he want to, create anything. He neither wrote, nor played, nor sculpted, nor painted. He did not even nurse the slightest interest in movie direction. Still, he viewed his job as a banker as just a shell for his spirit, just a place, like life, to live for a while. Why not be a banker, or a wood carver or a drugstore cashier, or anything else for that matter? Thus he quietly rebelled against ambition, upward mobility, manifest destiny, and all of his parents' monetary investments in his schooling heretofore. After all, why should the spirit be corrupted by allowing access to it? He kept, the best he could, body and soul apart.

His integrity, as he saw it, was greater than that of "the starving artist" who sacrificed his own life for his art and was ruled by the desire to create it. Art was a corruption of the soul, a gross translation of it. Whereas Matt's motives were purely elemental. Proudly, he was not a banker/poet like that pompous T. S. Eliot, but a banker, no more, no less.

"You wanna get a drink later?" Jacob said into the phone, leaning against the entrance to the 4, 5, and 6.

"I can't. I'm broke till the end of the week. You can come and watch *Nashville* if you want," said Mike.

"I'll buy the drinks. I don't know about *Nashville*."

"All right. Someplace in Brooklyn though," Mike said.

"When are you leaving work?"

"In a half hour probably. I'll call you when I'm out."

Jacob stopped for a burger at Soup Burg on Lex and 77th, and chewed and stared before wandering into Central Park as dusk settled. He thought about Heidi and then promptly forgot about her. An hour and a half later his phone rang.

"I just got home," Mike said. We're going to The Hat in DUMBO if you wanna meet us."

When Jacob arrived, Mike and Matt were silently eating dinner at the bar.

"What's up?" Jacob said.

Jacob ordered the salmon.

"You should eat a steak every now and then. It doesn't look good to surround yourself with so much pink. It's a bit effeminate, Jake," his father said in front of the waitress, before ordering the duck for himself.

"Why don't *you* get a steak then?" returned Jacob.

"At my age, I have nothing to prove."

"I'll have the braised quail," said his mother with a closed mouth smile, as she handed the menu back to the waitress.

Jacob's father was a snake-nut-can. That is, he looked like a can of nuts, but when you unscrewed the lid, a wire-spring snake jumped out. This combination of traditional snack outside and surprise-filled inside, he attributed to prep school. Having attended Wathen, as his father and his father had before him, and thoroughly absorbed its culture, the older man delighted in practical jokes, believing they built character on both ends of the gag. Thus he had endeavored to raise his son similarly, regarding Jacob less as a child and more of a freshman, and with that subjecting him to a series of initiatory hazings.

There was a downside to such a method, however. In prep school the upperclassmen eventually depart, leaving the freshmen who have successfully endured whatever trauma to assume the former's place, whereupon they can then perpetuate their joyous abuses onto the next incoming class. But from their family, Jacob's father would never graduate. Jacob, then, would always be freshman to the older man, would always be, until the day his father died—an eventuality even more intolerable to his mind than his father's overwhelming presence—the butt of every joke. And though his father encouraged mutiny in the boy, indeed hoped for it on his son's part, Jacob both knowing and refusing to know this, reacted by emotionally balling into an ever-ready defensive crouch. His father responded by calling him Gandhi.

"Dad—"

"I think it's time you started calling me Howard, Jake."

"Howard," he continued, though this of course threw him for yet another loop, "And how shall I refer to Mom now?"

"Mom is still fine," his mother broke in.

"Howard and Mom, Jake."

"Oh, Howard," she said smiling and grabbing his arm, "Why do you torture him like this?"

"No, Mom, it's fine. So, How. How's business?"

"Business is businesslike. And you? Have you thought at all about what you're going to do?"

"Well, my therapist recommends analysis, and I think that might be a good idea. Perhaps it will speed up the whole process."

"You know you can come work for me whenever you're ready."

"What would I be doing?"

"A little bit of this, a little bit of that at first, and then we'll see."

Jacob was filled with horror at the idea of his doing a little bit of this and a little bit of that for his father, and then seeing.

His mother interceded. "Don't pressure him, Howard. He needs time to figure out in what direction he wants to go. I think analysis might help. I'm for it, Jacob. You just take your time."

"All this time-taking. What the boy needs is to get his feet wet, Judy, do a little work without thinking so much about it. All this clarity, what good could possibly come from it? What is he going to be an astronaut? He just needs to work, that's all. Jake, no one decides what they're going to be; they just do, and then they are."

"Let's talk about something else," his mother said. "How is the apartment, do you need anything? I just bought these cute little potholders for you. You can stop by later and pick them up. They have the most adorable duck print."

"I don't know, Dad. I have some ideas. I've been working on this screenplay and I think it might turn out all right."

"Oh, that sounds lovely Jacob," his mother said. "What is it about?"

"It's about a guy who gets thrown out of Exeter for cheating on an exam, Latin or Greek, I haven't decided yet, but he doesn't tell his parents. He somehow manages to keep them from finding out for a while. Since it's only the middle of fall term though, what he does is, he secretly moves out to their summer house in Nantucket and works as a fry-cook at the club restaurant where he falls in love with a waitress from the lower classes. He brings her home on Christmas break to inform his parents of their pending nuptials, but the whole thing blows up when she sees how many antiques his parents own. There's this great scene where she starts crying and then lets him have it in front of a painting of a schooner. At the end, loveless, he decides to attend a vocational school in the inner city to learn welding or soldering or something, hoping he might get her back by becoming proficient in a trade. It's like a reverse Gatsby. I'm not sure if anyone dies though. Maybe his Aunt Marion." Jacob had not written a word.

"Well, I'd love to read it when you're finished," his mother said.

"I just started it though, so it will be some time before I can show you anything."

His father motioned to the waitress for more wine.

"All right, do that. Stew's friend Jarrel is a literary agent. When it's finished you'll send it to him."

"Yeah," Jacob said, "I don't know, we'll see. It might come out terrible."

"I'm sure it's excellent." His mother smiled. "So how are your friends, what are they up to?"

"I haven't been keeping up with them. Though I ran into Whit the other day on the M11. He's at Goldman now. Nice shoes and all that, but what a bore."

"That's too bad, but it can't be helped. His mother's exactly the same. I bumped into her at Citarella last week and she talked my ear off about what I can't remember. I was about to leave without buying anything and just come back later and do my shopping then, but luckily I was able to sneak off as she placed an order for a veal steak. What about the others? You used to have so many friends, Jacob."

"They were circumstantial, Mom. We have nothing in common anymore."

"Nonsense, they're your friends. You're just going through a phase." His mother waved it off.

"All friends are circumstantial, Jake," his father said with his fork. "That's why it's important to stay in touch. You never know when you might want to revisit certain circumstances, or worse, when you are without circumstances all together. One needs friends, Jacob."

"I suppose," Jacob responded, as a waiter, cake in hand, began singing "Happy Birthday."

Everyone in the restaurant turned toward Jacob, as the waiter placed the cake on the table exactly in front of him. His father announced, "Come on, Jake, blow out the candles!"

"Thank you," Jacob said quietly to the waiter, who then returned to the kitchen. "It's not my birthday, Dad," Jacob whispered across the table.

"Howard. I know. I wanted to surprise you. If I did it on your birthday, you'd have seen it coming a mile away."

If Jacob's nerves were a gong, his father's jokes were the mallet. His father smiled as Jacob rung.

Squirming in his chair now, Jacob grew smaller in direct proportion to his father's expanding smile. He had the fleeting thought that once he was small enough he might climb up onto his father's great chin, slide sideways through a gap in his massive teeth, and with a flashlight search the cave of his mouth. For what? His father laughed and as he did, Jacob felt himself bounce up and down, as if the restaurant floor were his father's tongue, and he and his mother this whole time had been sitting atop it.

"Jacob! It's just a joke," said his father, shaking his head. "You take after your mother."

"Yes," said Jacob, having once again found his father's antics more unnerving than humorous. His mother squeezed his arm.

It's not that he was humorless, as his father so often suggested, it was just that he felt he had always to be on guard around the older man, half expecting that as they would be leaving the restaurant later, some new surprise, impossible to anticipate, awaited. Maybe a group of pygmies, whom his father had hired just for kicks, would assail him as they rounded 57th and Park, one jumping on his back, as his father looked on, laughing good-naturedly.

For his part, his father, seeing how vulnerable and tightly wound his son was, thought these set-ups, besides being hilarious, therapeutic and would work as an antidote to his son's oversensitivity. If he surprised him enough, scared him enough, he'd eventually become inured to all that worried him.

With this in mind, when Jacob was growing up, his father had often jumped out from darkened rooms, eager to spook the boy and with that to cure him, making Jacob's trips up the stairs to bed every night a nightmare of anxious tiptoeing, not being sure if he was more afraid of the monsters that supposedly lurked in the shadows, or his father and more of his tireless good humor.

Instead of curing Jacob, unfortunately, his father's efforts only increased his general unease, which in turn spurred his father to devise ever new and ever more creative ways to scare the shit out of his son, hoping that once this metaphorical shit was out, it would be out for good.

Jacob blew out the candles.

The princess had already gone. But the dragon was in, his butler told me, and showed me into the morning room, where the two Jacobs were sitting before a tea table, their napkins already on their laps.

"It's you," Jacob said, as I walked in.

"I got held up," I said.

The other Jacob rolled his eyes and looked out the window, at the dark sweep of space and faraway galaxies. "It might rain," he said.

"The princess has gone," said the other Jacob.

I took the third chair at the table, the only one empty.

The other Jacobs sipped their tea and were quiet for a while.

"It might rain," Jacob said again, looking out the window, its blackness contrasting with the brightness of the creamy silk curtains framing it, the creamy patterned rug beneath our feet, and the creamy damask wallpaper punctuated by baroque paintings of fire-breathing dragons. A lone plant stood in the corner, a potted palm whose health was robust.

The china rattled lightly as Jacob brought the cup and saucer close to his face and blew across the teacup's surface. "I hope he brings egg salad. My favorite are the egg salad sandwiches."

"And scones," Jacob added after a pause, to fill the pause that was already gone.

"So long as there are scones all is well," said the other Jacob, and we all nodded.

"It has started to rain," said the dragon, as he walked in, stuffing his hands in the pockets of his smoking jacket. He closed the door behind him with his tail and continued toward the window, where the three of us joined him in looking out. Colorful shapes were beginning to form high in the sky and then, falling, landed among complementary shapes in the garden's topiary, leveling the gated courtyard fronted by the FDR. As each layer filled, it disappeared, revealing another level with more topiary.

It began to rain harder. The traffic on the FDR was stalled. Headlights glowed in the mist.

"Al Roker says to expect six inches of accumulation," said the dragon.

"I don't mind the rain," said Jacob.

"Neither do I," said the other Jacob.

"Neither do I," said I.

The dragon walked over to the fireplace, to the cream-colored settee before it and, lying down, put his feet up on the armrest facing us, his arms behind his head. He stretched and sighed. "What shall we do in the meantime?"

I went to the window and watched the Tetronic rain. Pulling my silver yo-yo from my pocket, I began in place.

"Do you have any movies?" asked the other Jacob.

The dragon shrugged. "I have riddles," he said. "What is the difference between a dragon and a dinosaur?"

The other Jacob guessed: "A dinosaur is real."

The dragon shook his head. "Then what am I? Guess again."

"Dragons have jobs," said the other Jacob.

"Do they? The princess has gone," the dragon responded. "I am retired, but am I not still a dragon? And before I got the job? Was I not a dragon then? Anyway, I did it pro bono. It's my castle, you know. It's been in my family for generations." He motioned to the paintings, to a dragon in a ruff. "She needed a place to crash, so I gave her the tower. I was about to rent it on Airbnb and then I thought, *What am I doing? I don't need the money.* Anyway, she's gone now, so I'll have to find something else to do. Archery maybe. Or tango. If I'm being honest, I've always wanted to try stand-up comedy. But is it too late? Am I too old? Can you see me in a nightclub?"

"Follow your dreams," said Jacob.

"That's an original idea," said the other Jacob.

"Adults always say things like, 'Just be yourself.' I've been hearing that since I was a kid," said the dragon, "as if that's any sort of advice. I want to yell at them, 'And who exactly is that?'"

"You are what you eat," said Jacob.

"Did Bob Hope eat Bob Hope?" asked the dragon.

"I had a salad earlier," said the other Jacob.

"I might go to law school," I said, stilling my yo-yo, winding it, and putting it back in my pocket. "I don't know. My dad wants me to."

"And what do *you* want?" asked Jacob.

"That's what you should be asking yourself," agreed the other Jacob.

The two looked at me. I felt my face grow hot from the attention, and my vision of the three of them melted a little. Jacob brought the teacup to his nose and sniffed. The other Jacob walked over to the plant and touched its leaves. The dragon yawned, picked his teeth.

"In college I wanted to be an existentialist," said Jacob, "but there's no money in it and even less meaning."

"Ha!" said the dragon.

"I wanted to be a poet," said the other Jacob. "In the old days you could get a job at court writing sonnets for the king and getting paid in wine, but these days it's mostly teaching." He shrugged. "Now I'm taking an editing class at the New York Film Academy."

"I always kind of wanted to be an actuary," said Jacob. "But I studied Latin and became a Latino, as was expected of me. I've recently started acting though. Little parts, on the side. I get the trades and go to all the open calls. I have tap shoes."

The dragon tapped his feet in the air, then rested them again. "In fifteenth-century France, acting was considered so shameful a vocation that actors were denied Christian burial rights unless they renounced their profession before their deaths, so that a lot of people's last words were, 'Wait, I'm a dentist.'" The dragon continued, "You could always do whatever needs to be done and then later, when you're finished with all of that, you can want to have done something different. Wanting doesn't have to come first, but can just as well come last. Regret is also tender."

"The Buddhists say the letting go of all desire is the only way to achieve happiness," I said. "But I don't want to be happy if it means not wanting to be happy."

"My father was very serious," said the dragon. "He told me he never did a thing he wanted his whole life. He only ever did what he had to. But then he also said, 'I worked hard so you'd have options. Whatever you want to do, I'll support you. So I took a pastry class and presented him with a cornetto. He ate it, marveled at its flakiness, but I could tell he was disappointed. He's gone now. He was in real estate when he was alive, mostly strip malls in Long Island. Probably, I should have gotten married."

"Were you in love?" Jacob asked.

"Sometimes. But more than getting married it was always my dream to get divorced. I should have liked to have five ex-wives. Full disclosure: I have Pluto Retrograde in the sign of Leo on my Ascendant. If you want, I can do your chart later," the dragon said to me. "But the riddle." He repeated: "What is the difference between a dragon and a dinosaur?"

I studied the dragon's face. His scales showed his age. He pulled a cigarette from a box inlaid with mother-of-pearl set out on the coffee table, then produced a silver lighter from out of his jacket pocket. I looked out the window, then at the two Jacobs, each of them occupied with their own thoughts, and then back at the dragon. I said, "What's the difference what the difference is?"

The dragon smiled, put the cigarette in his mouth, and lit the end. Blowing smoke from his nostrils, he laughed and said, "You win."

my ex-boyfriend

I loved a man who instead of a face, had a wheel of cheese, and instead of a wheel of cheese, had a tuba, and instead of a tuba, had three fish tacos, and instead of three fish tacos, had a pet elephant, and instead of a pet elephant, had a Carnevale mask, and instead of a Carnevale mask, had a bar of soap, and instead of a bar of soap, had a dictionary of dreams, and instead of a dictionary of dreams, had a gavel, and instead of a gavel, had a Ouija board, and instead of a Ouija board, had a crown, and instead of a crown, had a cracker, which he ate.

When he looked at me, instead of looking he sniffed, and when he sniffed, instead of sniffing he sang, and when he sang, instead of singing, he cried, and when he cried, instead of crying he danced, and when he danced, instead of dancing he dined out at a four-star restaurant with good Yelp reviews, and when he dined out at a four-star restaurant with good Yelp reviews he dined alone.

When he was alone, instead of being alone he was with me, and when he was with me, instead of being with me, he was with her, and when he was with her, instead of being with her he was alone at a four-star restaurant with good Yelp reviews.

* * *

When he was alone at a four-star restaurant with good Yelp reviews he was reminded of his youth, and when he was reminded of his youth he was reminded of the ocean, and when he was reminded of the ocean he was reminded of the beach, and when he was reminded of the beach he was reminded of me, and when he was reminded of me he was reminded of the first girl he ever loved, and when he was reminded of the first girl he ever loved he was reminded of her, which reminded him of me, which reminded him of something else.

When he was reminded of something else, he cried, but instead of crying he danced, and instead of dancing he consulted medical textbooks about little-known diseases he hoped not to catch, and instead of consulting medical textbooks about little-known diseases he hoped not to catch he held my hand in both of his hands, but instead of holding my hand in both of his hands he held a wheel of cheese, which is what he had instead of a face, and looked forlorn.

After, we broke up, but instead of breaking up we got married, then instead of getting married we went up in a balloon, and instead of going up in a balloon we kissed, and instead of kissing we put on our winter clothes, and instead of putting on our winter clothes we bought a small radio, and instead of buying a small radio we fell in love, and instead of falling in love, we got divorced.

When I see the ocean I see his face, and when I see his face I see a wheel of cheese, and when I see a wheel of cheese I see a tuba, and when I see a tuba I miss him most.

shelves

1 "I was having coffee with my subconscious. He was a peculiar-looking man. Small, with a waxed mustache and crossed legs. He repeatedly called me Escobar, though I told him, 'My name is not Escobar. It is Verskin.' And he said, 'What do you know?' And I said, 'I know my name.' And he just sat there twirling his waxed mustache, staring at me with contempt. Finally, 'Escobar,' he says to me, and at this I lose my temper and throw a cannoli at him, at my subconscious. 'My name is Verskin!' I cry. 'But you wish it were Escobar,' he whispers. 'No, I don't!' I answer. And then he says to me in this superior way, before he begins to sip again at his coffee, 'You don't know what you want, Escobar,' and I wake up. What do you think it means?" Peter asked, staring intently from his place on the couch, toward the yawning face of Freud, a tweedy-colored fox terrier.

His morning ritual: Dream therapy with Freud, followed by a session on the computer. He used to write poetry, but now limited himself to emails.

The great poet paused over the keyboard. "The weather is optimistic," he typed. "How are you, Mom?"

It was 8:45 a.m. in the small apartment in the small building in the small city, which happened to be very large. On a whim, he tried a couplet but was unable, as usual, to progress past a single line. Every day he would start with a fresh page, with the notion that today the sanctions on his writer's blockade would be lifted, that free trade of thought and language would again reign happily across all borders of the mind. He would begin, fingers intent, arched over the keyboard, like a magician straining to produce a rabbit. But no rabbit. "Not today." He shook his head at the computer screen. "In my heart, the embargo continues." He sighed and retreated from his desk.

He cleaned himself up and emerged from the small building, holding a portfolio. "I must visit my editor," he announced to himself, "and turn in this, my latest manuscript! If only art were as easy to construct as these flimsy pages," he grieved. "But then, it would not be art—alas, not one poem in all these five years . . ."

He boarded the 57th Street bus and took a seat in its accordion middle. The bus swiveled across town and stopped on Seventh Avenue, its doors opening to a woman. From the front entrance, fiery hair came waving toward him, then next to him, before resting on his shoulder like a butterfly, pausing.

He looked straight ahead as the bus started up again—an orchestra tuning before the opera, a garbled excitement, a rogue cello, intent violin, the sound of thoughts breaking within a person wishing to speak. He waited for the conductor to bring order to his voice, to point at him with his baton, his cue: Address her! You! Oh, shyness, Wagnerian! Oh, silence, music of my heart! She got off at the last stop.

Quickly, composing poems out of her hair, shards of words flying past and cutting him, he tore open his notebook to record, to tame, to harness the songs: "Red, red hair," he wrote, "how to construct?"

He exited, too, closing his notebook hurriedly, as the bus driver announced he would be taking his break and so all passengers should kindly "Get the hell off my bus!"

Stepping off, he watched her escape far down the street, red hair drifting like fire through a stone maze. She disappeared behind a corner. The wind against his face felt like a reproach. He crossed the street to wait for a bus going back, since he'd missed his stop.

There was nothing beautiful to stir him from his envelope of reserve on the return trip. His empty notebook remained secure in his pocket, and he did not chew the gum he did not have.

Standing at the foot of Management and Company, he looked all the way up to the spireless building's highest spire, a ritual glance with which he always prefaced his entry into the building's revolving doors. Sucked in through the entry valve, he was spit out on the inside, into a rose marble foyer that was ugly in a carefully planned way, then continued toward the elevator bank, ready to dispatch his responsibilities.

"Anton!" said the suited man. "You have finished this assignment even sooner than the last, how grateful our devoted customers shall be." The suited man walked out from behind his desk.

"My name is Peter."

"Of course," said the suited man. "And this, the final manuscript for the 2001 G-4 Easy to Stack, Pull, and Fold'em? I don't know how you do it. I find it all so frustrating, actually. I'll let you in on a little secret; I buy all my own furniture preassembled. I just don't have the patience for the kind of do-it-yourself convenience we here at Management and Company so amply provide," he said, pruning shears in hand.

Peter shifted.

"Well, I'll send this to the printer immediately. Gus Sanders in marketing will be pleased. They're already backed up with orders."

"You don't want to read it first, sir?"

"But why? Your work is always perfect. In your five years here at Management and Company, you've not made a single mistake.

You are a font of exuberant practicalities and possess an uncommon mastery over their application. I'm sure it's perfect," he said, winking at Peter. Then, turning to the plastic potted tree at his side, he gave a brief clip. "And besides, we're backed up," he repeated, as he began shuffling some papers on his desk with his free, ungloved hand.

This was Peter's cue that the meeting was over. He was preparing to take his leave when the suited man broke in. "Oh, and, Anton, I almost forgot. Since you are here, I have another assignment for you—Fold'em, Stack'em Chair and Coffee Table GTS-4. I was going to give it to Flemming, but—poor boy—he just can't keep up with you. You are the best writer we have on staff, Anton. Really."

"Thank you, sir, and it's Peter."

"Of course," said the suited man, as Peter exited the office.

☞2 It was five years ago that Peter Feinstein had not written a poem in over ninety days. He kept beginning poems and, when this didn't work he tried his hand at a new genre: "the poetical essay." A few of his attempts: "Phantom Cake: On Craving What Is Gone," "A Complete Theory of Fluorides," "The Elbow and Its Secrets," "Aglet: A Consideration," "Toward a Definition of Umami," "Ringtones of Our Forefathers," and "Modern Koala: Rise of the Twentieth-Century City Bear," all of them rhyming, all of them promising, all of them stalled. In desperation, he even tried a meditation on war, which proved finally fruitless, too, as all he knew of war was what he had read, thus prompting an effort toward a poem about war literature—equally unsuccessful.

Peter was without poetry.

He looked at his hands and buried his face in his grasp. It was the morning of his twenty-fifth year.

* * *

After high school Peter had done quite well. In the two years that followed, he had written and published his first book of poems, *Gerund,* which sold almost no copies. Peter accepted this philosophically, seeing it as a necessary step in his literary career. He applied, successfully, for a grant to complete his second book, which would be called *Growing Down.* It was to be about the childhoods of poets, his in particular, but written in iambic pentameter and from the perspective of a soft cheese. He would hint, throughout, at truffle. And he had been disciplined in that work up until this last ninety-day hit.

It began with a slight numbness in the fingertips, an odd tingle that cooled his usually feverish typing. Then it started to spread, from the fingers into his arms and then into his whole body, a pins-and-needles kind of thing, but at the cellular level, freezing him mid-stanza, casting him as a kind of ice sculpture of the writer at work. Peter moved freely, but his thoughts remained frozen within his mental double, who never left the computer, never looked up, and also never wrote.

The mornings met the evenings and those evenings met the mornings and those mornings met the evenings and so the numbness spread. And kept spreading across days, weeks, and soon months, until the day that Peter—sitting before his computer, sharing for a few moments the space of his double, wrists arched to act—stopped. He breathed and listened. His heart beat a Morse code that he could not decipher, a plea that he could not answer. The red light of his clock radio answered instead. The numbers blinked; the present shrugged. "What time is it?" the clock asked. The universe answered: It was time to get a job.

He rose from his desk as, he imagined, the first sea mammals had climbed upon the land—with gravitas and theme music suggestive of the moment's import. He pressed pause on his tape player. Then, spreading his arms to both sides, he began moving them in circles, before hopping up and down, too. Then he jumped. High! In the air, straining at the threshold of orbit, his

Shelves

arms a blur of furious revolutions, he would get a job, he determined, and join the waking world.

Peter cast off into a sea of concrete description and lived from there coolly among undisclosed metaphor and symbol. He would take a vacation from the figurative, he decided. He would no longer force imagery where others saw only architecture. Midtown spires would remain spires. The Statue of Liberty, merely a gift from France. The valves of the subway pumping commuters to and fro, he would regard only as a convenient twentieth-century construction on which work began in 1904, not as the city's cardiovascular system, nor as evidence of an urban Emersonian oversoul. Nor would he, he vowed, craft similes that would liken his morning cup of coffee to a milky bog, ambiguously promising through its caffeinated opacity. Nor regard his orange juice, as a river of citrus joyously bursting from the sensual delta of the carton Tropicana. Nor bagels, nor pickle brine, nor four hundred milligrams of folic acid in a gel cap, would he lasso into analogy. Not even the deep blue pin-holed swatch of fabric, which, discarded by some God, lay crumpled in a mass that at nights always fell skyward, dressing the unmade celestial bed glimpsable each nine p.m. on 57th Street, where he stood standing small at the floor of this gray Manhattan valley, out front of his tiny apartment for a few brief moments, a male copular gazing up as occasional gusts from city buses, like trade winds, blew his hair into his eyes, which, opened wide, panned the brief vista between building tops. He would not squeeze life into poetry with or without the pulp or added calcium, but would work, and live, literally.

Mornings held nothing but tea and toast, he noted, as he read the daily paper, searching the want ads for a suitable, practical position. And then one day he came to this: "Technical Writers needed to write instruction manuals. Visit Management and Co. at 444 Park Ave. for an interview today!"

*   *   *

Peter made it to 444 Park Avenue in somewhat of a sweat, despite the frigid air. The walls of the office were covered in a lima-bean-prior-to-boiling shade of wallpaper. It was an almost square room lined with folding chairs and a lavender leather sofa. He proceeded immediately to the receptionist who, staring out the only window, was vigilantly unoccupied.

"Excuse me," he said. Her gaze did not waver. "Excuse me," he repeated. "I am here for the interview. I am a writer," he said, straightening. She did not move, so he began again, "Excuse me—"

"I heard you. Please be patient."

"I apologize," he apologized, revolving slightly.

Another thirty seconds passed with his watching her watching before, sighing, she turned away from the window. Without a word, she began shuffling the papers on her desk. "Here," she said, handing him a messy pile. "Fill these out." He took the stack and looked around, then walked toward the empty leather couch. He was about to sit, was bent halfway when the receptionist's finger began to wag.

"What," Peter asked, still half-crouched, "I can't sit here?"

"Of course not," she said, and returned her attention to the window.

He took an unoccupied chair next to a large potted tree, the only plant in the room, and beside a young leather-clad girl with big black sunglasses who was also filling out forms. He removed his coat and was about to hang it on the vacant coat rack, when the receptionist began wagging her finger again, so he folded it instead and tried to stuff it beneath his seat. Sitting again on the flimsy folding chair, he produced a pen from his shirt pocket and assessed the work ahead. There were instructions written at the top of the page:

The science of prose construction demands attention to detail, a firm grasp of post-structuralism, and a descriptive prescience. Our writees are selected from a large pool of highly qualified applicators, making the hiring process at Management and Co. one of the most competitive in the field! Success in our prose industry depends heavily on our writees' compotency, as the pamphlets we produce are the bridge to customer satisfashions. This is not a job for the dabblededo or dreamer, but a position for the applicator committed to the craft of writing within a disciplined and professional environmental. BAs a must. MFAs preferred. Only serious writees need apply. Complete the preliminary test below if you are still interested in pursuing a career with us.

Match the figure pictured on the left with the description that best fits.

The page was covered with the following illustrations: a square with one rough edge, a cube with three rough edges, a cylinder, four screws, four washers, and a nail. Snatches of copy were clustered in numbered groups arranged vertically along the page's eastern margin. The options were tricky. Carefully, Peter considered his first answer before moving on to the rest of the exam, which comprised fifteen similar pages. After completing the test with, what he thought, relative ease, Peter waded across the carpeted room toward the receptionist, still motionless at her desk by the window.

"Excuse me." Peter cleared his throat. "Excuse me," Peter asked, "but, what now?

Reluctantly, the young woman turned from her point of interest outside and replied, "Huh?"

"What do I do now? I've finished filling out the forms." He motioned to the neat stack he'd placed on her desk.

She shrugged. "Wait—" she said, her attention arrested once more by the view. Then, turning back to him, "The application will be reviewed, and you will be called for an interview if there is any interest in your work."

"How will I be notified?"

"Verbally."

"Through what medium?"

"Air."

"By what means?"

"Aural."

"And when will that be?" he ventured politely.

"Hour, hour an' a half. After lunch, they'll call your name."

"May I leave and come back?"

She discharged him by unfastening her gaze and resuming her careful watch out the window.

Peter entered the elevator on the twenty-fifth floor and took it down to the lobby with a large UPS man. The large UPS man grunted as he entered the elevator, and Peter offered a half smile in acknowledgment of the human plight.

Peter did not know where he was going as he went. There was an expansive atrium in the foyer, so Peter circled this twice while he thought, and then decided to go to the Plaza, figuring he had just enough time to walk there, circle that atrium twice, and walk back.

The sidewalk was crowded. With thoughts of the office playing upon his mind, Peter walked, dodging others as they dodged him, too. Car horns, whirling police sirens, and growling diesel engines produced a cacophonous background silence, against which he dreamed.

Arriving at the Plaza at 59th and Fifth, shaking the cold from his shoulders, Peter entered the grand foyer.

Reentering the building of Management and Company, Peter looked at his watch, noticed he had three minutes left according to the secretary's estimation, and made one final loop of the atrium before re-boarding the elevator. He retook his seat by the large leafy potted plant and re-stowed his coat beneath his folding chair.

"Mr. Feinstein," said a voice emanating from a gray suit that had just appeared at the previously closed door. "Follow me," the gray suit said, before retreating into the office and shutting the door behind him.

Peter hesitated before opening the door. When he did, he found the suited man already at his desk.

"Please, knock before you enter my office, Mr. Feinstein."

"Yes, sir."

"Sit down," the suited man said, motioning to the carpeted floor, free of any chair. Peter looked at the floor puzzled, but not wanting to ask a stupid question and appear unqualified, sat Indian style on the spot where he imagined a chair would be were there one. The suited man rose, circled his desk, and then sat behind it once more.

Leaning back in his plush leather chair, he looked at Peter and showed him his teeth. After a moment, he pressed a button on his desk and barked, "Send them all in already; I have to go to the bathroom." Without breaking eye contact, the suited man gave him more teeth. Peter shifted uncomfortably on the floor.

The woman in dark oversize sunglasses and carefully messed hair; a teenage boy with baggy pants; an unrealistic blond man (were he a fictional character, he would not ring true); and a medium-size gray-haired septuagenarian male in a white short-sleeved button-down shirt, poly-fiber slacks, sturdy leather belt, and loafers, who looked as if he'd gone out expressly to buy a squash, entered the room. They, the other applicants, sat on the floor forming a row next to him.

The suited man opened a desk drawer from which he began to pull multiple green sleeves, each about a foot long. Piling them onto his desk, he addressed the group: "So, you want to be writers, do ya? You think you have something to say in a way that no one else can." He continued to pull one green sleeve out after another. "You're young, full of ideas. . . . I was young once. Last year, as a matter of fact. I ate clams by the beach with this ragtag blonde I picked up on the Jersey shore. My God, was she something. Broke my heart between her legs." He picked up a sleeve and removed a recorder from it.

He placed his fingers carefully over the air holes leaving the pinkies extended, and wet his lips. Bringing the instrument to his mouth, he began to play. It was a low, plaintive sonata; he trilled a G and then ascended to a D flat. Peter felt profoundly sad for the man. That ragtag blonde really *had* done him in. The sound of the recorder danced through the room, tiptoeing first across the surface of his skin and then crawling along the base of the rug where he sat before it lifted again, moving in graceful circles about the suited man. The suited man held out a final B flat and a tear. Laying the recorder back on his desk, he sighed a heavy sigh and looked down at the group.

The suited man began passing out recorders, and when he was finished sat behind his desk. "The best 'Hot Cross Buns' gets the job. Go down the line!"

One at a time the applicants began playing, while the suited man took out a set of shears and gardening gloves and began clipping the plastic tree next to his desk. When it was Peter's turn, he summoned all of his pent-up metaphors and channeled them into the three-note song. He played it a little bit jazzy at first, before breaking into an almost disco interlude, which nearly tipped into psychedelic funk, but then finished, at last, operatically. He lowered his recorder. He knew he had done well.

Peter looked up. Out of the tree, the suited man had sculpted a dinosaur. He removed his gardening gloves and laid the shears on his desk. "Well done, all of you. Unfortunately, there is only one position open." He began circling the room, slowly, with his hands clasped behind his back. He began again, "The science of prose construction is not for everyone. Writing is a lonesome occupation, requiring great discipline, the occasional fencing lesson, and a cumulonimbus mind. Not to mention, if you are offered a job here, you will have to let me cut your hair however and whenever I want. If you can't handle pressure, leave this office now!" The girl with the black sunglasses and carefully messed hair rose from the carpet and disappeared out the door.

"You four are some of the finest writers we have in this great city," he said, motioning toward a wall where a mural was painted of the view that might have been visible had there been a window.

"But this job requires more than great writing. It requires long hours; sixty-five, sometimes seventy minutes per; sleepless days; and an unwavering commitment to the firm," he thundered. "It requires mud, Chet, and fears." He motioned to an oil portrait of an elderly mustachioed man. "This is Chet. He handles billing and organizes the obstacle course at the company retreat. Terror on the tires, that boy." He leaned on his knuckles until they went white.

"You're probably all very tired. The interview process at Management and Company is, I know, a long one. But stay strong, my young idealists; we are entering the final phase.

"Again," he resumed his pacing, "to anyone who does not think they can handle the rigors of this firm, I encourage you to depart now without any hard, soft, or just right feelings."

The teenage boy with baggy pants rose and opened the door, vanishing beyond.

On the floor were three. The suited man surveyed them before once more pressing the button on his desk. "Bring in the Phase Three materials."

The receptionist drifted in and, without a sound, stopped directly behind the suited man. She pulled an argyle cravat from her dress sleeve, wrapped it over his eyes and tied it securely at the back. Then, from her dress pocket she handed him one paper donkey tail with tape stuck to its back. Addressing the assembled job applicants, she then said, "Stand up and don't move."

The last three applicants rose and froze as the blindfolded man, standing tall before them, began to say something in a tone of great importance. "As you youngsters begin to make your way through this world, you will learn, the sooner the better, that life, this vector of cells so susceptible to love and fat," he waved a hand up and down his body in explanation, "is driven by the thrusts of two opposing forces—Fate and Will. Sherri!" he broke off. "Take dictation: Remind me to sculpt a topiary of Grecian gods representing this dichotomy. Also, send Irv to Chinatown this afternoon to fetch more practice plants. Give him the car and also, ask him if he's gotten any leads yet on the name of that midget that's blackmailing my daughter-in-law. And once we're through here, get me a Cherry Coke and my William Butler Yeats Word Scramble."

"Yes, sir."

He resumed his tone: "Both of these forces work independently of each other and sometimes even against one another. These gods you can't yet see, which I plan to display over there where that ficus is—" He motioned toward the dinosaur. "Imagine one with the head of a giant owl and the body of a much smaller owl representing Fate, and the other, with the head of a tiny lion and the body of a really very large lion representing Will" —he raised a dynamic finger—"are inside of us." He exhaled audibly. "It is necessary that you learn to respect the boundaries of each, not to get into wars within yourself and all that, but to let each side have its say. When you learn to allow for this balance, life, like the planchette on a Ouija board, will steer itself. This is the same advice I gave to my son before he left for college. He is now the founder of the biggest peanut butter and jelly sandwich firm worldwide."

"I have already chosen one of you for this position. We shall see now if the fates agree with my decision. Sherri!" he said to the receptionist, which cued the young lady to begin spinning him by the shoulders. Spinning and spinning and spinning, until he stopped. Then, extending the hand holding the donkey tail straight out from his chest, he raised a leg deliberately and, wobbling, began walking toward the wall directly in front of him. The three applicants stood to his left watching.

Rapidly, Peter considered what the man had said, about the fates, about his own will. He was trying to understand that balance, trying to decide how much decision-making power he had after all, as the suited man inched inexorably toward the wall.

Peter was reviewing the situation, what had led him here, what the suited man had meant, when, before he'd even made the decision to, he found himself pumping his legs, moving them in long strides across the carpet in a race with the other two applicants, also making out madly for the suited man's destination. The three bumped and stumbled against one another until it was only Peter and the incorrigibly tall if poorly drawn blond man in the short lead. The blond reached out his long, false-ringing arm, attempting to push Peter out of the way.

Hit in the shoulder, Peter stumbled and fell to the floor, while the blond man, laying his back against the wall, opened his arms broadly at the last second to be tagged by the suited man upon the chest. The suited man extended the tail toward him, as Peter, on his knees shot a hand up, intercepting the paper tail, which came to rest exactly in the center of his palm.

Defeated, the blond lowered his arms, while the third man, still far behind, exited the office without a word, as if they did not have the squash he'd wanted. The suited man removed his blindfold excitedly and, grabbing hold of the hand with the tail still stuck to it, smiled, shaking Peter vigorously, and said, "Welcome to Management and Company, son."

Peter left the office extremely excited about his new job and his first foray into the exciting world of big business. He felt, finally, that he was on his way. It had been ninety days, and he did not need poetry; he had something more concrete, something practical, something pure; he had, at last, an assignment.

When Peter arrived home, the first thing he always did was clear the kitchen of all its furniture, dumping everything haphazardly into his bedroom and onto his bed. In the tiny kitchen, on the dirty linoleum tile next to the stove, he opened the box full of parts for the table and chairs, taking each part out and laying like ones together in piles along the floor.

He especially enjoyed this part. It was like a puzzle to him; he had all these pieces that were designed with a certain, now invisible, structure in mind, and he had to figure out how it would all hang together. From the pieces on the floor he would assemble a sort of destiny. It was like life, he thought, as he separated the piles; you are given all the pieces—a name, a body, a place—and you have to figure out what to do with it all, discern the overarching design. He held two oblong cylinders of wood and studied them for a moment. He wondered about destiny, if this, for example, was his, to make sense of strange objects for others. It certainly was a more noble profession, he thought on the bright side. Better than his past poetic waxings, which, from his position with the wood on the floor, now seemed disgustingly selfish—all the *I*s and *me*s he'd employed to make his poems rhyme; he winced. Yes, this certainly was more selfless.

He found a screw and inserted it into one of the cylinders, and looked at it, past it, around it trying to glean the larger idea. He thought of the woman on the bus from that morning, imagined what he might have said to her and what she might have said back, and then revised it all over again until it was perfect.

"It was tea and crepes this time. I was sitting at a table in a garden with my Unconscious. He was balding with an oily comb-over and a three-piece polyester suit, like that of a gym teacher chaperoning a high school prom in a 1979 driver's ed video describing the perils of operating a vehicle while intoxicated. 'I have to tell you something,' he said, dipping his mustache into his teacup. 'Okay,' I said, pouring a little more chocolate sauce onto my crepe. They were do-it-yourself crepes. All the materials were set out on the table. It was really very nice. 'What is it?' I said. 'I'm sorry, I can't tell you, I promised.' 'Don't be silly. Of course you can tell me.' He shook his finger at me. 'No,' he said finally.

"It went on like this for a very long time. And as it started to become dark, I became frustrated. Finally, I lunged at him across the table, yelling, 'I must know,' and began shaking him by the shoulders. 'Please,' he said as I shook him, 'my stomach is rather upset, don't jostle me,' and then I woke up."

Peter turned his head from the spot on the ceiling on which he'd been focusing for the better part of his narration to look at Freud, sitting silently with a stiff back on his desk chair.

It had been another long feverish night. Lately—he had been completing a new project every night—once he started, he could not pull himself away. He'd begin the work and then, at some point, disappear into it. Falling through time before landing on the next day, when he was finished he'd look at the clock and find it was five or six in the morning. He'd sleep for a few hours then, but that was it, just enough to dream.

He printed the manuscript and prepared to take it to Management and Company; he was eager for another assignment. He gathered his papers into his portfolio and began skirting the various shelving units he had constructed over the last few years during which he'd been with Management—they let him keep all of the products he worked on; it was one of the perks of the job—which were spread mostly unused throughout the apartment and in some places, for convenience, piled atop one another as in a furniture warehouse. Next to the door, a tall tower was developing from a table, a bookshelf, a CD rack, and a bar stool. He had to be careful when shutting the door because the tower would rock. It was slightly leaning.

On 57th, he began walking downstream. The wind beat his face and at one point caught the flat of his portfolio, turning it out like a sail, forcing him back a pace until he turned it again, cutting the air in half. On the corner of 56th, the sun beat down on a woman squatting with her pants around her ankles, a vein of liquid streaming from where she crouched. A truck growled. "Din't yo mama teach you no mannas?" she screamed back. "You sposta knock first!"

He arrived at the building of Management and Company, looked down to his feet, then scanned up to the highest stone as was his custom before proceeding through the revolving doors, careful not to impede its cycle in any way. He took the elevator up to twenty-five.

"Anton," said the suited man, shaking his head in the doorway. "Truly amazing!" he said regarding the manila envelope Peter had placed on his desk. "I shall get this to old Gus right away. He'll be so pleased. Poor Flemming," he sighed. "But what can one do, right, Anton?"

"There are few if any things each of us can do. Have you another assignment for me, sir?"

He pushed a button on his desk. "Sherri, bring in the GTS 28 Breakfast Nook for Anton. You know, Anton, it isn't necessary for you to come in every day. We could have these materials shipped to you."

"Yes, sir. But I'm afraid I prefer it this way, you see—"

"Come now, boy! There's nothing to fear but a pear itself, if you have that allergy. Do control yourself, Anton. In business, weakness must be monitored and minimized."

"Yes, sir. Sorry, sir."

"True love means never having to say that. If you love your job, quit the apologies."

Just then Sherri dragged a box through the door. "Good, Sherri. Thank you, Sherri."

Peter began loading the box onto his small foldable gurney (his Christmas bonus from Management and Company), when the suited man started shuffling the papers on his desk furiously, staring at Peter peevishly, with teeth.

"I can do this in the hall. Thank you, sir."

Peter wheeled his assignment gingerly out onto the street, weaving in and out of the stiffly lined faces moving urgently down the sidewalk, when he caught sight of a redness disappearing up the street. Hoping to catch it, he quickened his pace. He pursued the redness for a long avenue, until it dissolved into a sea of bodies and he gave up.

It took about an hour to carry the box the five flights up to where he lived. An hour including breaks now and then, during which he sat and shut his eyes. He felt comfortable taking his time because his neighbors were all at work at that hour. It was only one unemployed neighbor who would catch him occasionally laboring on the stairs. Mr. Smiley from 3B had passed him as he was rounding two and then, moments later, perhaps hearing Peter's heavy breathing and feeling guilty, returned with an offer to help.

"Thank you, but I'm fine. It will only take another forty-five minutes or so. You see, I need the exercise."

"Suit yourself," said Mr. Smiley, before disappearing in double steps up the stairs.

This dialogue with Mr. Smiley had occurred more than once, and the interaction was making Peter increasingly uncomfortable. Peter was not much for socializing. He had worked hard to cultivate an artist's temperament, which, in his youth he had felt was a prerequisite for the construction of poems. Solitude had been a plan he executed well. Mr. Smiley, though, was really becoming pushy.

"Please, let me help. It will be much faster this way."

"Thank you," he lied, "but I really do need the exercise. It is part of my regimen: every day I carry the box down and then carry it back up. If you helped, I would only be cheating myself, you see."

"Oh, well, okay," Mr. Smiley said, looking at the box skeptically, because it looked like a different box from yesterday's, and because he had never caught him before carrying the box down.

Peter added, "As I advance through the workout, I add weight, and therefore must change the box."

"Well, that makes sense." He paused. "You do know though, there is a New York Sports Club just across the street."

"I am morally opposed to running in place, believing it deleterious to the soul, Mr. Smiley."

Peter had seen his name on his mailbox. "I'd prefer to commit myself to practical labors and enjoy good health as a by-product of my efforts."

"Mmmm," considered Mr. Smiley. Mr. Smiley was very fit. He had been working out every day since he had lost his job and joined AA. He'd lost his job because of an alcohol-related escapade at the office Christmas party, which he couldn't actually remember. He had thought the Christmas party would be a safe place to act out, that there his "shenanigans" would go unnoticed, what with everyone else's.

The night came back to him in shadowy glimpses of his boss's face, enraged, yelling something—he could not make out what. Though he'd never exercised before he lost his job, after, he began working out regularly. He'd lift weights whenever he wanted a drink, which meant he lifted weights most of the day. "Well," he continued, "if you'd like a wheatgrass shake when you're finished with your workout, you ought to stop by. I make excellent wheatgrass shakes."

"Thank you, Mr. Smiley. Perhaps I will."

An hour later, after he had successfully maneuvered the new box into his apartment, and having looked in his refrigerator for a refreshing beverage and found none, he decided to go downstairs to see Mr. Smiley after all, figuring since he had given up art, perhaps it was time he let go of solitude, too.

Mr. Smiley blended an ample supply of shake for the both of them and told Peter all about his drink-related fallout at work, what he could remember of it anyway, and how he was now embarking on a totally healthy life and had never felt better. He took a deep breath through his nose, so that his nostrils flared like a dragon's. Then he made Peter guess his age.

"I don't know," Peter said.

But Mr. Smiley insisted: "Come on. Guess."

"Forty."

"Thirty-five!" Mr. Smiley said excitedly.

"I'm sorry, Mr. Smiley."

"Not at all. A month ago, I looked forty-five, so you see," Mr. Smiley said, not having to finish his sentence.

"Miraculous!" Peter said with the necessary zeal.

This became a regular appointment. Every afternoon, as Peter lifted his box up to his apartment on the fifth floor, Mr. Smiley would appear at his own doorway on three and invite him over for a vitamin shake once his workout was complete. After a while, Peter found this arrangement quite pleasant. Mr. Smiley did most of the talking, so Peter could relax, watching happily as Mr. Smiley made wide gesticulations in explanation of another of his stories. Then, when it was now and then requested of him, Peter would respond between sips of his shake, which he suspected, because of its repulsive taste, must indeed be very healthy.

In March, Mr. Smiley was still looking for a job. "The market's bad," he'd say on some days and shake a newspaper open to the want-ads, "but what can you do?" And Peter would say, "Indeed. There are few things one can do." Most of the time, though, Mr. Smiley was very upbeat. He always had a ready story of how he had, or he would, beat the odds. Mr. Smiley referred often to "the odds." "The odds" controlled everything, according to Mr. Smiley, but only mostly, he pointed out. He explained to Peter once, as he split the remains of shake between their still-full glasses, "Life is about navigating the exceptions," and Peter imagined himself climbing a tree.

In June, Mr. Smiley's unemployment checks would stop coming. But it was still May. Peter's dream therapy meanwhile was proving immensely fruitful. He felt all but cured of poetry now. Fleeting visions of the red-haired girl still arose from time to time when on his way to the office he'd imagined seeing her in some door. But that was not poetry—he would not succumb to that again. Instead, he imagined all of their encounters in prose, sometimes even in dramatic form with dialogue and stage directions: [*The red-haired girl sighs and exits stage left.*]

He knew at least not to mistake memory for the thing remembered, that memory was a metaphor, and of those he would never cure himself completely. Thus he understood, for he understood himself now, that if he did see her again he was unlikely to recognize her. Could one identify a person by their shadow? This he asked himself as he built desks and armchairs and coffee tables and consoles of fantastic convenience.

Hours or months passed with Peter lost inside of his work, unaware of time and his own ticking, until one day, a Monday, having looked from foot to stone and revolved without impediment, and ridden up the elevator of Management and Company to the twenty-fifth floor, and proceeded through the office door to Sherri by the window, he was announced and ushered into a startlingly silent room.

The suited man was at his desk, his head between his hands. Peter laid his latest manuscript on the desk. The suited man said nothing. Finally, Peter asked, "Have you another assignment for me, sir?"

"I've given it to Flemming."

The suited man rose and came from behind the desk, putting a hand on Peter's shoulder. "Peter," he began.

"It's—" Peter stopped his correction.

Shelves

"Peter, we've received some complaints from customer service. This is hard for me to say. It started with the GTS 1600 Mini-Bar. Customers . . . have been calling. They found your directions to be—how can I say this—less than adequate."

Peter flushed. "This is a blow, sir."

"When the first calls came, we assured them the instructions were infallible, reminded them to separate the pieces at the start so as not to confuse a cog for a screw and all that. But the calls kept coming, regarding ten models from this past March alone. It seems your instructions, though beautifully written, are misleading."

"Misleading?"

"We've recalled all ten models and have assembled a team, headed by Flemming, to evaluate the forty-five additional constructions you have written manuals for since March."

Peter sat down Indian style on the carpet, dumbfounded as the suited man walked a contemplative circle around him. He could not understand how, without his realizing it, his work could have taken such a turn. Especially when life, he felt, had really been swimming. Hadn't he finally found his place? Peter looked at his hands wondering how they could have deceived him.

"One family in Iowa is suing the company over your GTS 140 Shelving Unit. They claim it has caused nightmares in their youngest son. Another family in Salt Lake City has called the same unit pornographic and believe it to have caused their teenage daughter to become pregnant. Another mother in Idaho purchased the Children's Desk and Chair Set for their ten-year-old son, only to find once assembled, the material was strictly unusable; it came to resemble, she said, a nude and alarmingly angular woman."

"But that's madness, Mr.—"

"And they're not alone. A lawyer from Minneapolis is bringing a class action lawsuit against the company for the propagation of what they believe to be—how can I put this—pagan imagery. Of course, you see, Peter, how it would be impossible to keep you on under such circumstances. The entire company, too, has been placed under productive arrest—we are to cease all output until the matter is cleared in court. You may be asked to appear, but that won't be for some time, as the state is still gathering evidence."

Peter pushed on his knees, rose from his position on the floor, and said, "I don't know what to say, sir."

The suited man whipped around. "Say you'll get help, man!"

Peter drifted empty-handed through the streets toward his home, trying and failing to understand what had happened. When he got home, he wanted to talk to Freud about it, but he couldn't do that either, as Freud dealt only in dreams and refused to listen to anything that had taken place in waking life.

He sat on the linoleum floor of his kitchen with his back against the closed oven door and looked through the doorway, into the living room, where all of his designs reached toward the ceiling. It looked beautiful to him. Dozens of destinies in all different shapes and sizes, stacked on top of one another like the windows in the buildings across from his. He sat there for a while, thinking and staring at his work, until he fell asleep on the floor beneath the kitchen light.

He dreamed of the red-haired girl. They were playing a game of badminton and he was losing, but he was happy because she was smiling, and her hair was waving back and forth across her face as she swung. He kept missing when it came over to his side, and she laughed like a bell and called over the net across the grass, "Send it back, Anton! Send it back!"

He woke to the sound of the phone ringing. His phone never rang. He only kept it for emergencies. It was all the way on the other side of the room, so he had to climb over the stacks of furniture to get to it. First, a mountain of chairs lying over each other at discrete right angles, then three consoles piled vertically into a tower, and then across two end tables leaning against each other diagonally, supported underneath by a shoe rack and a breakfast nook. The phone was on the floor in the corner, beneath a set of shelves.

By the time he got there, sitting atop a chair that was stacked above a tower of others just like it, the ringing stopped. He looked out the window; it happened to be in front of him. Then the phone began to ring again. He climbed down and picked up the receiver.

"Hello?"

"Is this Mr. Verskin?" a woman's metallic voice asked.

"How may I assist you?"

"My name is Phoebe Caldwell. I'm a reporter for the *New York Mercury,* and I was wondering if I could ask you a few questions about the Management and Company case."

"I don't know that I have answers."

"Mr. Verskin—"

"Please," he interrupted her, "Call me Anton."

"All right then, Anton. How long have you been working for Management and Company?"

Over the next few weeks, he received many calls from many different newspapers, big city papers and little ones, too, from places he'd not heard of. They all wanted to know why he did it, if it was a prank, or was he disgruntled, mentally ill, had he ever been in prison, did he feel remorse over the lives he had adversely affected, about the divorces his furniture was said to have caused, about one girl's running away from her family in Milwaukee to become a soothsayer in New York City while studying film at NYU. He told them all he didn't know anything about that.

"I just did my job," he answered. "My job was to write instruction manuals. I can't help it if some people are not happy with the way things turn out. Life is like that." He thought for a while and then added. "Destiny sometimes appears differently in the picture on the box."

One Monday, he received a call from a woman named only Jane.

She was an art critic for the *New York Herald* who wanted to meet with him to discuss his work: "May I visit you at your studio?"

"It's a one bedroom."

She appeared at one p.m. with auburn hair, jeans, and a crisp white shirt and blue sport coat. Sunlight streamed through the apartment, casting a jungle of shadows through the furniture stacked in the den.

"This is very exciting for me. I'm a great fan of your work," she said, shaking his hand and filling her eyes with the room. I have three of your pieces and think they're magnificent. Not since the armory show of 1913 has the art world been so profoundly shaken," she said placing a hand on the GTS 22 next to her.

"I don't keep food in the apartment," he said. "I'm afraid I can't offer you anything."

He followed her down the stoop on their way to lunch, and her hair, when it met the sun, flashed a fiery red.

They had lunch at a restaurant on the corner of 57th and Tenth Avenue. She asked him many questions while making notes in a little pad. Then she told him she had a friend with a gallery who was desperate to give him a show.

On the sidewalk, after lunch, they stood facing each other while the river of people cut past on both sides. Her hair was blazing when he said, "I've seen you before. Yes, I've seen you." And taking her hand and opening it, he kissed her palm and then her eyes. She studied him for a moment and squinted into the sun. "I know," she said finally, arriving at his mouth.

He looked for her column in the paper some Sundays later, while she sat in the next room talking to Freud.

The article began, "Not since the retroactive revelation of paint by number has a movement so radically upset the art world. Anton Verskin constructs destinies, he'll say if you ask him, 'I just put the pieces together, and write the instructions for how they best fit.' His work began selling at Kmart under the guise of simple assembly-required furniture. The buzz began in controversy as people in the Midwest who had sought only to reorganize their shoe closets found themselves instead building monuments to his despair.

"Formerly a poet, Verskin's work has sold out of Kmart now and will soon be exhibited at the Jacques Flanheim Gallery on Madison Avenue. Meanwhile, Management and Company awaits trial for having forced the disturbingly abstract images on consumers across the country. The company, whose manufacturing plant is currently closed, is now working closely with MoMA to launch a retrospective of Verskin's work from his five years in the company's service."

Next to the article, three of his designs were pictured accompanied by their requisite "instructions."

"'The genius of his work, of course, is that it is do-it-yourself art,' remarked Anne Douglass, PhD, art history chair at Columbia University. 'Note the near elegiac quality of his instructions for this desk unit: "Fit screw securely into cylinder or your table will be wobbly, and life will forever seem a question with too many answers. Tighten screw and look for five minutes out the nearest window. What don't you see? Repeat steps five and six and then slide the drawer back so that it appears as a mouth speaking to you from the deep. Fill the drawer with what it says."'"

☞ ENVOI

Having fallen through time and woken up together, Jane and Anton determined they were in love. They married in a garden along the Hudson shortly after his first show.

Cannoli were served at the reception, which was followed immediately by a badminton tournament played between the wedding parties.

After, Anton, Freud, and Jane took up residence at the Plaza, where Anton was named Artist-in-Residence-in-Perpetuity. Downstairs in the main foyer, there is a permanent installation of his GTS-22 Handi-Table, before which tourists are regularly photographed.

Mr. Smiley never found a job but decided, after Anton left, to start his own business. He calls it "The Moving Gym" and it's the biggest exercise craze to hit North America. His business serves as a moving company for recent arrivals to New York City as well as a workout regimen for those seeking a sense of purpose in their fitness routines.

If you hire The Moving Gym, a team of gym members will assemble at your door, ready to carry your furniture and bric-a-brac—depending on their fitness level—to your new home. To qualify for service, however, you must be moving to a walkup.

Pictured recently on the cover of *Forbes*, Mr. Smiley was quizzed by an eager journalist about his innovative business plan. In the interview, he thanked his still-close friend, the famous instructional artist Anton Verskin, for giving him the idea. Anton, when called for comment, responded by saying, "This is his destiny, all of ours, to swing from tree to tree, looking for footholds in exceptions."

the autobiography
of gertrude stein

"It takes a lot of time to be a genius, you have to sit around so much doing nothing, really doing nothing."
—Gertrude Stein, *Everybody's Autobiography*

I think I was a genius in my last life that is that I was the author of *The Autobiography of Alice B. Toklas* who was Gertrude Stein which is partially why I quit my job. Burger King is no place to cultivate genius.

I have a friend named Jacob who is very fond of Hemingway and so I told him one day I said Jacob, in the end Hemingway was just an imitation of himself and your imitation is just as good as his so your being him is really no different than his being him so you might as well be him. He agreed and so now we are they. He quit his job too. The men's department at Saks is no place to cultivate genius.

Every Tuesday he brings his manuscripts over for me to critique and I cross out everything but for the *c* in his name. He needs to make his prose more lean, I tell him, striking through all the superfluous letters.

After I quit my job in order to claim my destiny and trust fund, I decided to make a salon of my apartment, just like Gertrude Stein's in Paris but with fewer omelets. Stein's cook only made omelets, but if she didn't like the dinner guests, instead of breaking the eggs, she'd fry them whole. References to omelets in *The Autobiography*: 137.

Another of my friends is a conceptual artist, and we began our relationship after I cut his hair. He is called Fred. You may have caught his last piece, displayed just next to my stoop from January 25–March 12, a sculpture made of found objects, which was widely misunderstood before it was removed as trash. Genius is always widely misunderstood.

I met Fred outside my apartment late one night on my way home from a visit with my boyfriend Jeff's. I call him Jeff's because he's always saying things like "that's mine." He is plagued by that horrid sense of entitlement that defines his whole generation. I'll light a cigarette and accidentally pocket his lighter and he'll start in with his millenialisms. I'm a bit older than Jeff's so one day I said to him, "Jeff's, yours is a misplaced generation. You're lost now but will very likely turn up later in someone's pocket turning a good dollar."

Jeff's smokes a lot of pot and has throat nodules, which is what inspired him to start his own line of edibles. He spends most of his time making artisanal pot brownies, which he sells on a motor coach that roams the city. In honor of the nodules, he writes things on paper instead of speaking, his prose terse but good: "Iris, give me back my lighter."

So I was on my way home one night when I happened upon Fred lying beneath his latest piece. Arresting! Moved by this work and the rogue leg that I didn't see jutting out beneath it I fell down, dropping my glass flask of $5.99 whiskey. Lying there, stunned for a moment, I told him, "You're the real thing." He answered by holding out his cup. Artists are our truest capitalists, and so I became his patron.

Prior to our arrangement, his work scattered the city. His latest piece, which I commissioned, is installed within the walls of my burgeoning salon. It cost me some, but if you have to choose between buying a new dress or buying a new piece of art, I always say get both. I turned to show Fred its flattering cut after I got back from Bloomingdale's. He answered me with an approving growl, before I handed him his new horizontally striped shirt.

When the rest of the avant-garde pays visit—Wyndham from the gas company (whose given name is Lloyd), Juan from Time Warner Cable (I call him Gris)—they at first pretend not to notice the shocking piece, though I can tell it has profoundly disturbed them. When they do finally look at it, they almost always agree that it is interesting. A shopping cart sitting unapologetically in the center of the room, with old scarves and clothes and Fred himself bursting out of it yelling unintelligibly!

I admit that I also did not understand it in the beginning. Bumping into it on my way into the kitchenette, I asked Fred would he mind reinstalling it out of the walkway. Fred shook his cup resolutely, and I blushed at my own stupidity before depositing a fiver.

I wrote a profile on him, which will soon be published in *The New Yorker,* though I haven't heard anything back on that front yet. In the meantime I've showed Fred some of my writings, too, which have been greatly influenced by his work. Fred is trying out a kind a visual octagonalism, and my new short stories also have eight sides. It was then that Fred offered to make my portrait.

When the avant-garde visit, they say it looks nothing like me. This enrages Fred who, upon hearing this, pops his head out of the shopping cart and informs them that one day it will. This disconcerted me at first, as it is a paint by number of a T. rex. I do enjoy red meat, however, and his artistic antennae must have picked that up.

My dog, Leo, didn't like it at all at first, though I think now he is coming around. He has a very well-developed aesthetic sense, Leo does, a holdover from his last life, I suppose, when he was Leo Stein, Gertrude's—my—brother. Despite his keen eye, Leo is not an artist himself, and I can tell he harbors some resentment toward me because of it—why should I be a genius and he only terrier? Well, it is the way it is the way it is the.

About my writing you must be curious. I work mostly at night, all through the night—a whole half hour—and never revise. I find it impossible to write for more than a half hour at a time ever since I learned that sitting is the new smoking. What I do is drink quite a lot of coffee while standing, and then I stare at Fred's "shopping cart" and listen to his beer-soaked snores emanating musically from within his fascinating concept.

Fred's work has provided me with no end of inspiration. Indeed it was his wheezing that gave me the idea for my first book, which I had privately printed (publishers today are so afraid of the experimental). It's going to be serialized in *The New Yorker* (as soon as they get back to me) and is called *The Autobiography of the Autobiographer*. Three thousand pages! All of them blank! Every one of my friends at the dog run assured me it was genius, as did the salon members, but publishers these days want only what has come before. Such is the plight of the genius in any age.

The publisher Mead initially showed some interest, but they wanted to cut it by three quarters, line the pages, use a spiral binding, and not pay me or acknowledge my authorship, which I refused. Art does not compromise.

Thus I had one thousand copies printed at my own expense. In addition to my small trust, I have a good sum of money that should be arriving any day now from my patron, Ed McMahon. I've never met Mr. McMahon, but his letters arrive faithfully, ever encouraging of my linguistic experiments.

I keep the books in boxes surrounding my bed, which has come to resemble a rather interesting little fort. Indeed, if the state ever comes for me (as they did for Uncle Francis and Aunt Mathilde), be they incited by my subversive language and innovative narrative structure and how both challenge the status quo and thus the law itself, I feel quite confident that I'll be able to hole up for a good stretch behind my books. I have begun collecting canned goods, too, in the event of the inevitability, should the time of my arrest present itself without warning. Fortress aside, I have sold a few.

Three Lives bookstore around the corner judiciously took on consignment three of my soon-to-be valuable first editions. I like to go and look in on them from time to time. It makes me tremendously happy to see my work out in the world, shaking things up. I had been going every day, looking at them through the window for a variety of hours to counteract the smoking, which I recently learned is the new sitting, until finally the store security guard came out and said he'd notified the police. "You can ban me, but you cannot ban my books!" I told him. Then he asked me to leave, as I was "blocking the window display."

The truth is, I pitied him. He obviously didn't know who I was. Charitable, I told him. I said do you know who I am and he said no who are you and I said I am I because my little dog knows me. I could see he was impressed and felt nervous about how to respond, so I shook his hand and told him it was lovely meeting anybody and left.

Modern art aside, I get my ideas primarily from supermarkets. My second book was a novel entitled *Pickled Pickles*. The first one hundred words is *rutabaga*. If you read it out loud you will see exactly what I mean. If Saussure is correct about the signifier never approaching the signified, why not say *rutabaga*?

About my process, you will want to know more: In the mornings, after I have finished a new piece, I show it to Leo, whose artistic sensibility I trust completely. I gave him *Pickles* to review last Wednesday and three hours later found it in the corner under a smudge of poop. Leo sat in the corner opposite looking livid with folded arms. Critics can be cruel, hostile even, when they see genius on the rise, envious perhaps, for genius be they not!

Unfortunately that is the case with Leo. He is jealous of my recent successes, of my being a genius, of my running a fashionable salon, of the Supercut I gave Fred that first night. But whatever the friction my work may cause between my barking brother and me, I owe it to posterity. The experiment must continue!

But now I must interrupt the day's labor. Fred, Jacob, Leo, and I (Jeff's and I are on a break) are attending an art opening in only an hour, from time to time a thing we do. And though the work we see is for the most part laughable—oh, how we laugh—on the drinks table they have these tiny little pretzels, of which I have grown quite fond.

agnes decides it's time

"I have my reasons," she said, adjusting her glasses. She stuffed her hands into the pockets of her capacious slacks.

"What are your reasons?" he asked kindly, when he might easily have assumed.

He knew he was handsome, but now, preparing himself to listen, he was reminded that he was also humble, which contributed to his great opinion of himself.

"I don't have any," she said, stealing a hand from her pocket to push her glasses up her nose. "I bet Kara likes your sandy hair and Tania likes your blue eyes. Michelle thinks you're good in Speech and Debate and Grace is impressed that you're captain of the swim team. Each of them likes some particular thing about you. Having one or more reasons, they love you more or less."

He touched her hair.

"I'm speaking," she said irritably, regarding his hand.

He withdrew his hand.

"I, on the other hand, like nothing about you, Kevin. I have zero reasons for liking you. And it is this absence of fondness that suggests the possibility of something long lasting: As I have no reason to love you, I shall never have a reason to stop. We might marry, though I'm not ready yet to discuss that. You may now," she motioned, "with my hair."

He raised his hand and touched her hair as before.

She studied his eyes and said, "We will have sex."

She turned and walked toward the twin bed, removed her capacious slacks followed by her white cotton underwear. She sat down facing him.

He looked at her sitting on the bed. Her red-framed glasses too large; her upper half obscured by a black turtleneck; her legs, pale and spindly and joined at the knees, on which her hands rested palms down.

She took off her glasses and folded them onto the dresser, then placed her legs on the bed and lay down on her back. "I'm ready now."

philip and penelope in a variety of tenses

Dear Professor,

I really enjoyed your lecture yesterday on Heidegger and the existential imagination. It got me thinking: Am I becoming too serious with Philip?

Last night he prepared a candlelight dinner. He served chicken, plugged in the candles, and went on to explain the whole difference between us: "The light's just the same as wax candles. Only these never burn out. My sister gave 'em to me for Christmas."

"Yes, just the same," I said sadly. As everyone knows, candles are romantic only because they're consumed by their own fire. "When the robots take over, they will never die or fall in love," I said then, before the perfected light switched off. Philip works with computers and had set the candles on a timer.

It's true I could never love him, but I do not dislove him either. See you Thursday!

—Penelope

P.S. We met at the birthday party of a mutual friend. That was on Saturday, and we've been together ever since. He's in the other room right now, preparing our breakfast with a state-of-the-art egg boiler.

P.P.S. I've enrolled in a creative writing class at the Y. I thought I might try to extend my critical faculties toward an aesthetic disregard for the self and just sort of see where it goes.

Dear Professor,

Gilgamesh is an asshole. I hope this won't affect our friendship. I've had it with these monster myths and am starting to think they're just a way to avoid talking about one's feelings.

Yesterday Philip suggested we stop seeing other people. Panicked, I started talking about Homer. Slyly, he moved the conversation toward Horace—"I think I'm coming down with something; my throat's a little Horace"—and suddenly I'm in a committed relationship.

He asks to see me every day and then looks forlornly into my eyes, as if he had something very important to tell me. I say, "What is it, Philip? Have you something to say?" Then he pauses, looks down, and says, "I was thinking about dinner. What should we eat?"

I've gained five pounds since we met—the weight of belief. I'm sure the existentialists were very thin. Sartre's *Nausea* implies as much. I'm sure de Beauvoir and Sartre took their meals separately, as eating in front of another could be seen as an admission of weakness. What an awful thing to admit that you're hungry, that you lack something as essential as a sandwich.

For a while I couldn't even nibble a cracker near Philip; I was skeptical of him. Yesterday I ate a leg of lamb off the bone. Our relationship is evolving. Philip and I eat elaborate dinners now with many courses. He chews and looks at me. He has nice eyes.

Best,

Penelope

P.S. I attended the first session of the workshop yesterday. The instructor had us go round the room to introduce ourselves and offer a little about what we hoped to get out of the class. The woman to my left, Felicia, explained that Pottery was already closed. A difficult young man with a freckly scowl, Sean (pronounced "Larry"), confessed his girlfriend dumped him a month ago, that she was a bitch anyway, that high school is lame, and that he's partial to E. E. Cummings.

The instructor claims to have known him. E.E., I mean. That's how he refers to him. He says they were in the same graduating class at their primary school in Utah, and that E.E. was a real asshole most of the time, but that they still got on rather well together, and that he felt even then an inkling of his difficulty to punctuate. Cummings stuttered terribly according to the instructor and, in fact, there is only one *E* in his name.

When it was my turn I offered that I was Penelope and that I wanted to learn to write short stories in hopes of improving my wanton abandon during sexual encounters. The instructor seems very supportive.

Have to go now. Philip is looking peevish. We're having dinner together again tonight!

Dear Professor,

He's told me three times now, I think, though am not
sure. He said once in bed, "I love you!" Not sure of his
articulation over the percussion, I smiled and continued moving. Then, after a weekend apart, while
speaking of his croquet score and forking a well-done
steak, he let escape, "God, I love you!" Not sure if he
meant the divine or me, I smiled and his mouth turned
down. I was asleep once, the third time, and am not
sure if I was awake or asleep, actually, when he said,
"I love you, Penelope." My eyes were closed, which is
supposed to heighten one's hearing, but I couldn't be
sure with the air-conditioner on. I said, "What?"

I've been trying to keep my ears open since; I try
not to lie with my ear pressed against his shoulder, in
order to verify the sounds and where they come from
when they do. I angle my head just so.

I've told him beautiful things, too—"Philip, I hate
every minute of you," I confessed yesterday, just in case
I heard him wrong, figuring unrequited hate is prefer-
able to unrequited love. I've already told him during
sex, overheated and irrational perhaps, "Philip, I
know I should perhaps not say this in the heat of the
moment, but I have, however, Philip, developed a
rather fond feeling for the likes of you." I closed my
eyes after. I don't remember his response.

Yours,
Penelope

P.S. I'm sorry you think writing workshops are for
hacks, but I am enjoying the sense of community the
group offers, as well as this flirtation with the right

side of the brain. It is, at the very least, harmless, I think. Do you agree with my instructor, by the way, that "the artist creates his own moral universe?"

Dear Professor,

Thank you for googling my writing instructor and for offering to have him followed. Though I don't believe such precautions to be necessary, I appreciate your concern for my intellectual growth. Yes, I agree one's influences must be handpicked, but I don't see that his will have any deleterious effect on my "burgeoning sense of metaphor," as you put it. And yes, I know he is married, and no, I have not allowed him to touch my breasts "metaphorically speaking or otherwise." Believe me that the warning is not needed. But if it helps you to rest, I will take care to watch out for "the roaming appendages of his moral universe."

Sincerely,
Penelope

Dear Professor,

I've been thinking a good deal about Neoplatonism and how it could work for me; I ordered the entire series of cassettes. I was up late last night and saw your infomercial on PBS. It came on right after the Pasta Pot and before the Ionic Breeze Air Purifier.

I couldn't sleep. Still can't sleep. Up all night lately trying to figure things out with Philip, trying not to call him. Philip told me I should keep him guessing.

So I had just gotten off the phone (I ordered the Pasta Pot. I already have the Ionic Breeze—it doesn't work), when I saw your ad. It will arrive in three to five business days. For now, I am reading from your list: Aurelius's *Meditations*. I copied into my notebook, "It is possible to be happy even in a palace." I opened, too, Virgil's *Aeneid*, hoping for some advice on how to proceed with Philip, whether or not I should perform oral sex on him, but there was nothing usable. The rhyme scheme was interesting, however.

Kind regards,
Penelope

P.S. I am not being seduced by the bohemian "this and that," don't worry. The rigors of academia can hold their own against the "flaccid force of ill-executed feeling," as you put it. But, does modernity hinge on casual sex? And do I even want to be modern? One wonders particularly when reading capsule biographies on collectible bookmarks.

Dear Professor,

I think you were a little hard on Harold yesterday in class. With regard to the Romantics: I rather like Byron, though Coleridge, too, sings in me a suitable sound—it's totally relatable. I often feel as if I were carrying a dead fowl round my neck. Doesn't everybody?

Harold and I discussed your hair after class over coffee. "Those white flames!" I said. He made some salient points. He completely agreed with me, by the way, that Gilgamesh is an asshole. Harold has some interesting ideas. They are largely similar to my own. He suggested we meet again next week to discuss the Dante. Philip refuses to talk with me about Dante.

Best,
Penelope

Dear Professor,

I received your cassette tapes in the post yesterday. I listen to them while I sleep with the idea that they might subconsciously affect my decision-making patterns and with that my sexual prosody. Philip does not like this. He feels your voice disrupts the rhythm of our lovemaking. He often has songs in his head, and he claims your voice is dissonant. I guess. He says it does not match my own sound.

Philip believes people emit sounds. Very minute vibrations, he says, of varying frequency. I asked him what my song was, whether it was popular, a rag, or an aria, for example, trying to get at his feelings for me. He kept his mouth tight. He did say it becomes louder during sex, however.

He doesn't know this, but I hid a tape recorder beneath the bed last night and listened to it this morning after he left for work. But I noticed nothing over the usual sound of headboard and box spring and a few verbs he likes to use. I don't know. Does my body make a sound when I sit for your lectures?

Philip and Penelope Go to Bed for the First Time

He said, "What's your favorite color?"

He said, "What do you say when you meet new persons?"

He said, "How old were you when you learned to ride a bicycle?"

He said, "Whom do you love more, your mother or your father?"

"What's your favorite flower, food, and/or cassette tape?"

"How often do you have your hair trimmed, and do you answer the hairdresser honestly when she asks how you are doing?"

"Do you read the paper, the late or early edition, which section first?"

"Do you fly in your dreams and/or breathe underwater?"

"Have you ever suffered from amnesia, Tunisia, or the company of women named Felicia?"

"If you were a verb, would you be transitive or intransitive?"

"Are you better at charades or forensics at parties?"

"Have you always liked cartoons, science fiction, and your hair to be long?"

"What would your name be if it started with a Q?"

"Do you believe that children should be made to work in factories?"

"Does candy make you live longer? Cigarettes? That quart of whiskey?"

"Do you own a separate towel just for the beach?"

"When you eat clams, is it the clam or the breading of which you are fond? Or is it the overriding sense of boardwalks?"

"What is it about boardwalks?"

"Why do they make you take those tests for scoliosis in grade school if only to tell you, 'Yeah, you have it, there's nothing we can do?'"

"Can I take this off? And this? And this?"

Philip and Penelope in Bed After the First Time

"What's wrong?"

"I love you," she said, her eyes wet and trembling.

Penelope in the First Person

To Sharon in Central Park:

"We stopped at a deli yesterday to get matches, and I was saying about the Joseph Campbell program on Channel Thirteen, the episode called 'Love and the Goddess' in which Joseph Campbell tells Bill Moyers about early documentation of romantic love. How the troubadours were the first to sing of it, and that love is a kind of agony. 'The anguish of being totally alive,' I paraphrased next to the pork rinds. 'Love is a pain, Philip. You see?' I told him. 'Should we get anything else? A soda, or juice or something? A pain, so true,' I said. Hold on. Isn't Sheep Meadow *that* way? I'm sorry, what were we talking about?"

To Aspiniza at Grand Central Bar:

"Wednesday morning we walked across town together on his way to work, and I asked him if he believed in spontaneous human combustion. I was saying how it was actually a reasonable possibility, as there are monks in Tibet who can dry wet towels on their backs by willing hot temperatures. He pointed to the probability of witchcraft or trickery, the ubiquitous influence of Tony Robbins cassette tapes, but I offered further and more centrally that 'People blush, don't they? Their body heat rises with a disturbance of mood? If one becomes embarrassed, the face might flush—this is true?' He conceded. 'Well,' I said, 'There you are! Imagine being so embarrassed or ashamed that beyond blushing you become enflamed!' I leapt over a pothole. We were under the scaffolding on Twelfth and so I told him, 'I know that's how I'll go. I'll be giving a speech at the Policemen's Benevolent Association, where I've become a member, and upon stuttering my closing words, I'll burst into flames. How do you think you're going to bite it?' Are we staying by the way? Should I order another drink?"

To Charmaigne at the diner:
"On Friday night we'd just left the movie theater on Fourteenth and were walking through Union Square. We saw that new zombie movie and I asked Philip if he was afraid. Of zombies. He said there was no such thing, and I explained to him about that being how they get you. 'That's how they get you,' I explained. Where is our waiter? 'Because you never expect a zombie to lean over and bite you. The zombie apocalypse is the result of a faithless world. A lack of belief in zombies is what brings on zombies. It's an allegory. The question follows: When God dies will he become a zombie? According to Nietzsche, God died in 1882 and we were left with existentialism. In the twenty-first century, God un-dies and we are left with absurdism and the zombie rom-com. The movie was quite realistic in my opinion,' I told him. So that was Friday. Then we had dinner. But enough about me, how are things with you and Craig?"

Penelope Thinking on the Subway Platform

I love the way his teeth are corroded as a result of a childhood smoking habit while caddying golf clubs for gentlemen in Connecticut. That he takes good care these days, brushing them meticulously with the electric instrument morning and night, while mine are white and I sometimes pretend to forget to floss before we go to sleep, but talk to him while his mouth is full of paste. That he gives me these large cups of coffee in the morning and fries toast on a skillet because there isn't much room for appliances. How he keeps a book on mixing cocktails in the freezer, stores his pots and pans in the oven, and moves his dish rack with forethought to the closet where he keeps the bar and grill. I love this about him; when he suggests a nightcap then has two, when he removes the dice in order to get at the microwave. He lets me reheat my coffee in the microwave—the cups are too large and I have to because I can't drink all the coffee fast enough—while he dresses for work. I sit on the couch and sip my coffee and eat my toast and reread the books I've given him and sometimes pause to linger over the spice rack, which is over the stove. "I've never met a man with so many spices," I said yesterday, regarding the jar of dill next to the curry powder. "You've never met a man like me," he said pumping air into his bicycle tires, the bicycle next to the refrigerator next to the oven.

Words and Phrases Penelope Likes

"Hell's bells"

"Trousers"

Use of the pronoun "one" with regard to matters personal, e.g., "One thinks one left the stove on," Penelope says to Philip when saying goodbye at the airport. Or, "One loves one."

"For that matter"

"Furthermore"

"Disease"—as in a state of discomfort. "I am dis-eased," she pronounces at a cocktail party where she does not know the host.

"Nevertheless"

"And," when feeling particularly moved by the romantic implications of conjunctions.

"Really!" (Instead of "Really?" Not to be confused with "Really.")

Words and Phrases Philip Makes Use Of

"The fact of the matter" with regard to his opinions.

"The truth of the matter" with regard to the opinions of others.

"Moreover" when Penelope is sitting too close.

"Furthermore" when she is still sitting too close.

"It's not the heat, it's the humidity," in summary of the human plight.

"Perhaps" when prefacing a negative response.

"If"

"I smoke like a fish that smokes a lot."

"I drink like a chimney that drinks a lot."

Exclamations of joy or appreciation such as "Great!" "Fantastic," or "Wowsers."

"Wonderbar" intimating the joy of candy. Not, however, "Wunderbar."

"Love" as in the statements: "I love you; I love salad." "There's nothing I love more than an individually wrapped bite-size Snickers bar, and you." And "God, I love steak, and also you," he'll confess at a BBQ on Tuesday.

General: Slipping popular song lyrics into casual conversation without prompting the raising of eyebrows, e.g., Penelope is pouring coffee in the morning and asks Philip if he would like some more. He responds, "Fill me up, Buttercup."

Penelope and Philip Have an Argument

PENELOPE: Stop calling me "Turbo."

PHILIP: I thought you liked it when I called you "Turbo."

PENELOPE: Yes, because I thought that nickname was just for me. It made me sick to hear you go around calling everyone "Turbo" at the party last night. (*Penelope begins making the bed.*) It sounds stupid and it's impersonal. Nicknames are supposed to be personal, Philip.

PHILIP: What's the big deal?

PENELOPE (*raising her voice*): How would you like it if I went around calling you and everyone we know "Felix?" "Felix!" "Felix!" You wouldn't like it, would you?

PHILIP: I wouldn't mind it, but the truth of the matter is I'd much rather be called "Turbo."

Penelope in Her Notebook during Friday's Lecture

What is it about him? The dangerous sense of cholesterol?

Penelope Writes to Harold, Not Sure of Her Intention

Dear lover of many broken things (drain pipes, chronology, the history of lunar eclipses, and the YMCA),

> I'm sorry, Harold. I'm not sure why I called you that.
>
> My new boyfriend has come on like a rash. At least, I think he's my boyfriend. I'm certainly showing all the symptoms. My plan is not to scratch him for a week and see if he goes away all by himself. Harold: Am I in love?
>
> I read an interesting critique of Sartre yesterday. That though his ideas claimed revolution and the death of god—not the French death that makes women cry after sex, but Nietzsche's—his writing (take *Nausea*, for example) is really quite staid. Absolutely! The point seems obvious now. Otherwise, how are you?
>
> Send me a note with some tidings of your gait (how

you're walking these days—slow, fast, or with a deci-
sive freak out of the hip),

Penelope

P.S. Have begun signing my letters on the left side of
the page in order to encourage right brain thinking.

Philip and Penelope Going to Bed

Penelope lay on the bed in her underwear. "Let's say I say, 'I like
those trousers on you. Those trousers are nice,' but really, they are
only okay. And also, in a Saussurian sense, what do I even mean by
trousers? You know? I mean, when I try to tell you how I feel, the
words slip and become their own thing. The signifier and the signified can't connect... I've been thinking about our relationship."
Philip took off his pants.
"One gets an odd sense when one kisses one, as if life were a
personal matter," she said toward the ceiling.
Penelope continued to recline with her hands behind her head.
"You seem to love me. And stones," she added, furrowing her
brow, noting his vast collection of the less popular tectosilicates
on the dresser.
"And I am like a stone"—she got up to dress the bed—"I'm certainly more mineral than animal, that's true. And perhaps there
in lies your interest. Nevertheless—how one wishes one could be
less." She slipped beneath the bedcovers and he slipped beneath
the bedcovers and found her hips, then her mouth. She blushed,
looking at him, "Do I talk too much, Philip?"

Philip Receives a Postcard from Penelope on Wednesday Afternoon

"I dreamt of you yesterday. You were in the kitchen demonstrating again how to separate the egg whites."

Philip and Penelope Continue to Argue

"You're so argumentative!"
  "You are!"
  "You speak too loudly!"
  "I can't hear you when you mumble!"

Views of Philip Chewing

"I disagree," she said examining the coffee.
  "MMMmmm," he chewed.

"If your lips were made of paper," she typed over Instant Messenger at noon, "I am sure that I could fold them more than seven times in half."
  Philip chewed on his lunch break.

"I dislike the smell of gasoline," she said at the gas station, regarding the Dipsy Doodles in his hand.
  He chewed and unlocked the car door.

"Most men would insist on carrying my suitcase, but not you. I wonder, is it the weight or the principle, or the weight of the principle?" she asked while waiting for the bus.
  Philip bit an apple and, looking off to see if the bus was coming, he chewed.

"My mother thinks you're argumentative, too," she said after the waiter took the bread away.

He thought about this while he chewed.

Penelope Meets with Her Professor over Lunch to Discuss the Dante

"Philip is all the time. I love him now, which is everything."

"Kierkegaard will clear that right up. Rub some on your elbow."

"I feel as if I were being flung through the air, toward a recycling dump of plastics and glass, and will have to crash eventually, hopefully, sorted."

"Landfills are at the heart of every great relationship. The Acropolis was built over a landfill, just like that ski resort in Vermont they featured on *60 Minutes*. The Greek lovers were famous. God's gift to the people, the olive from which they made oil had a multitude of uses—a place to dip bread, to unstick stubborn windows, soap, and lube to be exported in clay urns decorated with lovers of the ancient variety."

"I have decided to stop swimming in Philip's dramatic pauses. Is this the end or can there be something more?"

"A question I often ask myself at faculty meetings—should there be more Dante on the syllabus? The red-haired dean rejected my proposal, Penelope."

"Philip is leaving me and you speak of Beatrice?"

Penelope and Philip Agree to See Other People

"How was work today?"

"Fine."

Penelope: How It Is with Harold

"I don't love you particularly."
  "What?"
  "Nothing." Penelope regarded Harold's ears.
  The waves rushed.
  "I love you," Harold said, next to the fish shack.
  "What?"

Philip: How It Is with Mona

"Fuck me slowly at first, then a little faster, but not too fast, just a little faster. After a while, three measures in two-four time maybe, three or four at your discretion, actually, make it three or five, even numbers are inartistic." (Mona played the viola in a garage orchestra that rehearsed at her pregnant friend Mary's house in Connecticut. Her husband, though, was reaching his limit with the group.) "Then begin the syncopation. Like a heartbeat. Wait, before we begin, let me feel your heart to see if that's right. No, no, yours is too slow. You'll have to speed it up some or the whole thing will be lost and I won't be able to come. But not too fast either, because then I get anxious and start to think about work. God, my boss is on my case lately. The Frye design! I should quit."

Philip put her hand on his penis. He moved it and she continued to speak. He took her hand off. Philip put on a condom.

"Yes, yes, to the left, to the right, there, now double up, one Mississippi, count Philip, you're not counting! One Mississippi— your heart's beating too fast! There! There! There!"

Philip heard sounds when he was with a woman, not necessarily audible, but feel-able, and from the sound he knew whether or not he was in love. Penelope's sound was quiet, the sound of the ocean bed. The silence occasionally punctuated by a sniffle. "Sometimes I hear her sniffling when I'm at work," he'd told Lozario at happy hour.

Philip got up and walked over to the bathroom. He could hear behind him the faint echo of Beethoven's "Ode to Joy" emanating off Mona from the bed. Of all compositions! He shut the door and pulled off the condom; threw it in the toilet.

Dinner with Friends

She'd had food in her teeth. After he told her he needed time, she'd smiled over her plate to make it easy for him. And she'd had food in her teeth. Philip thought: Who could ever love her, her with food in her teeth? The image was burned in his mind. She looked ridiculous, pathetic. He thought about it over dinner the next night. "But who of us hasn't after all, at one time or another had food inopportunely caught in one's teeth? My teeth are not flawless." He picked his teeth with a toothpick as he sat down to dinner with friends. His friends tried to get his attention, but he was given to his thoughts. He was thinking of her, Penelope, that she did look beautiful, however, for example, when she didn't know he was looking and began to pick her nose. How ridiculous, how pathetic! Who could ever love her? Her with her finger in her nose? Did he want her back?

Philip and Penelope Run into Each Other on the Street after Three Months

"Destiny or Divine Punishment?" Penelope asked at the corner of a stone edifice.

"Coincidence," Philip answered.

"In a series on Channel Thirteen, Moyers and Campbell discuss the idea of courtly love as sung by the European troubadours of the twelfth and thirteenth centuries. Campbell asserts that prior to that time the idea of marriage solely for personal love, marriage as a person-to-person thing, did not exist as a social system. There had always been isolated incidences of it, but after that time it became 'the ideal,' at any rate, of love in the Western world. And Campbell points out that this is what makes the West unique: That the individual is taught to have faith in the validity of his own experience 'against the monolithic system.' Further, he goes on to discuss love as a kind of agony, a sublime agony . . ."

"I know," Philip said. "You told me."

She regarded the building next to her. She was about to say something else.

Philip touched the tips of her fingers with his. Her hands with his.

He looked at her.

She smiled a little.

Philip took a long breath, then bent to the line of her mouth.

Pornography

Penelope asked Philip if he had any pornography and gave him mischievous eyes on the couch Saturday afternoon. After some coaxing he produced a film. "It was a gift," he supplied, "from the manufacturer of pornographic videos to which I subscribe." They debated for some time whether they should or should not watch it. Philip didn't want to, "I don't think it's a good idea." But Penelope insisted.

Penelope watched with widening eyes. After Philip and Penelope made love, after she came three times and moaned unusually loudly, she said, tears brimming, "Do you like her more than me?"

Penelope Conceives of a Poem and Brings It to the Workshop

"The protagonist reminds one of a jellyfish," said Sean, disgusted.

"It reminds me of the Grecian urn," said the woman from the Y.

"It's electric," said the instructor excitedly. "But Penelope, the voice seems to me a bit subjective. Perhaps you might consider removing all of the vowels. I think you'll be well surprised at how it tightens the prose while not compromising the character of the initial impetus to express."

The class nodded and agreed she might lose the vowels.

Philip in the Morning When Penelope Walks in

Philip sat naked in bed. The radio on his lap, he adjusted the antenna to the Charlie Parker program he enjoyed every morning—they had been playing nothing but Charlie Parker for the last fifteen years. They played Charlie Parker and thought about Charlie Parker and talked about Charlie Parker every morning over the radio. Philip was thinking about Charlie Parker when Penelope opened the door. "Yikes," he said, startled from his aggressive tuning. Penelope squinted, he thought, looking at her through the doorframe.

"When I say 'Yikes' it means, 'I love you.' What did you mean?" Penelope asked.

"You startled me."

Philip in the First Person

To Guillermo laying down his bike in the park:
"Women emit sounds. It's nothing like sonar. It's like music, all different kinds of music. For you, it's a woman's scent that catches you; it's something like that, that she can't help. The sound that comes from each woman, especially after, is unique. Most of them don't know that they can be heard. They don't know they have a sound. But I hear it. Sometimes it's all I hear. And when I love a woman the song stays with me all day. Another drink?"

To Michael downstairs on their lunch break:
"Last night Penelope and I watched a documentary on commercial fishing boats off of Sheepshead Bay. Then we went to bed. I'm exhausted. She hits me when I snore. What'd you do last night?"

To Clive in the kitchen during the Super Bowl:
"I think she wants to get married. She keeps talking about spontaneous human combustion. Brings it into every conversation. It intimates finality. Reproductive expiration dates. Five-year plans. Clocks. She looks at babies on the subway for a very long time. She speaks of the future in pointed metaphors. She wants me to make our weekend plans way in advance. Unwavering. I don't know. I don't know. I'm not sure that I'm ready. She wants me to save her, take her to seven o'clock movies. This guacamole is really good. Did Janie make it? You're a lucky man, Clive."

Penelope Brings a Short Story to the Writing Workshop and Receives Tough Rebukes. Sean, in a Loud Voice, Says, "It's Pronounced Larry!"

HARBINGERS

We spent a weekend on Long Island. I took him to my parents' empty house. It was a cold weekend after a hot week in the city, in the fever of which we'd planned to run from last weekend's spree spent together whiskey soaked in a summer house in the Catskills, where his "I could spend a lifetime with you" turned into "not another minute."

But then in the back seat of the car on the way home his foot touched mine, and we passed the jar of vodka orange till we were in love again. His friends rode in front, and we all confessed to shameful acts: pornography collections, cheating at backgammon, stolen chewing gum. . . . No one mentioned any hearts. I offered the pack of Juicy Fruit I lifted from a drugstore when I was twelve, which I carry with me always—you have to steal to own. The chewing gum is nonrefundable and therefore mine. I keep it close in my breast pocket. The wrapper's lost its shape.

We raced toward the city in the back of a Jeep, and he looked at me as if he were renting space in my heart and was happy with the furnishings, though how long he would stay he didn't know.

"Damn it!" He had thrown the whiskey down into the creek out back of the house in the Catskills. "I hate you when you drink. I often enjoy being around you," he minced, "but I have . . . reservations." He cupped his hands at the water's edge. Scotch and water. There was no ice in the house.

All the things you love are all the things you hate. I thought of Zeno's paradox and turned away so as not to show my tears. I'm tired of paradoxes. "When I leave you're going to miss me, and when I return you will suffer under my cold and practiced shoulder. My shoulder is used to, you see, low temperatures," I did not say but warned him with my silence. The water trickled by and I put my feet in to feel it rush past without us. "I like you, you know," I said and shrugged.

We didn't break up, but raced back into the city, had a nightcap, and kissed hard with our mouths closed.

The next week was long and we decided together to see the beaches of Long Island. On Saturday and Sunday, we shivered in the sand. The beach was deserted but for the lifeguard above us. Philip, next to me, fell asleep on his side; I filled his ear with sand. I told him then in low tones how it was with me. Taking his silence for agreement, I tickled his chin to make him nod yes, before I lay down next to him and listened to his breath mingle with the wind.

On Sunday we traveled the same route to the beach. Heading east on the Southern State, tangled in conversation, we got lost. Turning around in the parking lot of the boarded up Pilgrim State Asylum, I sang on about shock treatments and my illustrious family history. "What?" I said lightly, responding to his raised eyebrows. "I thought everyone's family was crazy. That's what people say, isn't it?"

"Not literally."

"You're too much with the details. There's the service road."

On the beach I kissed him. Then I looked away, pretending for a few minutes that I didn't know him, that I hardly wanted him. He grasped me around the waist, the way men do if you don't look at them for long enough in just the right way. He kissed the back of my neck. His breath was hot. "I must have you," he almost would have said. The wind blew.

We took the Long Island Rail Road home to Manhattan after that and just one stop in, our peanut butter jar began to leak its leaky contents. Gin and Lemonade were sweating out the lid. So we raced to catch it with our mouths before it fell, drank it fast and then regarded the fine weekend. We were tired and became quiet.

He read *Popular Mechanics,* and I looked out the window. The train stopped five minutes into his article and five minutes into my seventh cloud from the left. The weekend was over and the heat began pouring in. We kissed in the stillness. An announcement from the conductor sounded over the loudspeaker. Then men came through the car and ordered all the passengers out, forward or backward.

We trudged along with our weekend bags; I don't remember if we trudged forward or backward. What I remember is asking one of the police officers we passed on the way to the next car, "Why has the train been stopped?"

"A man has thrown himself onto the tracks."

Philip and Penelope Have an Argument about Their Relationship

"Work is good, I guess. Though I wish I was working on a different project."

"Were," corrected Penelope.

"The movie was good. But I wish it was better."

"Were," scowled Penelope.

"My father's in town tonight. You ought to meet him. Can you come to dinner? I know it's a pain. I wish he was coming next week, when I wouldn't be so busy."

"Were," she continued to twirl her pasta.

"I love you, Penelope."

"Were," she sat across from him.

Philip and Penelope Have a Philosophical Discussion Late at Night

"Do you think you'd still like me if I were a woman and you were a man? I mean do you think we'd get along?" asked Philip.

"I often ask myself a similar thing. I ask: 'If Philip were a break-fast food, would he be high in cholesterol?'"

"Must you answer every question with a question?"

"Must you?"

"It's like that rule about paintings, how a true work of art should be just as beautiful turned upside down. I don't think we'd be beautiful upside down. The good kind of cholesterol or the bad kind of cholesterol?"

"Artery clogging. You're already pretty artery clogging. I think we'd be wonderful upside down," she said, leaving the room.

Philip Watching Penelope Cry

The spaghetti was long. She held back. The water glass in front of her mouth. "Of course, of course." Her eyes wiggling, she put the glass down. "I . . ." looking away, looking back, at the spaghetti, at the water glass, the inescapable appetizer. Why hadn't it arrived yet? She looked off toward the kitchen. She laughed. "The service here is terrible."

Philip to Penelope in the Back of a Cab

Penelope looked out the window. The car wended around Columbus Circle. The trees were green and the sky nine o'clock blue. The wind rose; you could see through the window the sound of the leaves. Philip looked at her, the blue dress with the gift-wrapped box on her lap. "I'm just not sure."

3

Dear Penelope,

I apologize for not correcting your letter. I should have understood immediately that it was a test. Of course you would never allow yourself to punctuate so haphazardly. Still, I thought perhaps you were so excited by your treatise on carbs and how this excludes your seeing me again that you forgot yourself and misplaced a semicolon.

I am grateful that you have begun responding to me, at least. And more, for the care you took in returning my previous letter, which you corrected. But red ink is so harsh, honey! Couldn't you at least use blue? I poured my heart out and my letter came back bleeding. And while I value your critique on the prose style I've employed to win you back, it left me with so little to warm my hands on. I've run my fingers over your inserted commas so much that the paper is worn in places that required my additional punctuation. Is this as close as you will allow me to get to you? Still, I must insist that some of your commas are a matter of taste and not form, but have it your way. Whatever it takes.

Also, just to clarify, my not finding your strategically placed errors in your own letter does not mean, as you wrote, "that one doesn't like one enough. That one doesn't care enough to find fault with one, that one doesn't think about one in detail or look at one closely enough." Anyway, you told me I was too judgmental the last we spoke. I believe your exact words were,

"You're a judgmental prick." You see, I do pay attention! How was I to take that, honey?

> Your's,
> Philip

P.S. I wish I was next to you right now.

Dear Penelope,

> My "insistence," as you say, on not using the subjunc-
> tive in reference to my wishing I WERE with you, was
> not intended as an act of "aggression." I'm sorry you
> took my mistake for arrogance. Yes, I understand you
> haven't yet made up your mind. It was only a grammat-
> ical error; the copula is tricky. You have a point about
> the heart of every joke housing a kernel of truth, and
> that, further, at the heart of every spelling and gram-
> mar mistake lies the true feelings of the letter writer.
> But can't you allow that this one time it was an honest
> mistake? The subjunctive mood is complicated and I
> often confuse it with the conditional. Can we meet to
> discuss this?

> Miss you,
> Philip

P.S. Yes, I was aware of the unnecessary apostrophe in
the closing of my last letter and, no, it was not put there
to mock you, your sense of the modern, your taste in
clothes, or your skills in the kitchen, as you said. I just
miss you and since you won't allow me to see you, I
knew if I extended a wrongly placed apostrophe you

would not be able to resist drawing a circle around it. How I wish you would draw a circle around me. I guess it was manipulative on my part. I'm sorry (but not really).

Dear Penelope,

I know you'd never consent to my telephoning, and seeing me in person, you've said, is out of the question. As you explained, "[You] [are] having trouble inhabiting a sense of I with regard to [me] right now." But letters are so slow. Why can't we at least email? I understand you "need time to think," but I'm running out of stamps, and the post office is always closed by the time I finish work, and I have to go on my lunch break, and then I am hungry all day. Do you really want me to be hungry all day?

–Philip

Dear Penelope,

Thank you for sending me a sandwich with your last letter. It was very thoughtful. It showed me despite your coolness that you still care. It was a bit soggy and bruised by the time it arrived, but you know I like a sandwich to ripen. Everyone on line at the post office was jealous of my turkey/honey mustard. It was sweet, like you.

Love,
Philip

Dear Penelope,

I know, I know. You've told me a million times that tense is important. I apologize for ending my previous letter so ambiguously. Though isn't ambiguity the essence of poetry? Didn't you tell me this? You read me a passage of Nemerov's over the phone that night after Jacob's party, the night we met.

I had been talking with Eugene when you asked my opinion of the weather. I told you my theory of humidity. I remember I found you strange but asked your name anyway. You ran off before I got it—Jacob wanted to introduce you to Richard. I admit I was jealous, though I didn't realize it at the time. Later, I spotted you putting on your coat. "I still don't know your name," I said. Do you remember? "Will you write it down?" I asked, and gave you the back of a receipt. Beside your phone number you wrote, "To Be Continued." God, you're difficult! Anyway, let me clarify: I love you and I loved you. Is that wrong? I mean, grammatically?

Love, loved,
Philip

P.S. Thank you for sending me another copy of Strunk and White. I agree it is invaluable. The passages on "hopefully" and "lay vs. lie" are among my favorites, too. Perhaps we might have a drink some time and read to each other from the set of common errors?

Dear Penelope,

You asked about the future. If I *will* love you, etc. But I am afraid of making a mistake, mixing tenses. How can I tell you? You want so much. Can it be enough, today and yesterday, for now? Can't we start again here? Perhaps we can develop a new dictionary together. You've told me language is mutable. You said so at the Italian place on Tenth Street after you won the swimming trophy. Dear, how can I describe the future today when the words might not be in active use tomorrow? What if the grammar changes? What if everything becomes "bootylicious?" Will you fault me for that, too? Just let me hold you again. Can I?

In a variety of tenses,
Philip

Dear Philip,

Okay.

—Penelope

P.S. Please don't read what I've crossed out.

a fortune of cookies

One day you'll put a pen down with your right hand and pick it up with your left, and your writing will be illegible.

One day you'll go outside and, realizing you forgot your umbrella, go back inside to get it.

One day you'll go outside and, realizing you forgot your umbrella, will not go back inside but buy a small one on the street that will immediately break.

One day everyone you've ever loved will return to you and say, "I heard you on Alec Baldwin's *Here's the Thing.*"

One day Paula Abdul's "Straight Up" will be the national anthem and no one will know why.

One day you will watch Nick at Nite with your significant other and get an idea for a TV show called *Insignificant Others,* but will stay together for another year.

One hour you will feel hungry again.

One day you will realize that you hate the winter because you fear what you don't understand.

One day you will realize you hate the winter because you are the winter.

One day you will buy a warmer coat and realize you never hated the winter but were just cold.

One day your mother will ask you how the writing's going and you'll say, "fine" and she'll pause and say, "maybe you should consider teaching."

One day you will not trust the calorie count listed on the wrapper.

One day your ex will send you a text that says "hi" and you will think for a long time before you text "hi" back and then instantly regret it.

One day you will get high with your roommate and ask, "Who is General Tso and was he an effective military leader?"

One day you will wonder if it's okay to order Chinese food two days in a row.

One day you will lose all interest in Gertrude Stein and say so belligerently after you get too drunk at a literary party where everyone has published except for you.

One day you will buy Dipsy Doodles from a vending machine, though you have never liked Dipsy Doodles and there were plenty of better options.

One day you will have 2,341 unread emails.

One day you'll realize that "one day" was yesterday.

One day you will adopt an elephant online and feel disappointed because they don't mail it to you, but just once a month withdraw money electronically from your bank account for the elephant's food.

One day you will understand that even if they did mail you the elephant, where would you put it?

One day you will contact your favorite Chinese restaurant and ask them what *they* want.

One day you will contact the Chinese restaurant, mention their great fortune cookies, and, after asking who writes them, say, "Wow, he's really talented. He should come write for my TV show."

One day you will think to yourself, "If only I could meet someone who understands me as well as this fortune cookie."

One day you will realize you have met someone who understands you as well as this fortune cookie when your father, who is Dick Wolf, introduces you to his new protégé who no longer writes fortune cookies but works on a mega hit TV show, and so was able to move out of his parents' basement.

One day he will look into your eyes and tell you that he has three MFA degrees—one in classical Spanish guitar, another in pottery, and a third in salmon fishing, but none in creative writing. You will wonder how he knows you so well, considering you are not a fish, a clay pot, or a Spanish guitar. He will tell you he has always known you, kiss you, and then propose.

One day after you're married, your husband, who is now the showrunner of his own TV mega hit, will take you in his arms and say, "Life is a comedy for those who think and a tragedy for those who feel," and you will ask, "What about *Alf?*"

One day he will answer, "*Alf* is a comedy for those who feel and a tragedy for those who think, and it's about time for a reboot." He will make a lot of money.

One day someone else will write the messages in these fortune cookies, but they won't be as good.

aboard the shehrazad

At five feet, seven inches and with a slightly extravagant build, he was much too large for the small wicker basket in which he lay naked with his wrists and ankles negligently bound. I was traveling south on board the Shehrazad, an Egyptian cruise liner that passes between Aswan and Luxor every three days on the Nile. It was noon and I was sunning myself off the ship's prow with Ebo, the ship' s cook, when I spotted a shiny reflective thing amid the bulrush along the eastern bank, what turned out to be the nubile flesh of Mr. Jacob Augustus Blau.

I picked up my binoculars, then sent Ebo inside to fetch my grappling hook. Following a few less than successful attempts, I hooked the basket and pulled it aboard. Standing over the still unconscious figure, I instructed Ebo to go to my stateroom where he'd likely find Albert, my butler, perusing my collection of *InStyle* magazines. "Tell him to stop opening all the fragrance samples. Then ask him to bring my smelling salts, the guest Speedo, and a bottle of Captain Morgan's nonalcoholic rum."

Albert arrived on deck in a gale of sighs that is typical of him and with the requested provisions. I immediately attended to business, resuscitating Jacob with the salts, refreshing myself with the Captain's N.A., and then, once Jacob had fully regained his senses, inviting him to don the guest Speedo. It was red and, just as I'd anticipated, went very well with his pale olive complexion.

"It provides a nice contrast to the brown in his hair. Don't you think so, Albert?"

"An impeccable combination. Madame has chosen wisely."

Jacob blushed.

I asked him his name, where he'd come from, what he was doing naked in the bulrush with his wrists and ankles bound, if my husband had sent him.

"Jacob Augustus Blau, freelance medical anthropologist." He pressed a hand to his naked breast. "I'm afraid I haven't any cards. I split my time between New Hampshire and Princeton. I don't think I know your husband. Unless—on a recent visit to Phuket, where I'd gone to research local varieties of Lorynx root, I met a piece of animated granite going by the name of Bing. He was a traveling salesman and tried to sell me a countertop with eyes— his sister. Unable to settle on a mutually acceptable price, he finally broke down, confessing to me that his whole family had fallen on hard times. After his parents accepted a high-interest loan from an infernal spirit named Sammael, whom they'd been unable to pay in due course, Sammael demanded payment via the contract's auxiliary clause, which promised that their children, he, and the rest of his brothers and sisters work as a staircase in Sammael's East Hampton summer home until the debt could be satisfied. He and his sister had recently broken away in hopes of making enough money to buy their siblings' freedom. Their efforts so far, however, had met with little success. Was that your husband?"

"No."

Jacob nodded. He had no memory of how or why he had arrived in the bulrush, he went on, though I suspected he knew much more than he was telling. He spoke guardedly and his discomfort even in disclosing where he lived and what he did was easily gleaned. His caution, however, illustrated a commendable prudence, for I was a stranger to him then and he was very far from home.

As a show of goodwill, I offered him use of my Coppertone Coconut Oil SPF –36. "It magnifies UV rays up to twice their standard concentration, producing tanning results that were previously available only on Mars. I bought it in the ship's gift shop."

He thanked me with a flourish and rubbed some on the bridge of his nose and across his shoulders, before confessing that what he really could use was some food.

I thought for a moment. "Albert. Have a room made up for Mr. Blau next to mine, then see that he finds his way to the dining compartment for an early supper at eight p.m. Mr. Blau," I turned back to him and shook his hand, "I never eat before eight p.m." I motioned to my figure. "It keeps me young. I shall see you at eight, Mr. Blau. You'll find some soda crackers, mixed nuts, cookies, and champagne in your room to tide you over. I suggest you avoid the cookies, however. They're made of a rare combination of time and space gathered from the eastern arm of our galaxy and have a tendency to upset the stomach if consumed this side of the equator either before or after 9:31 p.m. on the dot. Some people explode. Albert, be sure and find Mr. Blau a dinner jacket. You will not be allowed into the dining compartment without one, I'm afraid. And pants."

The sun had moved only two inches in the sky since I'd first spotted Mr. Blau, gleaming and bulbous among the reeds. I judged from its new position that it was two o' clock. Still peak sunbathing hours. So I remained on deck with Ebo, who'd been peevishly silent for the duration of the rescue. Then at four p.m. Ebo and I retired as well, he to the galley to resume his afternoon kitchen duties, and I to my room to stretch and prepare my costume for the evening ahead.

At eight p.m., the percussion section announced our entrance into the dining compartment. We entered from the kitchen. Kashta, my Nubian dance partner, sashayed first. The three-piece band, composed of bongos, clarinet, and lute strung with refined pig guts, was assembled behind the dance floor facing the dinner tables. Kashta—in black leather pants (acquired for an excellent price at a bazaar in Alexandria, so he informed me) under a traditional Bishari blouse that he wore unbuttoned to the navel in order to show off the oversize gold cartouche on which was inscribed in hieroglyphics, BIG PIMPIN' KASHTA, his rapper name—danced with a cane in an otherwise traditional Bishari style, clearing a path as he moved through the crowd of mostly English and American tourists. With Kashta finally in full view on the dance floor, the lights dimmed, and the music quieted as well, so that only the bongos sounded now, low and steady, like the sound of your heart in your ears when holding your breath under water.

Concealed behind the kitchen door, I waited the usual fifteen seconds for the heartbeats of the audience to sync up with the drum, and then I kicked the door open and the lights went out completely, before they were turned on again at a blinding wattage. The clarinet player screamed, the lute player howled, Kashta fell back as if struck by an angry God, and the audience gasped. The music sprang up again louder and even more hectic than before, and it was then that I began making my way via hips unstoppable, through the parted crowd to join Kashta where he lay, folded backward from his knees in ecstatic paralysis.

Arriving adjacent Kashta on my knees as well, so that I faced the audience while he, hinged back, faced the ceiling, the torrential melody of clarinet and lute softened, and with its quieting, the frequency of my shaking quickened so that my shimmy became a shiver. Slowly, I shivered back, positioning myself identically to the already prostrate Kashta. Then I quickened my shiver further still, so that its frequency became so narrow, so tight, so uncommonly fast that to the naked eye I looked as if I'd stopped dancing altogether, as if I were only standing very still but had for some reason become blurry—a technique I learned in Madagascar last year at the Discothèque Haute Plateux where the after party for

Antananarivo's Annual Tumbling Festival was being held. A nice young Malagasy named Fankanonikaka handed me a glow stick before teaching me the Fuzzy.

At the surrounding tables, members of the audience one at a time began rubbing their eyes, confusing the blurry effect of my dancing for a lapse in their vision. Without slowing, I lowered myself further still until, lying beside Kashta, I was like a hot inscrutable letter on the bottom row of a dizzying eye chart.

Reactivating Kashta with the touch of my hand, we both began "fuzzing," and as the music grew louder, together we rose up. The audience began cheering confusedly, as if to mourn and cele-brate our death and subsequent rebirth before them on the dance floor. On the swell of clarinet, we shivered until we were upright and then, slowing our shakes to the pace of a moderate heart, we slowed ourselves more still until we were like peanut butter being poured. Kashta and I commenced the back flips. The crowd burst into wild, unrestrained applause and screams, as they always do at this point in the routine.

I should point out that the back flips are not an authentic part of the Bishari style of dance, but audiences love it, so we do it anyway. When the number was finished, Kashta escorted me off the dance floor to the corner booth where Mr. Blau sat among my entourage. Kashta bowed and I bowed in return. The sur-rounding guests applauded once more before Kashta returned to the stage alone to begin his snake charming routine. I remained standing before the table as Albert lit a cigarillo and placed it smoking between my rouged lips.

My entourage: Mr. Blau, Ebo, Albert, and a cockatiel that'd been bread to grow feathers resembling an elegantly fitted tux-edo. The cockatiel belonged to Albert and was called by Albert "Little Albert," and introduced as Albert's butler. Albert had had Little Albert for just under a year and had recently decided to hire Little Albert a "Littler Albert" to work as *his* butler for the bird's upcoming birthday. I'd been invited to act as godmother to our newest addition, which had been pre-ordered on Amazon and, according to the merchant, awaited us at port in Aswan.

I exhaled a long plume of smoke in the shape of a Chinese dragon—a trick I learned in the opium dens of Newark, New Jersey. Before I could take my seat, Mr. Blau rose, took my hand in his, and began commending me on my performance, referring to it as "satanic in the best sense, yet puzzlingly without malice or artificial grape flavoring—in short, divine." He kissed my hand.

I found his old-fashioned manners charming and resolved then and there to have him come work for me, though I would not broach the subject officially until after 9:31 p.m., when the cookies would have been fully digested.

"And you, Mr. Blau, are more elegant tonight then when we first met, if it is even possible. The tuxedo Albert selected suits you well."

"Merci, je l'aime vachement beaucoup."

"I'm the one that knitted it," Albert interrupted irritably. "Perhaps I'm the one Madame should be complimenting."

"Oh, Albert."

Albert sighed loudly.

I reached out and touched Jacob's lapel. "Very fine work, Albert. As always." I winked at Jacob. "The dining room doesn't require guests to wear a fez, but I thought it might give you a little something extra."

"Vero, a voluptuous obvius!"

"I beg your pardon?"

"A delightful accessory! And it is your pardon for which I must beg. The mater's from Rome, you see—Latin is my mother tongue and I sometimes slip back into it." Jacob fingered his tassel. "I've always delighted in hats, so says Mater. Though, I hope you'll not take offence if I correct you; this is not technically a 'fez' but a 'fezuala.' Notice the length of the tassel and width of the fringe. It's a style of fez particular to the Ginglo tribe of the Democratic Republic of the Conga, frequently confused with the more widely known fez made popular by the Ottomans. The Ginglo use it to store their cold medication, which is their predominant form of currency.

"How interesting."

"I spent a semester among them in my sophomore year," he shrugged. "It was a very exciting time in the village of Blotom. As you may remember they were campaigning to host the 2004 Olympics. A silly idea in retrospect, as the village boundaries are much too unstable to make a persuasive bid on the games. The map in those parts is constantly changing as the tribal population is given to excessive gambling. Sad situation on the whole. And where is the UN on this? Nowhere, of course. When they run out of cold medication, they ante up the land with the result that their borders shift more frequently than the Aegean tide. In the brief time I was there, the village was relegated to its smallest ever—five square feet in total—so that during the three terrible days it took Pikatnha, a fearsome boy of ten and the Ginglo's leader, to win back his people's land from Norquoise, ruler of the neighboring Flaux tribe, in a double or nothing tournament of Caribbean Poker, all twelve of the townspeople including me were made to stand very close together for fear of accidentally crossing the Ginglo-Flaux border, a serious crime resulting in trial by ordeal." Jacob shook his head. "I'm boring you. Forgive me. You must be exhausted from your performance."

I motioned for the others to make room for me at the center of the booth. Albert sighed and slid over. Little Albert remained indifferently mute on his perch beside the porthole. Ebo adjusted his position, all the while directing a glare toward Jacob. I wiggled into the booth, careful not to catch my sequined bikini bottom on the decorative buttons of the booth's seat cushions.

The entertainment continued up front with Kashta's comedy act, "The Irrepressible Snake Charmer," in which Kashta tries via a series of unsuccessful pickup lines to get the snake, costumed to resemble a saloon girl of the American Old West, to go to bed with him. Kashta spent ten years waiting tables at a resort in the American Catskills and his act bears the stamp. The tourists love him for it, however. It seems he's hit upon the perfect combination of Egyptology and Americana to make them feel at once excited by the African exotic and comforted by the cultural markers of home.

All the while the first course was being served discreetly. With silver tongs, the tuxedoed waiters lay tiny baguettes before each of us along with prepackaged single servings of butter produced right here at a factory in Egypt by a company called The Wrath of Cow. The baguettes were so fresh they seemed almost to scream in pain when you cut them open, and then sigh at the application of the native butter, spread like a healing balm against their injuries. Jacob voiced his concurrent guilt and appreciation.

"This bread is marvelous. Sort of a bittersweet quality to it," he said, brushing away a hint of tears. "Reminds me of the Kaiser's rolls. I spent some time in Russia last winter after a misunderstanding involving a stolen veal chop. Served a month in a mostly charming gulag before the Kaiser discovered my whereabouts and sent a pardon. Poor man was miserable with grief over the mistake. I told him there were no hard feelings as it did wonders for my diet. Much better than that cleanse I tried last year while visiting Tim, an old college chum who's moved out to LA to act—you might know him from the Clearasil ads. I didn't lose a pound on that. But where was I? Yes, the Kaiser had the most marvelous rolls! Much like these, but with considerably less sensitivity to the butter knife. Composed of a more hard-hearted genus of grain, as I remember, though still wonderfully crispy."

"And how is the Kaiser, still married to that Chinese?"

"Couldn't say," he answered before taking another bite and continuing. "That was some months ago, and I haven't been home to collect my mail."

Then the soup arrived, followed by an appetizer of fried octopus lips served with a red caviar, which we were encouraged to paint across the lips like the gloss on an impertinent harlot. Jacob remarked on its similarity to a dish he'd once consumed at a feast held before the mouth of the Stuttering Volcano on the tiny island of Cataract, which "sits squarely in the middle of the Indian Ocean, marring an otherwise uninterrupted stretch of blue when viewed from above, much like a floater, which is how it got its name. The natives themselves call their island "Kelg."

"I can't say I've heard of it. Is the swimming any good?"

"Not bad, but what the island's best known for is its barbecue."

"I thought you said it was the octopus lips that reminded you of one of their dishes," Ebo broke in suspiciously,

"Ah yes, that's true. The fried lips I had at the Hilton, where I stayed for a night after my flight was delayed, so I'm not sure if it's in fact a native dish or just served ubiquitously at every Hilton, as is their pizza, which, incidentally—" he stuck his tongue out to suggest his meaning.

Then the wasp tagine arrived, followed by a heart of lettuce arranged on a platter beside a stethoscope. I motioned for Jacob to do the honors. He put the stethoscope to his ears and the other end to the lettuce and listened for five seconds. "Still beating," he announced. "I prefer mine well." He looked around the table as if to gather our agreement. I interceded with the waiter. "Have Lars throw it on the fire another five minutes, would you?" I winked at Jacob with both eyes simultaneously for stronger effect.

The entertainment continued through the rest of dinner, obviating the need to manufacture chatter where it did not flow naturally. I watched Mr. Blau delightedly consume one dish after the next, his emotions changing with each course so that to watch his face as he chewed was an experience akin to reading one of the great European novels of the twentieth century. It was a provocative, moving, and intellectual read that for a while demanded my full attention.

When the entertainment had finally concluded, the lights came on brighter and the waiters descended in full force upon the tables, removing the dinner plates, glasses, empty platters. . . . Just before they removed Jacob's, he speared a final morsel, disappeared it into his mouth, and chewed the final chapter of Thomas Mann's *The Magic Mountain*. I regretted the young hero's sad end and sipped my water.

"Incandescent prose!" Jacob gurgled, and placed a hand before his mouth. "Heavens! Excuse me."

"What's that?"

"My apologies. I'm afraid I blurbed. Sometimes when I have gas, my body involuntarily expels it in short bursts of favorable book-jacket copy. Terribly sorry."

"It's the wasps," I told him. "They're a bit hard on the untrained stomach."

"The spirit of Jane Austen is alive and well in this saucy new novel of modern Manhattan mores! Two parts Austen, one part Wharton, shaken and served up in a frothy pink cocktail that contemporary female readers will not be able to resist!" Jacob covered his mouth again and blushed. "Terribly, terribly sorry," he continued.

I signaled Albert to send for the Tums. After a minute, a waiter deposited a small hill of colorful tablets onto our table. Mr. Blau selected one yellow and one pink and nodded his thanks.

"I'll have one, too," I said to make him feel comfortable. I popped a blue one into my mouth and chewed.

When the waitstaff had cleared the last dish, I stood up and began to clap. The rest of the dining room joined me in applause.

Ebo stood up and made a slight bow to the room.

Coffee and tea were served along with the cookies—it was 9:31 p.m.—and Mr. Blau expressed his delight.

"The food is really something!" he said.

"A bright new star named de Groot for the Target Corporation—the caterers. Our Ebo here is chef by proxy."

"De Groot is my uncle," said Ebo. "I've been with the company since my tenth birthday, when I was given my first lesson on the ritual tenderization of a 'screaming lemon tart.'"

"I employ de Groot chefs exclusively on all my ships."

"Your ships?"

Ebo intruded another angry look at Jacob.

"Yes. I own the fleet. That's why they let me perform. They have to," I laughed. Everyone laughed.

"Madame's dancing is hardly tolerated. You have gifts!" said Albert.

"You were really on tonight," added Ebo, before scowling again at Jacob.

Jacob took a sip of wine and then with his napkin wiped the two corners of his mouth. "A fascinating business, shipping. Did you major in tourism in college or did you just sort of fall into it?"

"Oh, no. I just bought the fleet last year." I lowered my voice. "Complications with my husband, you know. I needed to get my money into something solid, so I thought, boats! I didn't go to college. I educated myself by visiting the great libraries of the world! I do, however, have an Associates in typing." I showed him the Katharine Gibbs pin I had stuck into my sequined bikini top. "Education is everything to me."

Jacob nodded. An awkward silence fell over the table. Ebo continued to glower in Jacob's direction. Albert wiped some crumbs from Little Albert's beak.

"Ebo," Jacob began with a warm smile, "That means 'Born on Wednesday,' does it not?"

Ebo gritted his teeth. "Tuesday" he pronounced carefully.

Jacob tipped an imaginary fedora, leaving his fezuela undisturbed. "My sincerest apologies for the mistake, *ya'akh* Ebo. My knowledge of Egyptian culture is sorely limited, I'm afraid. My work focuses primarily on island life clustered around the tectonic ridges and deals little with civilizations of the continent."

Clearing his throat, Jacob rose and addressed the table. "Please excuse me while I visit the men's room." Bowing slightly, he turned to depart.

As soon as Jacob was out of earshot, Ebo exploded. "I don't trust that man! He knew perfectly well what my name meant!"

"Ebo," I said, calmly spearing a slice of pear from the fruit plate the waiter had just set down, "Re-lax."

"I left my wife for you!" he cried, raising his voice.

"Only for a few minutes; she's right over there." I nodded to Ebo's wife, overseeing service on the other side of the dining room. "Now, I'll have no more of this foolishness! What do you think, Albert, did you also find the peas to be a little too soft tonight?"

"I like them softer than Madame does."

"That's true."

"I'm leaving," Ebo said and threw his napkin down on the table.

Jacob returned just as Ebo sulked off.

"Where's Ebo going?"

I shrugged. "Tell me, Jacob, more about your work. And please, allow yourself a good stretch. Albert, fetch some more cushions so that we might recline as we digest. Also, let them know they can bring out the water pipe whenever they're ready. The smoke swims freer through the body if you're lying down, I find," I explained to Jacob, as I worked to make myself more comfortable among the cushions. Jacob remained standing, mentally negotiating his position.

"Albert, fetch some more cushions and then tell them inside to bring out the water pipe," Albert repeated to "Little Albert" who, without responding, remained listless by the porthole. Albert stared at Little Albert and then, after a moment, let out a great sigh and retreated to fetch the pillows. Before he left, he picked up the whole table and brought it with him.

When he returned a moment later it was with a fresh table that sat lower to the ground. The tuxedoed staff followed and arranged the water pipe, an assortment of perfumed tobaccos named for the Proustian memories they promised to induce in the smoker, and a new fruit plate on the table's surface. When all was settled, Albert hoisted the mute cockatiel onto his shoulder and disappeared again into the next room, all the while giving orders to "Little Albert" perched quietly beside his ear.

I made myself as horizontal as possible among the pillows stacked into the velveted booth and encouraged Jacob, still standing awkwardly, to do the same on the adjacent seat. Jacob worked the cushions while I loaded the pipe with a tobacco called "Combray," which gave off the mellow fragrance of insomnia, a longing for one's mother, petit madeleines dipped in tea, and Hawthorne. Resting sideways now on a brief hill of silk-covered down, Jacob politely accepted the pipe from me. Inhaling more than he expected, he coughed winsomely. I smiled and suggested he soothe his throat with a piece of sweet melon.

We passed the pipe between us in silence for a few minutes. Jacob soon relaxed and began, without having to be questioned, to tell me a little bit more about himself and his strange work.

"A medical anthropologist . . . Is that, like, a private detective or something?"

"Precisely," he went on. He spoke of the adventures his research opened to him for a whole hour without cease but for the one interruption of a bejeweled dowager escorted by her tuxedoed companion who, while leaving the dining room, stopped at our table to offer their compliments on the evening's entertainment. I shook hands with them both, as I always do, and asked them where they were from, what brought them to Egypt, and so on, and then had Albert give them a signed black-and-white glossy of Kashta and me posing before a small, festively decorated intergalactic void—leftover PR pics from our old act—before they drifted off with the rest of their company waiting by the exit.

Eventually the dining room was completely empty but for Jacob, satiated and shining under the rooms glittering chandeliers; me, held rapt by his story of wrestling magicked dust mites that expanded to an unfathomable size last year in the illegal boxing rings of a small village in New Guinea; and a rudimentary staff

of forty waiters lined up silently against the far wall in anticipation of our next request. Catching sight of them, I gave instructions that they all feel free to smoke their cigarettes and chat
quietly among themselves if they so wished. The forty bowed and
lit up one at a time.

Then it was my turn. Jacob asked about my work, what I was
doing in Egypt alone but for Albert, Little Albert, and Ebo—
whom, he warned me, he didn't trust. I told him Ebo was harmless if just a little bit immature. "He's only nineteen, you know.
And he's quite dear to me, really, like the third cousin twice
removed I never had. Anyway, relationships require patience and
understanding," I went on. And then, for some reason, though I'd
never before answered even the most relentless reporters who to
this day dog me, I felt an easiness with Jacob, an immediate confidence, and wisely or unwisely, I found myself relating to him
the previously secret events that had lead to my hushed arrival in
Cairo two summers ago and my current life among the crew of the
Shehrazad.

"For more than a year, I've been living aboard the Shehrazad, by
nights dancing incognito as one half of the popular act, 'Felicia
and Kashta's Coconut Dreams,' and by day hiding from my husband and his lawyers who hunt me even now. After a close call
with my husband's trackers last winter in Zanzibar, I was compelled to assume my stage name and alias, 'Felicia von Hips Unstoppable.' My real name is Iris Smyles," I confessed, before I
began again, this time reaching back further still toward a much
earlier moment in my tale, as a means to explain why and how it
was that I came to Egypt so many months before.

"My husband, or ex-husband, as I am trying now to make him,
is a notorious global trader in illegal laser pointers. You must
believe me when I tell you, though, that I knew nothing of his
criminal activities when I accepted his proposal. Back then, the
patent on his pointers was still pending, and he had assured me

without hesitation that board approval was only a formality. I was naïve. I know that now. But I was just a girl when we met and had difficulty discerning between the real world and what I wished of it. Foolish? Of course. I believed myself in love.

"And my fiancé's behavior presented no obstacle to this idea. He was very careful at that time to behave exactly as he seemed to know I wanted him to. Seduced by his terrifically thin mustaches, by the gleam of his pinky ring, and the sibilance of his S's, I was unable to see him for what he truly was. Sadly, I was only able to recognize his falseness after our relationship was consummated—after, when the shiny surface of his expert courtship wore off, and the person I imagined I'd given myself to seemed all at once to vanish in my arms.

"He was my first, Mr. Blau. I cried for days after without knowing why. I had expected tenderness, you see. But none of that matters now. How I reproached myself afterward for being so easily fooled. How I reproached him for having been the one to fool me. Alone in our icy matrimony, I had no one even to share my grief with. I couldn't confide in my parents for fear of disappointing them. I had been so proud to release them from the infelicitous financial burden of caring for an unwed daughter. Having proved myself a dutiful child by marrying quickly and well, I couldn't bear to tell them that my sole accomplishment up to that point, my gainful marriage, was a sham—so I turned to alcohol for consolation, the bottle my only friend.

"And then one day my tears—which for months had fallen in seemingly endless supply—ran out. Amid this new dryness, the quiet of a rocky cliff where once a fervid waterfall ran without cease, I reconsidered my situation. But this time, instead of regretting all the twists and turns that had lead to my terrible mistake, I began thinking of what I could do to make life better. In short, I decided to grow up. Though the past could not be altered, the future was still well within my influence. And so, leaving my youthful illusions behind me, I made it my mission to be a good wife to my husband despite my lack of true of affection for him.

"To begin, I forced myself to stop reflecting on the elegant carnation that decorated my husband's lapel on the day that he proposed, a memory that pained me the more for how I'd cherished it. We were standing in my father's rose garden and he was bathed in so wondrous a light. I'd lovingly replayed the episode every day leading up to our wedding. The sunlight then was so unlike the fluorescent overhead that lit him now, each morning during breakfast as he belched the alphabet backwards from Z to A in a coarse song that seemed to have no end, for as soon as he finished, he'd start over again in Spanish. One at a time, I plucked such memories from my mind, as I would the pretty dandelion weeds that as a child I'd confused for flowers decorating a field of grass, which they would soon destroy. Careful now to weed my mind of its most beautiful and potentially most destructive fantasies, I resolved to live reasonably. Despite his failings both as lover and at table, I would devote myself to him and to the success of our marriage. This I vowed. Then people started dying.

"The laser pointers were not only defective but found to be highly dangerous and summarily banned by the American Board of Health. In addition to their mechanical deficiencies, tests revealed many of the pointers to be infected with Mad Cow, a disease which, at that time, had nearly the whole of the British Empire locked in its terrifying grip. A 'Cease Production' order followed, with specific instructions for the safe destruction of all remaining pointers along with a punch-list detailing the conditions under which their ashes should be quarantined.

"My husband, however, had sunk all of his money into their manufacture. To destroy them would mean the end of him financially. An end, he decided, he could not allow. Ignoring the board of health then, he enacted a heinous plan to smuggle the pointers out of the country and into secret warehouses all over the world. There he had them relabeled under a fake patent before having them shipped back to dollar stores across the United States. In tempting displays arranged artfully beside each checkout counter, they'd be purchased on impulse by unsuspecting American citizens, undocumented aliens, and foreign travelers on short-term tourist visas who too tragically had strayed from an otherwise strict budget. One sale at a time, it continued, this quiet massacre of thousands. And as his wife, I was expected to say nothing and look the other way.

"But how could I? The belching I had reluctantly trained myself to abide, but murder was another matter. So I confronted him. In a fit of either great bravery or profound stupidity, I told him I would not play Lady Macbeth in this tragedy he was writing for us all. 'I will not stand by,' I said, 'while innocent people seeking only a bargain on a novelty keychain'—many of the laser pointers came attached to a key ring—'go blind or worse' (I'm not sure how the thing caused fatalities exactly), 'just so you can turn a profit!' He warned me to keep my mouth shut, told me that if I liked life and had no plans for its immediate conclusion, I'd do well to keep my nose out of his affairs.

"I went to the authorities anyway and gave them what I knew; it wasn't even a choice. He was tipped off, however, by Sally, my secretary with whom, I didn't know at the time, my husband had been having an affair. And then, just before the police arrived, just before he made his escape, standing in our kitchen with a furious flourish of his hands, he vowed vengeance against me and disappeared. I fired Sally a few days later. She'd already packed her things and was preparing to move in with her brother Joe in Staten Island. Last I heard she was selling tires at his walk-in automotive.

"Things got quiet for a while and I assumed it was all over. Months passed, then a year, followed by more months, before my husband turned up under a new name and with a new face. He'd been living in Bolivia, he said, with our three children, who by this time were fully grown. He'd had extensive plastic surgery so that even his fingerprints were untraceable. I had no recourse to any authorities because as far as the US government was concerned the name of the man standing before me was Escobar Sanchez, noted Latin American singing sensation and unofficial ambassador to the Latin pop explosion that was just then having a moment on the Billboard Hot 100. Further, there was the additional complication of our children.

"How could I abandon them to this maniac, especially as I had already missed out on so much of their childhoods? My motherly instincts kicked in, and I asked Escobar to move back in to the Connecticut house, over which I, unable to live with Escobar but unwilling to move away for the sake of our kids, anchored my dirigible full time.

"There, floating above my former home, I remained with Albert, whom I'd hired immediately after my husband's disappearance, to serve as my bodyguard/butler/fencing partner and amanuensis. Albert, whom you've already met tonight, would in time also become my most trusted companion."

Albert's head peeked out of the kitchen. I blew him a kiss and he caught it with his hand. "Are you getting all of this, Albert?"

Albert waved his notebook and smiled boyishly.

"Albert transcribes all of my conversations," I explained to Jacob. "He's writing an oral history of my life. Literature is the last line of defense, I believe, against the aloof, amnesiac Shylock called Eternity. For the high-interest rate on Eternity's great loan—life!—which can only ever fully be repaid with one's death, is the daily erosion of one's memories. Death visits us when we forget, Mr. Blau, ushering us at first slowly, so that we don't know it, into a cold, rushing, disordered river that ends in a waterfall of violent oblivion. And if not by land then by sea it will come, for death is also a great car wreck! A violent undoing of life that according to insurance company statistics is inevitable if you spend any time at all on the road—which is why I float." I made a scribbling gesture in the air for Albert to be sure and get that last line word for word.

"Make a note to edit some tomorrow morning as well," I whispered into my sequined bikini top.

"But how can he hear us?"

"I'm wired with a microphone." I pointed to the small microphone stuck into my bikini top beside my Katharine Gibbs pin.

"I see," Jacob marveled. "I assumed it was for the performance."

"That, and posterity."

I nodded my dismissal to Albert, and he retreated once again into the kitchen.

"I found Albert," I continued, "by responding to an ad he'd placed in the *London Review of Books*. It was worded with such elegance I shall never forget it: 'Experienced butler seeks full-time butling position. Résumé available upon request. Pay is negotiable,' I recited nostalgically, waving my hand like a conductor before an intimate orchestra of one. "He was the only person I interviewed. I hired him on the spot and have never once regretted it. It's hard now to remember what my life was like before he came into it. We've been through quite a lot, you know."

"Oh?" Jacob asked, his eyebrows curling into supine question marks before, leaning closer, he commenced another go at the water pipe.

"Well, when I first met Albert he was very sick, you see. During his interview, when I asked him why he left his former employers, all he could say was, 'They were a bunch of phonies.' When I asked him to supply a reason for such a judgment, he was unable to say more. Instead, he produced a doctor's note and handed it to me. The note described a strange illness, a very rare form of Asperger's syndrome—Salinger's—that rendered him incapable of communicating through any means other than literary allusion. Unsuited to most types of work as a result, it was the prolific P. G. Wodehouse, I soon discovered, that had indirectly enabled Albert to successfully pursue a career in 'butling' thus far.

"My heart went out to him, as I'd gone through a brief spell of this sort of thing myself when as a child I saw the movie *Working*

Girl with Melanie Griffith and was unable, for weeks on end, to stop speaking in Hollywood business lingo. To my parents'dismay I spoke ceaselessly of 'number crunching' and 'a rumored merger with Trask Industries.' I developed a terrible fever that proved resistant to every manner of treatment. Though the fever eventually subsided on its own, and with it so did the lingo, the horror of that time has never left me and, even now, sends a shiver through my body. It was only natural that Albert's plight should strike a chord. I felt compelled to keep him with me, to try to help him in any way that I could.

"So I hired him—along with a team of ten doctors to see about his condition. Nothing worked, however, except for Albert who, though peculiar in his eclectic references to Stendhal, Cervantes, "Pussy" Wharton, and Rabelais, proved quite excellent at the table where the ten therapists sat nightly, stuffing themselves greedily as they discussed Albert's vexing disease. The following months saw the publication of five scholarly papers, six failed clinical trials, and three international medical summits that I hosted in my own home, but no improvement in Albert himself. At last I decided to get rid of the whole lot of them. Firing all of the doctors, I began treating Albert myself. My approach was simple: I would convince him that we were participating in our own original literary work, so that anything he or I might say to each other could thus be considered literary dialogue and would upon utterance automatically allude to the work in which we were the main characters."

"Did it work?"

"After only three days of Revision Therapy, Albert, declared incurable by the ten, was cured. Indeed, the only vestige of his disease was a frequent sighing, which, he informed me, was characteristic of his namesake's protagonist." I shrugged. "We celebrated with a trip to Red Lobster."

"I'm a great lover of their complimentary biscuits! But tell me, did you publish your study? I feel I've read about this before."

"You're referring to a paper published under the name 'Kraus-Milpood,' I suspect."

"Of course!"

"I couldn't use my real name for it was around this time that Escobar returned, along with his threats, requiring me to keep a low profile. It was around this time, too, that Albert and I, as I mentioned, fled to the dirigible up above the Connecticut house. It was then that I purchased Little Albert as a means of making Albert's transition from land to sky less rocky—poor Albert had already been through so much, I feared the sudden change in altitude might effect a relapse. Happily, Little Albert proved to be a stabilizing influence on Albert as well as a loveable companion to us both.

"Months passed this way, with Albert letting down the rope ladder each afternoon, from sky-kitchen to land-kitchen, in order that I try for some quality time with the children. Despite my best efforts, however, my relationship with the children remained strained. First, because they spoke almost no English, and second, because I became more and more suspicious that they were not actually mine. I hated myself for thinking it, but the fact was they looked nothing like me. They, all three, wore mustaches and identical three-piece suits in a cut and color I never would have chosen for them. Also, they, all three of them, were at least fifteen years my senior.

"Try as I might, I simply could not find my way to like them. Though I was loath to admit it, they gave me the creeps. They were always popping up, three heads in a row outside my kitchen window as if to imitate the eerie effect of a Magritte painting. They were always muttering to one another, too, but when I'd ask any one of them to repeat what he'd said, this time a bit slower so that I might consult my Spanish-to-English dictionary, they'd just clam up and look at me suspiciously, their eyes darting back and forth among themselves, as they twirled their dark mustaches in horrifying synchronicity.

"At first I reproached myself for being a bad mother—what kind of mother does not love her own sons after all? But then, finally—after watching a movie marathon on the Lifetime Movie Network and recognizing a host of similarities in the stories of beautiful, wealthy women married to men whom they'd only *thought* they know—I decided something was just not right in all of this. There were too many strange coincidences. Too many details that just did not add up. For one, I had no memory of giving birth.

"When Escobar informed me of the children's existence, he'd intimated that I'd carried and delivered the three as triplets in an alcoholic blackout that had lasted nine months, that if I didn't remember it was as a result of my ferocious drunkenness. In the throes of a formidable addiction at that time, I was reluctant to admit to him or to anyone else that I did not in fact remember the detail for fear of acknowledging what this and so many other recent blackouts implied. So I went along with everything, not ready yet to confess to him or to myself that I had a problem, afraid that if I said it out loud, I'd be forced to stop. And frightened further, that even if forced to, I couldn't.

"But then, at the gentle and persistent encouragement of Albert, who wished only to help me as I had helped him, I decided to stop of my own volition. On a Sunday, terrified of leaving my vodka-stocked dirigible for even an hour, with the help of Albert, I made it out to visit a well respected hypnotist on Manhattan's Lower East Side who, most surprisingly, was able to cure me right then and there by placing me inside a large decorative box before an audience assembled for a matinee performance of terrifying magic. With the help of Flossie, his beautiful assistant, the hypnotist sawed me in half, showed the audience evidence of his incision, and then reassembled me as if nothing had happened, except that a lot had—I was cured of my alcoholism!

"My head clear finally and with Albert by my side, I began to investigate the increasingly suspicious behavior of my three sons.

Last spring, after days of searching the local library's microfiche collection—we'd floated the dirigible over and let down a ladder accessing the fire escape—Albert and I uncovered their true identities.

"They were not my sons at all, but three former members of one of the earlier incarnations of the famed Latin boy band Menudo, and also three of the most notorious criminals then at work in Bolivia. Known by authorities and by their underworld peers as 'The Children,' they are wanted the world over for smuggling, drug trafficking, falsifying documents, hosting illegal Botox parties, and nine counts of murder.

"Fearing for our safety, Albert and I abandoned the house that very day, cutting rope beneath us and charting a course for Zanzibar, where, once safely ensconced, we called in tips to all relevant United States authorities including the CIA, FBI, FDA, the American Board of Health, the US Patent Office, the Bolivian Consulate, and the international nationally syndicated radio show Casey Kasem's Top 40.

"One month later, after a near run-in with Escobar's cronies in Zanzibar, I changed my name to Felicia and took refuge aboard the Shehrazad, where I've remained since, save for the occasional shopping trip in Luxor. Escobar and The Children are currently under investigation and facing trial for a host of crimes that could put them away for life. Until the district attorney has closed the book on them, however, Albert and I must remain abroad. It's not so bad." I popped a grape into my mouth and chewed, watching Jacob all the while.

"Certainly not!" Jacob broke in jovially.

"I enjoy my life here very much, Mr. Blau," I said snapping a finger at the forty waiters to suggest their dismissal. They bowed one at a time like dominoes and filed out. "Send Albert in, if you see him," I told the last one before he disappeared. "I have my dancing to look forward to in the evenings, and I am able to run all of my stateside businesses by proxy.

"If anything good came from my ill-fated marriage, it was this new life I have made in business. For, unable to throw myself into the care and maintenance of husband and home following my disastrous betrothal all those years ago, and equally unwilling to resume my former life under the care of my parents, out of necessity I threw myself into work and found, quite by accident, that it was not my husband who had an entrepreneurial flare, but, most ironically, it was I.

"Speaking candidly if not a little coarsely, Mr. Blau, the financial burdens of a divorce are great, greater even than the burden sadly assumed by the parents of an unwed daughter. But I'd be lying if I didn't confess that it gives me great pleasure to be able to shoulder this burden by myself, while still having plenty of money left over to pay for my parents' archery camp tuition and Medieval Stoning Festival tickets, or whatever else those two crazy kids next get themselves into. In Florida for the time being, they've taken up Armenian Shuffleboard!

"I don't wish to brag, but I know of no other way to show off. The fact is, business is booming! Why, just last year, I opened a new Smyles Family Roller Rink in Levittown, Long Island, which is doing great. And the Smyles Meat Processing Plant in Winnipeg is producing excellent profits as well. Only one month ago, I acquired the patent on a new invention, which I plan to pitch to Congress as a potential solution to the current housing crisis I hear is plaguing America's western territories. I call it 'Bouillon Housing.' Wait just a second, I'll show you. Albert, bring in the prototype," I whispered into my bikini top.

Albert emerged from the kitchen, came toward us and placed a tiny yellow cube on the table between Mr. Blau and myself. "Imagine for a moment, Mr. Blau, that a cube of dried broth measuring only two-point-five cubic inches could grow to a two-story, three-bedroom house with the application of only a teaspoon of water?

"Of course, the land to accommodate such a house must still be bought—Thank you, Albert. You can take it away—but the possibilities of such technology are great, no? The only stumbling block as of now is how to mask the pungent chicken soup odor that permeates all the resulting edifices. But I have a stateside team researching solutions as we speak and have no reason to expect they won't come up with something useful.

"The project that is closest to my heart, however, what is most exciting to me at this time, is my magazine. Just a few short months ago I acquired a small, nearly defunct trade paper called *Fish* being published out of Western Colorado and distributed for free among the local fishmongers. I don't suppose you've heard of it."

"No."

"No, not yet. No, of course you haven't. Why would you have? The magazine is still fish heavy, but since our rebrand—we are now called *Smyles & Fish*—we're publishing more and more general interest articles. 'If Love Means Never Having to Say You're Sorry, What's Hate?' and 'Top Ten Reasons to Stop Shooting Deer and Start Strangling Them.' That sort of thing. The fishmongeratti are so far on board with the new direction, thank god, but we've also begun to attract a more mainstream reader.

"And, though some say literature is dead, last month we launched a new fiction section with a word jumble by Jonathan Franzen. I don't know about you, but there's nothing I love more than curling up with a good word jumble. The arts are everything to me, Mr. Blau. Also recipes. Ours was the first publication, incidentally, to instruct readers on how to make lava cake, even if they don't live near an active volcano. The title was, let me see if I remember, ah yes: 'Let Them Eat Carrera Marble!'"

"More tasty and less fattening than molten chocolate, I understand." Jacob touched the fabric over his belly. "I saw something about it on *The Today Show*."

"They've been good to us, that show. Al Roker is on our board."

"The prognosticator?"

"He reads the taffy before our Tuesday meetings. Charming man."

"There's a special place in Hell for weathermen, according to Dante. I've always wanted to go," said Jacob. "Have you been?"

"Not yet. There's a new resort being built on the Eastern coast of the eighth circle to which I'm hoping to send one of our reviewers."

"The beaches are fantastic," said Jacob, "but don't drink the water."

"Perhaps you will investigate for us. We could use a man of your discernment on our staff. We publish a great many reviews, you see, along with our weekly Worst Seller List. 'All successful novels resemble one another. All unsuccessful novels are unsuccessful in their own way'—there's a bit of Tolstoy for you. We'd do better as a people to celebrate failure, I've always thought. The grand disaster, the profound delusion, the noble loss, the architecture of folly—here is the province of the holy, Mr. Blau. Here is art. What is the world after all but a series of mistakes made to correct the last? Evolution, God's apologia."

Jacob shifted on his elbow, adjusting the pillow beneath him.

"It is venal to suggest that God's creation should not also be subject to review. If the world is his art, let it stand to scrutiny. Let us measure it along a range of one to five stars with instructions to 'must see' or 'stay home' in a column of well-constructed prose set below the critic's daguerreotype.

"'Criticism for criticism's sake,' wrote Walter Pater, whose *Studies in the History of the Renaissance* our reviewer gave two thumbs up, despite his feeling that the fourth chapter was 'too minty.' The second half of our magazine is a review of the first half."

"Turtles all the way down." Jacob nodded.

"Speaking of, in the last issue we ran a really great review of a cosmetics company that tests its products solely on the cuter animals. I wrote it myself, actually—"

"This tobacco, if I may interrupt you, Ms. Smyles, reminds me of the sap of a particular tree I've come upon only in my travels along the western bank of Bashtagu— an island off the coast of the Cape of Good Horn, you may remember—from which they manufacture the most wonderful pancake syrup."

"Very perceptive, Mr. Blau. This tobacco is in fact coated with the sap of the Balagerawa tree from the very island of which you speak. I haven't tried their syrup. Should I?"

"Must," Jacob said solemnly, inhaling from the pipe again before letting a plume of smoke dance playfully out from his mouth, like a chain of ghostly maidens frolicking hand in hand and visible only by moonlight in the clearings of a Scottish wood intimating by their presence the terrible curse that has long enshrouded this particular forest and extends to any and all who dare trespass its forbidding borders. "Please," Jacob pressed me, "tell me more about this wonderful magazine of yours. I'm fascinated."

"Circulation was nearly dead when I bought it, but now we're up to something like two or three-dozen subscribers. Of course, it's only a hobby, but then, so was the bowling alley and nuclear power plant in the beginning, both of which now number among my most thriving enterprises. So who knows where it will all go?" I disappeared another grape into my mouth before I went on. "In any case, the response so far has been promising." I shrugged. "And what's more, Jacob, if I may call you Jacob—"

"Of course."

"I've found that on board the Shehrazad one meets a much greater variety of persons than one could ever hope to meet while floating in one's dirigible over the richly varied Red Lobsters of Connecticut as I used to. Indeed, I'd say the early success of the magazine is in large part owed to my running it from this ship. Chance meetings in this dining room alone have enabled me to

multiply my editorial staff three times over already. Ebo, for example, edits Fine Dining."

Jacob smiled. And then sucking deeply on the water pipe,
pulling much longer this time than he had each time before,
he exhaled a plume of smoke so billowing and thick, that for a
moment I could not see him. The perfumed cloud grew larger
and larger until it consumed the whole chandeliered dining room
in which we two lay, briefly silent, consumed the kitchen next to
us with its bustling staff still cleaning up from dinner, consumed
all seventy-five passengers asleep or preparing for sleep in their
cabins, consumed their dreams, their stowed luggage, their dinner jackets left to drape over state room chairs, their silk chiffon
gowns crumpled romantically on the floor, the discarded tissue
paper from a husband's gift to his good wife of a gold-plated collector's bottle of Coppertone Coconut Oil SPF –35, consumed the
initialed cufflinks left out negligently on top of a dresser to roll all
night back and forth in soft accord with the river's quiet undula-
tions, consumed the entire ship with all its festive lights, the prow
where I lay earlier sunning myself in exception of a wooden mermaid, consumed in a great white mist, for just a moment, the Nile
itself.

The story I told Jacob that night involved many more details than
I am able to document here, what with the trial of my ex-husband
and The Children still pending. When I was finally finished, however, Jacob vowed to keep my secrets and in collateral confidence,
began unfolding the true tale of his own arrival in the bulrush,
what he'd claimed earlier to have had no memory of, and which,
for matters of international security, can neither be revealed at
this time. When he was finished relating his tale, we sealed our
confidence in a sacred pact—we split the warm chocolate cake
with a scoop of vanilla ice cream from off the dessert menu and
said, "I promise."

"I'm not an actor, but I have played one on TV," Jacob confessed during the evening's final round of Truth or Dare. Albert had just rejoined us after having lifted his shirt and shaken his belly at the captain. "There you have it," he sighed before our table. "Madame has got what Madame wanted," he said amid Jacob's and my conspiratorial giggle. Albert bowed slightly, then left for the kitchen.

It was then that I formally offered Jacob a position on my staff. "My magazine is looking for a critic, as I may have mentioned, to review a variety of goods and services. My aim is to cover everything, from the recent spike in 'whale blubber coat' sales, to this season's unexpected 'indoor hat' trend."

"Indoor hats?"

"For the gentleman who likes a warm head but does not wish to insult his host by keeping his hat on while inside. The indoor hat looks just like hair, obviating the need for its polite removal."

"Isn't that just a toupee?" Jacob quizzed me.

"Precisely the kind of question to pose in your first review. But you'll be asked to review more than just today's fashions. Anything from batteries and vacation destinations, to foodie trends, automotive parts, and experimental vaccines. The whole kit and caboodle," I articulated carefully.

Jacob looked at me. He seemed to be thinking. Candlelight danced in his eyes though there were no candles anywhere in the room.

"My boy, a worldly one such as yourself could do well in such a position," I told him, locking eyes. "Of course, it pays nothing monetarily speaking, but, then, I can't see you as one to put price before adventure. Or have I misjudged you?"

The candlelight still dancing in his eyes performed the Tarantella. "Also, you'll get free reviewer's copies," I threw in.

"Can I choose my own subjects?"

"Of course!" I said broadly. "Naturally, each and every column will be of your very own choosing, save for those occasional assignments that won't be, which you must not question. Failure to complete such assignments will result in the permanent termination of your contract with *Smyles & Fish* as well as your life. Please be advised further that in death *Smyles & Fish* will maintain exclusive North American rights over any printed material you produce while in our employ, after, and before the given term of such employment. Should you at any time be reincarnated under the same or different name or species, by signing this document you agree to forfeit your rights to any and all material produced at that time as well," I said, reciting the fine print.

Jacob nodded, "Sounds fair."

"Upon signing this," I said, as Albert leaned down proffering a sliver tray on which the contracts had been artfully arranged beside a glowing fountain pen, "prepare to be dispatched to exotic locales all over the globe, as well as some local B. Dalton's and North American shopping malls to review the performances of various Santa Clauses featured in seasonal shopping displays, and report back to our readers of your findings in an upbeat column of one thousand words or less, give or take three or four thousand."

Jacob signed.

"Albert, return to my room and print up some business cards on my portable Epson. The cards should read, 'Jacob Augustus Blau, Capricious Critic and Staff Medical Anthropologist at *Smyles & Fish*.'"

Albert disappeared once more, leaving Jacob and I silent as we waited for his return. I brushed a bit of dust that had caught on one of my sequins, and then with a cloth napkin cleaned the surface of my tiny microphone and Katharine Gibbs pin.

Jacob stood up, sauntered toward the adjacent table, and kneeled down to pluck a coin he'd spotted on the floor beneath it. I watched him bite into it thoughtfully. "A gold amalgam, I'm afraid," he said, studying it. "I collected coins as a boy." He laid the coin on the table between us before laying himself down on the cushions as before. He smiled.

Albert reappeared in the doorway and came toward us, conveying a small father-of-pearl box. Leaning over, he opened the top, then nodded for Jacob to reach in. Jacob plucked a card.

Studying it, he said, "I like the silver ink. Mined from the mouth of the Catalwan River, I presume."

"Ork Blood," Albert said slowly.

Suddenly, Ebo burst through the kitchen screaming in a crazed Arabic and waving his arms wildly, followed by his wife, who, taking him by the hand began singing softly, so as to calm him, a native lullaby. She nodded to me and I nodded back as the two quietly went back through the kitchen door.

"My parents will be thrilled when I tell them I have a job," Jacob said. "They think I've extended my studies just to avoid working."

"I'm sorry, Mr. Blau, but your parents cannot know of your affiliation with *Smyles & Fish*. No one can, at least for now, lest Escobar and his fearsome Children trace you back to me. I'd have to sell the ships. Perhaps move again. And I like it here, Jacob. You do understand," I said, pressing his hand.

Thus began the first year of my long and profitable relationship with Mr. Jacob Augustus Blau. Though we would communicate via email, post, telegram, Morse, carrier pigeon, two cans tied together with string, bicycle messenger, a variety of psychic channels, email, Facebook, MySpace, Friendster, LinkedIn, hi5, Twitter, and Skype, I would not see him in person again for some time, as Albert and I were forced, because of the legal proceedings, to remain aboard the Shehrazad. Indeed, a whole year would pass before we'd sit once more face-to-face, alone and under cover of night in a Moroccan coffee shop in lower Manhattan, where I, disguised as a fern placed purposefully to liven up a dead corner of the room, had arranged for our meeting.

Following the successful launch of the *Smyles & Fish* theme park in Western Ontario, I'd called the meeting with Jacob to discuss construction of his wax figure double. As I write this reminiscence, a team of twelve biologists, three physicians, fifteen artists, one active cosmetologist and another consulting, and twenty non-specific effectuators culled from the nation's top colleges and research institutes, and headed by Little Albert, is at work on the wax statue which will include scale wax organs, wax skeletal and muscular tissue, and a working wax circulatory system which will naturally be invisible beneath the wax epidermis and outermost Speedo cuticle.

Pending FDA and American Board of Health approval, clearance with both US and Canadian patent offices, permission from all affiliated licensing organizations sponsored by the International Theme Parks Commission, and the successful negotiation of a new contract with the current Waxworks Union Rep, the statue's unveiling—set to take place at the center of the park's food court on a wax plinth at the apex of Eli Whitney's All-American Cotton Candy Gin™, a Ho Hos® vendor, and the entrance to the ever popular International House of Poisonous Blowfish— is slated for this June.

exquisite **bachelor**

Last night I dreamed everyone was here for the wrong reasons. I was an aspiring dental hygienist from North Dakota on a TV show featuring twenty-five surrealists and a Texan named Fred who were all living together in a house in Hollywood, competing for my hand. Some, like Man Ray, wanted only my hand.

"For a collage," he explained, before kissing it.

It was the cocktail party before the third Rose Ceremony and I was nervous, unsure of whom among the remaining twelve to send home.

"What a peculiar name, Man Ray."

"They call me Man Ray because I shoot Man beams from my Man eyes," he said, leaning in.

Magritte appeared in the doorway. "Can I steal you for a second?" he asked with his back to me. He'd placed a pair of sunglasses over his hair and was raising them up and down provocatively.

Ray rolled his eyes. Magritte took his place on the sofa.

"Non," he said, handing me one of two mirrors. "That way," he said, suggesting I face away from him. "I learned this trick from my barber. Look in your mirror," he instructed me, "and find my eyes looking into my mirror looking into yours."

Our eyes met in the glass. "May I kiss you?" he asked after a long pause. He leaned in. So did I. The glass was cool against my lips. When I opened my eyes he was gone.

In his place sat Aragon. I dropped the mirror and turned to him.

Aragon stared ahead and said nothing.

"I feel our relationship is not moving as quickly as my relationship with some of the others. I know so little about you. What is it that you do again?"

"I'm a writer," he hissed. "I nap."

I smiled and laid a hand on his knee. "You seem upset."

"It is not my intention to throw anyone under the bus, but you ought to get rid of Gide. He is 'a bothersome bore' and not here for the right reasons."

Dalí appeared. "May I steal her?" he asked, mustaching his twirl.

"You may borrow her," Aragon snapped. "It's not stealing if you obtain permission. If you need me," Aragon said, "I shall be in the fantasy suite, preparing my treatise."

Dalí proffered his arm. "Come!" he said, leading me into the kicthen. On the stove bright flames licked a festival of silvery pots. One at a time Dalí removed their lids revealing clocks, all the clocks in the house, boiling in their juices. He took my hand, brought it to his chest. "Can you feel me ticking? You've melted my heart, the way I've melted these clocks."

"Beat it, Dalí!" said Aragon from the doorway.

"I wanted to give you something," Aragon continued, coming closer. "My last book."

I read the title aloud: "*Irene's Cunt.*"

"It's the collected sex columns I wrote for *Men's Health*. Irene's my ex. I spit on her bourgeois nothingness; she married a doctor—ha!—as if we aren't all going to die anyway. If you marry me, I will write only of your cunt, of its snapping teeth, its lettuce-like hair . . . " He was on his knees, waxing vegetarian, when Pierre Reverdy walked in.

"Can I steal you?"

Aragon growled.

"I want to marry my best friend," I told Pierre once we were alone.

Pierre replied, "'The more the relationship between two juxtaposed realities is distant and true, the stronger the [marriage].'"

"Opposites attract, in other words." He nodded and kissed my hand.

"Artaud calls the Rose Ceremony 'The Theater of Cruelty.' Do you think I'm cruel?" I asked Pierre.

"Just enough," he said, his lips grazing mine.

André Breton walked in. "I need to talk to you about the drama in the house. Aragon sent a nasty letter to Fred."

"Fred, the part-time personal trainer and children's party magician from Texas?"

"The one."

He removed a folded page from his breast pocket and began reading: "'Dear Scumbag: I find you to be obscene, asinine, and above all, lying and cowardly. I have no intention of arguing with a lardhead. The mere idea of your kind of trash stinks . . . and you yourself . . . smell to high heaven. I'm telling you this very gently: I respectfully stop up my nose in the presence of your goatee.'" He refolded the page and placed it back in his pocket.

"I don't think Aragon is here for the right reasons," he continued. "I've drawn up a second manifesto detailing the right reasons." From out of his breast pocket, he produced a second sheet. "Shall I read it?"

I closed my eyes. When I opened them I saw Magritte holding a pipe. "This is not a pipe," he said and walked out.

Voices in the hallway drifted into the living room. I edged closer and found Breton hunched in close conspiracy with one of the show's producers. "'I believe in the future resolution of dream and reality,'" Breton confessed. "'A surreality, so to speak, I am aiming for its conquest.' If she does not choose me, I think I've got a good shot at being the next Bachelor."

I returned to the kitchen to check on the clocks, then remembered the old axiom—a watched clock never boils. When after ten minutes no one had come to steal me, I wandered into the living room, where all the bachelors were gathered before Aragon, who was reading aloud from the 'Treatise on Style' he'd written for *GQ*.

"Mustaches out. Sock garters in. Long pants out. Cravats in . . . Automatic writing out!" he said, casting a serious eye about the room.

I shook the ice in my empty glass. Startled, one of the men on the sofa turned, revealing the head of a rooster.

With his beak pointing straight at me, Ernst rose up in full tuxedo.

He rushed to my side and whispered in my ear: "Tell me your dreams!"

"I'm an aspiring dental hygienist and am hoping, once I finish school, to find a position within a good practice and get married and start a family."

"No, from last night!" Ernst said, leading me out to the patio.

"But I never remember my dreams."

"Then I must take you to the fantasy suite!"

"I'm not that kind of girl."

"We will sleep together and when we wake, we'll write down what we've seen. The path to the soul is through the unconscious. There the soul will find its mate. I love you!" he appended quickly.

"'What is [love] anyway?'" Aragon boomed, appearing, skeptical, in the doorway. "'Let me begin by explaining what [love] is not . . . [Love] is not the poison of strong souls, nor is it strong fish glue . . . [Love] is not a lantern, nor does it come to those who wait. . . . It is not horrified by ghostly apparitions. It is not surprised by a pianist. . . . Nor—as one might be tempted to conclude from all this—is it a state of mind.'"

"What is it, then?" Dalí inquired, exiting the kitchen.

"'It is not the rosin of wit nor the cuckoo of perfect timing,'" Aragon answered. "'It is not the telephone of days gone by. Nor is it a way of recouping oneself, and I ask you, is it possible to recoup oneself?'"

Ray shrugged and threw back what was left in his glass.

"'[Love] is not a clown,'" Aragon went on, motioning to Fred, who was making his way toward us. "'Not a swallow, not speaking Latin, not falling asleep on one's feet,'" he motioned to Gide, whose eyes were closing from drink. "'It is not nincompoop, not dandelion, not—'"

"Come with me!" Fred said suddenly, sweeping me over to the pool.

"Watch!" he began, once I'd sat down. From his right pocket, he removed a long string of colored handkerchiefs, then began stuffing them into his mouth and removing them again from his left pocket. Then he crouched low beside me and took the arm of my chair between his teeth, lifting me in it, high off the ground. After a moment, he put me down and confessed:

"In my dreams, I am a contestant on a game show, but I do not know the rules or the prize. I am living in a house with twenty-five competitors and every day one of us is sent home. We are judged by vague if exacting criteria. I am attacked from all sides. I say things like, 'Don't throw me under the bus,' 'This is who I am as a designer,' 'It is like a fairy tale,' and wake up screaming. Am I dreaming now?" He pinched me. "Can you feel that? Let me take you away from here, out into the real world where we can appear in *People* magazine shopping for groceries like a normal couple, and together plan a modest, nationally televised wedding."

Just then, we were interrupted by a foghorn. "Come," I said, standing up. "The Rose Ceremony is upon us." The foghorn blared, blending into the sound of my alarm clock. I hit snooze. Two, three more times I snoozed, each time returning to that Hollywood house, to those exquisite bachelors, to my choice.

"Aragon is still in love with his ex . . ."

"How do you know?"

"He's been writing about her again . . . *Irene's Cunt Deux* . . ."

I tossed and turned.

"'There is only one difference between a mad man and me,'" Dalí announced, staring into my eyes. "'I am not mad.'"

I turned and tossed.

The Rose Ceremony, the theater of cruelty. Magritte among the others, with a sheet over his face. One after another I call their names: Artaud, Ernst, Duchamp . . . "Will you accept this rose?" I do not call Aragon's name and he leaves, climbing into a glossy black limo. Inside, tears stain his face as he speaks, no longer to me, but to a camera:

"She asked me, 'What color are your dreams?' A fool's question . . . Her dreams were blue . . . I am not the man of them, apparently. I am not blue. I do not blame her her stupidity, just as I do not blame a flower its leaves. She is not for me . . . I try to believe someone is, though often I feel like 'a man who does not hold the key to a door that does not exist.' And now I am humiliated again. 'One might wonder what bizarre advantage I stand to gain by this incomprehensible trampling. One might wander,' and one might learn when one tunes in four weeks from now for a very special episode of 'The Men Tell All.'"

veterans of future wars

"We're a lost generation," I told Jacob, cradling the phone between my ear and shoulder.

I was painting my nails a dusty pink and explaining how we're like the young veterans of WWI who, upon returning home, found the war had altered and alienated them irrevocably. After the horrors of the front, how could they possibly be expected to find jobs and settle down to normal life?

"It's the same with us," I said, finishing off my left pinkie. "NYU changes you."

"Listen," Jacob said after a few seconds, "I'm watching *The Simpsons*. What time should I meet you?"

Five hours later I was sitting next to him at Gramercy Tavern.

"Three cubes," Jacob said with a frown, before turning to me.

"Maybe I should move," I said. "Go to graduate school in the Midwest. Or a top-tier mental institution, like that Anne Sexton hospital in Pennsylvania. I could spend a year there, write a memoir about my breakdown, sell it to Hollywood. I checked their website. They don't even require the GRE."

Jacob sipped his Irish whiskey. "I'm done with school. You couldn't pay me to go back."

"Or to get a job, apparently."

"Actually," he said, "I've been thinking a lot about what I'd like to do. I know I want to make films, but in terms of a day job, I thought I might act."

I nodded slowly. "So your fallback plan is to be a celebrity. Makes sense."

"I have star quality. I should exploit it."

I shook my empty glass. "Yeah. I should probably be a star, too. Just until I get back on my feet."

"You want another?"

"Does the pope shit in the woods?"

"I don't think so."

"Yes, I want another. Three cubes." Jacob addressed the tuxedoed bartender.

We'd decided last Monday to stop going to nightclubs. That was kid stuff. We decided instead to go exclusively to old New York watering holes: a sophisticated bar in Grand Central terminal, a modest but dignified hotel bar in Gramercy, places where you'd receive a ticket in exchange of your coat and the bartender would call you sir or madam, appreciating the fact that you'd specified the number of ice cubes you wanted in your drink. Places where you felt comfortable signing a credit card receipt, the credit card your parents had given you to buy course books in college and had not yet taken away. I regarded the oak paneling.

"Was the Lost Generation before or after the Greatest Generation?" I asked.

"Lost, Greatest, Boomer, X."

"What are we?"

"End of X, beginning of Y. They're going in alphabetical order now. Like hurricanes," said Jacob.

"What's your favorite hurricane?"

"Gloria's unrivaled."

"Gloria's overrated." I sipped my drink. "I prefer '38."

"What was that one called?

"Hurricane of '38. They didn't start naming them until the fifties. I saw a show about it on the Weather Channel."

"I didn't know they had shows. I thought it was just weather."

We were definitely maturing, and the rest, career and all that, would soon follow. Because these sophisticated haunts closed early, though, we'd often find ourselves on the street a little after eleven, buzzed just the right amount, but not ready yet to go home. And so, last Monday, the very same Monday on which we'd vowed to quit the night forever, we ended up at one of those terrible clubs downtown we said we'd outgrown and promised to leave behind, at one of those awful hip places where, some time after midnight Jacob was forcefully ejected after attempting to scale a decorative wall, one of those lounges hemmed in by a velvet rope in lieu of a moat, and a man with a clipboard instead of a dragon, where I'd gotten sick in the bathroom and then passed out on a velvet banquette, one of those loud colorful strobe affairs where I lost my purse again and ruined the new pencil skirt that had made me look so grown up.

I straightened my freshly pressed pencil skirt, opened my notebook, and wrote something down.

"What are you writing?"

I read aloud: "Amateur actors are like volunteer firemen, except instead of saving your life, for a few hours they ruin it."

"You didn't like the play?"

"I hate the theater. I was thinking of becoming a theater critic."

"Greta looked good."

In a small black box theater one hour earlier, Greta, an acquaintance from college, had entered stage left—naked.

"Hurricanes were given girls names exclusively until 1978," I reverted. "Then they started alternating them with boys names. I think we should be called Generation Hurricane."

"Generation Excel spreadsheet."

"Generation I Love You But I'm Not In Love with You."

"Generation It's Not Me It's You."

"Generation Wind-Blown Penis."

"That'll catch on," said Jacob.

I spotted myself in the mirror behind the bar. "The worst thing you can be is a poet, then literary magazine editor, then actor," I announced.

"You write poetry and majored in acting."

"You don't have to attack me. Should we get something to eat?"

"Not here though. Let's pay."

I threw back what was left in my glass. "Fine. But if you're not going to pay for my drinks, you better not try and kiss me later."

It was three a.m. when he tried last week. He'd just finished showing me the holes in his kitchen wall where he'd hung all the pots and pans. "I felt really good about their placement, so I went and had lunch at that new sushi place around the corner to celebrate, and when I got back my roommate had taken them all down. She said I had no right to hang them without consulting her." He shrugged. "I thought it would be cool to have all the pots and pans where we could see them."

"That would have been cool," I agreed, staring at the scarred blank wall.

A few minutes later, we were kissing on a foldout sofa in his living room when I pulled away and mentioned rumors of a Second Avenue subway.

"They've been planning it for years," Jacob said, then closed his eyes and leaned in.

I listed the pros and cons of the proposed line.

"You are aware that we just kissed," Jacob sighed, and sat upright with his eyes open again.

"I'm sorry. I value our friendship too much."

"That?" He stood up.

"Thanks again for letting me crash on your couch. I can't see spending money on a cab. Do you have anything I could sleep in?" I asked, stretching out.

He rolled his eyes and left the room.

"You're the best," I said after he threw a white T-shirt at me. "Wait!"

"What?" he said, halfway through the door.

"Fix me a drink? I'm worried I won't sleep."

Standing before the wall with all its sad holes, Jacob poured a miserly inch of his prized Bushmills. He handed me the glass. "I've measured how much is left in the bottle, so if you drink more I'll know."

He went to his room and shut the door.

In the morning we went out for breakfast. After discussing Schopenhauer's porcupines, Gertrude Stein's problem with railroads—"She said that's where America went wrong"—and reprising one of our go-to topics—the ubiquity of the Hostess snack cake ("Seriously, who's eating all these Twinkies? They don't even advertise!")—we decided we should have a radio show and made plans to get it underway no later than Monday morning, when we'd call each other to figure out the next steps. Since neither of us had jobs, we agreed, we needed to create our own opportunities.

On Monday, neither of us called the other and we never spoke of "the radio show" again.

We ate standing up at a pizza place nearby.

I looked out the window. It looked cold. "Ever since graduation everyone loves to brag about getting up early. It's always, 'I can't come out, I've got to get up early.' You notice that?"

"I don't have anything to get up for," said Jacob. "I can stay out as late as I want."

"The life of a star."

"It's just a day job."

"You think I should run for president? Just until I get back on my feet?"

"I wouldn't vote for you."

I threw my paper plate in the trash. "Whose party is it again?"

"Friend of Jason's friend Jason."

"Have I met Jason?"

"I think you dated him."

* * *

We walked over to Third Avenue, where we tried and failed to hail a cab. I shivered and struggled to light a cigarette in the wind as Jacob wrestled the traffic. Two cars stopped, but once Jacob said where we were going—"Astoria"—they shook their heads and drove on.

The cigarette burned down. I took a last drag, threw it away, and stuffed my cold hands in my coat pockets, crunching my shoulders to my neck, like an actor playing me in a movie about me.

"He says he'll take us!" Jacob yelled a moment later. He held the door open as I ran over.

The cab dumped us outside a two-family house in Queens, in front of which we found Alex swaying in the wind, like a thin tree that had lost its leaves.

"What's up?" Jacob asked.

"I forgot to buy beer. I'm trying to remember which way to the deli," Alex said not quite looking at us.

"We should pick up a six-pack, too," I told Jacob.

Jacob pointed. "I think I saw a deli a couple blocks that way."

We began walking three abreast. "You must be freezing," I said, noting Alex's bare arms. He wore only a T-shirt, jeans, and black worn-in Converse.

"It's supposed to snow later, you know," Jacob added. "Like, a lot."

Alex shrugged and began explaining his pre-Copernican attitude toward weather, how he believed it revolved around him. I searched his face to see if he was serious and he shot back an odd look, like a sensitive potato chip who'd made the difficult decision to leave the bag.

Jacob and I had both had classes with Alex, but neither of us knew him all that well. That he was a Cinema Studies major was most of what I remembered about him, and that he'd started losing his hair early, in freshman year. He wasn't losing it exactly; a patchy beard was coming in at approximately the same rate that his hair was falling out, as if the hairs on his head were migrating south. Colonizing his chin, I remember thinking while he read something aloud during a poetry workshop.

"We saw Greta," Jacob said. "Naked."

Alex looked at me.

I nodded.

The play starred five acquaintances from our graduating class, Greta among them. I'd been less interested in her nudity than with her program bio, and had spent most of the performance poring over it and all the others, trying to determine which if any of our former classmates were fairing worse than I.

"Cool," said Alex happily, without asking why.

We found the deli and proceeded immediately to the back. Alex opened the refrigerator door, and said, "Ladies first."

For a second I thought he expected me to climb in. I pulled a six-pack of Bud Light and thanked him. He gave me his potato chip face.

We paid for our beers separately then waited for Jacob who was still in the rear, searching for a particular brand. When he couldn't find the brand he wanted, he came up front to ask the cashier who, speaking little English, followed him to the refrigerator to consult. Alex and I went outside.

"What have you been up to?" I asked, looking up the sidewalk at nothing and then at him.

"Not much. Got a job as a production assistant on *Law & Order*. Getting coffee and whatever needs getting. Mariska Hargitay's nice."

"I don't watch TV."

"Me neither." Alex looked toward the deli door. "What have you been up to?"

"I am, as they say, 'between jobs.'"

"That's rough. What were you doing before?"

"I was unemployed. Anyway, my main priority right now is finishing my novel."

"That's awesome. I can't wait to read it."

"Read what?"

"The novel."

"Oh, right."

"What's it about?"

I was, in theory, writing a novel. "Desolation and redemption at a local bar," I heard myself say. "It's a novel of ideas. The main character sells human hair to wig shops in Hell's Kitchen while he drinks himself to death and works on his novel." I hadn't written a word.

"I saved one of your poems," Alex said.

"Really?"

"Yeah, I still read it from time to time. I like the part where you write," he closed his eyes, "'taste penis.'" He opened them.

"That's weird," I perked up. "I'm like the poet laureate of oral sex." Jacob emerged.

"What'd you get?" I asked.

"Heineken," he frowned. "They didn't have what I wanted."

"Buddhists believe that all unhappiness has its source in desire. Eliminate desire and you eliminate suffering," said Alex. "I learned that at Clown College. My grandparents gave me a pile of money for graduation, so I went down to Florida for the summer and invested it all in this three-month intensive. I learned to juggle, swallow fire. . . . I just felt like, shit, everyone goes to Europe after they graduate, you know? But how many people become carnies?" Alex looked off into the distance and began nodding at something he saw there. "I met some amazing people."

"There's a lot more to clowning than face paint and big shoes," Alex explained on the way back to the house. "It's really a philosophy, which is really a science. Isaac Newton called himself 'a natural philosopher,' you know."

Alex began counting on his fingers. "Newton was a clown.

Einstein was a clown. Carl Sagan was a clown. Stephen Hawking is a clown. . . ." He cited the law of conservation of matter with regard to the disappearing of small objects, then explained how special relativity is the secret to getting so many clowns in such a small car. "String Theory is changing everything. Also that show on Fox. Have you seen it? They call him 'the Masked Magician.' He wears a mask and explains how all the tricks are done. Before a magician teaches you, you have to swear an oath not to teach anyone outside the magic community, so it's a pretty big deal. He's a traitor to the guild."

"I saw that once while visiting my parents. When he started explaining how to cut a woman in half, I left the room and told my parents what I thought of them."

Alex made a slight theatrical bow. "You know I was a vegetarian in school?"

I nodded. I didn't know.

"But then I realized six days ago that eating meat is not the problem; it's not beef, but our whole society—nobody believes in anything anymore. My parents are getting a divorce."

We arrived at the apartment and proceeded through a low metal gate, where we fell in behind a group of strangers on their way to the same place. Jacob went up ahead of us and held the screen door for a girl with a gold star stuck below her eye where a beauty mark might be; her legs were bare beneath her coat and she had a hula hoop slung over her shoulder. "It's my birthday," she said to him and stuck out her bottom lip. "I'm old. I'm twenty-three." A snowflake fell on my nose.

Alex and I were last. He held the door and with a flourish waved me in, as if I were the last colorful handkerchief he were stuffing into a top hat, as if I were the rabbit he'd pull out a moment later on the other side. For a second I hesitated, worried about how we'd get home at the end of the night, thinking to say something, maybe make a plan for leaving, an exit strategy, but when I looked at him, he smiled in this funny way and I forgot.

"You're so pretty," he said sadly, before pulling a quarter from behind my ear. He handed it to me.

"Thanks."

Then he began straightening his imaginary tie and, placing a sure hand at the small of my back, he grinned, kissed me on the cheek, and together we disappeared into the hat.

"No shoes allowed!" said Jason's girlfriend's best friend's friend, as soon as I walked in. She pointed to my feet.

"But they're new."

"We're trying to keep the carpets clean," she said, opening the front door and motioning to the pile of footwear we'd ignored on our way in.

"Just take off your shoes," Jacob said. "What's the big deal?"

Reluctantly, I peeled off my heels and deposited them on top of the stack. Jacob looked at my feet—bloody and blistered and swollen around the toes—then at me. "What the hell happened to you?"

"You should see the other guy. Let's get a drink."

We wandered in, my feet leaving a bloody trail behind me.

The room was dark but for a dim halogen lamp lighting a far corner, and some red and white Christmas lights draped haphazardly along the perimeter of two framed pictures: George Bellows's "A Knock-Out" and three dozing women in flowing robes of gold and white. Albert Joseph Moore's "Dreamers," it said under the women, from the Metropolitan Museum. The prints hung above a dark blue futon, now occupied by the girl with the gold star and a thin mustachioed boy with his arm slung over her neck. Her face was buried in a red cup, as he gestured toward a friend with his free hand. "Don't even think about it!" he said, smiling aggressively. "Don't even think about it!"

Alex was already by the far window, sentried next to a potted plant his same height, studying its leaves.

"Edward!" someone yelled, as a disheveled sandy-haired boy pushed his way through the crowd. His hair, damp at the front, stuck to his forehead.

The mustachioed boy took his arm from the girl on the sofa and began to clap, chanting with everyone else. "Ed-ward! Ed-ward!"

Edward looked around, extended his arms just above his shoulders, as if he were trying to embrace God, then began to drink from one of the two bottles of Colt 45 duct-taped to his hands.

"That must be the kitchen," Jacob said, motioning to the lit room from where Edward had just emerged. We squeezed through the crowd and into the kitchen, then slid by a few more people holding red cups at half-mast.

Jacob opened the fridge and began rearranging the beer, putting his six-pack all the way in the back and reinstalling a twelve-pack of Budweiser up front. Then he shut the door and began opening the cabinets until, on a high shelf, he found a bottle of whiskey and a tall water glass.

"They don't have lowball glasses," he said, pouring. When he was finished, he took a sip and looked at me. "You want some?"

"Does a bear occupy the highest office of the Catholic Church and lead a decades-long pedophilia cover up?"

"Hold on." He put his own glass down, opened the cabinet, and reached up to the high shelf to where he'd re-hid the whiskey.

I found a red cup and dug out some of the ice melting in the sink.

"I think the girl with the gold star is into me," Jacob said, pouring. Someone bumped me from behind.

"I'm gonna make a move," he said, and disappeared into the next room.

I re-hid the whiskey, then leaned against the counter, feeling the back of my shirt become wet. Brushing at the damp, I looked at the two guys across from me.

"You can't just say *Gone with the Wind* is the best movie ever made. You have to back it up with proof," one said to the other.

"*Gone with the Wind* is the best movie ever made. The proof is the movie itself."

"Oh my god, I'm not having this argument with you again."

"You were great in the play," I said, recognizing one of them from Greta's show. He turned, then turned again.

"Your first fan, Reginald!" said his friend.

"I'm Reginald Monty the third. This is Jim."

"No last name for Jim?" said Jim.

"Cher doesn't have a last name, why should you?"

"If I could turn back time," Jim sang, before taking my hand and bringing it to his lips. "I love your outfit," said Jim. "So Fragonard."

I was wearing a beige pencil skirt with a blue oxford shirt rolled to the elbows. "Thanks. I love your tiara."

Jim touched it lightly. "You see, Reginald Monty the third? Everyone loves my tiara but you."

"I love your tiara. I told you. I just don't think it goes well with that shirt, is all."

I studied Jim's shirt, a crisp blue plaid, and wondered if I was partying.

> Party, To Party. What does it mean? What does it require? What elusive substance is it that marks the difference between attending a party and partying in the verb? Between the dead, man-shaped material on Dr. Frankenstein's slab, and the live, air-breathing monster vowing to kill all those the doctor loves, and prompting the doctor to hunt his wretched Adam to the ends of the earth and his own very life?

> 1. In order to party, one must always be leaving. Though you don't have to leave a party in order to party, you must always be on the verge of leaving either the party

as a whole or the person or group with whom you are partying. If you remain in the same place or talk to the same person, you are not partying but merely in attendance at a party.

2. In order to leave a party or a person at a party politely, one's departure must be made in the service of a mission greater than one's preference: Doctor Frankenstein would love to stay and chat more about your one-man show, but his creature is a threat to all of mankind and so he must pursue his bane into the darkest reaches of the Arctic's icy heart. "Excuse me, I've got to find the ladies room." "Excuse me, I'm desperate for another drink." "Excuse me, I created this monster and it's up to me to destroy it."

"What are you writing?" Jim asked.

I put my notebook and pen back in my purse. "Notes for my novel."

"Cool. What's it about?"

"The main character is called Herlett Floog. She's an amateur phlebotomist living in New Mexico."

"What happens to her?"

"Very little. It's a novel of ideas."

"Jim's a phlebotomist," said Reginald Monty III.

"I'm intrigued," said Jim. "How can one be an amateur phlebotomist?"

"By collecting blood samples in a nonprofessional capacity."

"So it's a thriller," said Jim, rubbing his hands together and flashing his eyes.

"Sort of. The thrills are existential. The book opens with the discovery that God is dead, and the plot follows Man as he searches for the killer, which is actually just a distraction from his own search for meaning. In the end, Herlett realizes life has no meaning except what one puts into it, which she writes into the novel that the reader holds in his hands." I sipped my whiskey. "Imagine a detective story with no body, no clues, no action, and no detective, and you have my book."

Jim nodded. "Cool."

"In the movie version, Tom Hanks should play Man and God should be played by Tracey Ullman," said Reginald Monty the third.

"God is dead, Reginald Monty. There'd be nothing for her to do," said Jim.

"You could have scenes in flashback," Reginald said.

"Oh my god, I love this song," I said, before hurrying into the living room, where Jacob was already standing in the middle of a crowd.

Someone turned up the volume. Jacob turned up a shoulder.

I shimmied toward him and began nodding on the downbeat.

Jacob circled as I shook my hips. Then he started throwing his hands at me like an aggressive Reiki masseur, and I danced back hard, as if I were being healed.

"When did you learn the worm?" I panted in the kitchen after.

Hands on hips, head down, Jacob breathed and leaned against the sink. "Last night. Couldn't sleep."

I reached up into the high cabinet, pulled out the secret whiskey, and poured. I handed him a new glass, leaned against the fridge, and looked out at the party. "Who *are* all these people?"

"Party filler."

I caught my breath and took a sip.

"Packing peanuts," Jacob went on.

"And who are we?" I said, biting the rim of my cup.

"You're a lamp and I'm a cheese grater."

I leaned on my elbows and rested my chin in my hands. "This party sucks. I want to fall in love."

He shrugged. "Maybe next weekend."

* * *

"I hate that they won't let us wear our shoes," Larry complained, looking up at me.

"Eh," said Jacob. "I don't mind being short so long as the woman I'm with is tall. I used to hate it, but then I realized as long as one person is able to carry the other, it doesn't really matter who picks up whom. What matters only is that one be able to carry the other to safety in the event of volcanic eruption. Lava! That's what I'm worried about."

"A lot of leading men are short," I said.

"Robert Redford's practically an elf," said Jacob.

"When he's not acting he sneaks into the homes of struggling cobblers and repairs their shoes," I said.

"There's Jonathan," said Larry, motioning toward the door.

Jonathan, tall, mainly in the torso, was quietly removing his shoes. I'd never had any classes with him, but knew him through Jacob, with whom he'd become good friends freshman year after Jonathan stole his girlfriend.

"I'm gonna be the bigger person," Jacob said in the dining hall the day after Margot dumped him for Jonathan. Later that afternoon, Jacob showed up to Jonathan's dorm room and loaned him a copy of *The Plague*. After another month, Margot dumped Jonathan, and Jonathan and Jacob read *To the Lighthouse*.

"What happens if you step in lava? Do you catch fire or, like, start to melt from the feet up? And how long does it take?" I asked.

"I'm trying to be the bigger person, but he's making it really hard," Jacob said again at the diner last week, this time referring to the V. S. Naipaul incident—Jonathan had overridden Jacob's book club choice, forcing him to read *A House for Mr. Biswas*. This had become their relationship's leitmotif: that Jonathan was taller, and that Jacob was the bigger person.

"I think it's instantaneous," said Larry.

The book club was extremely exclusive and had only two members, who were also its founders: Jonathan and Jacob. They were reading *A Vindication of the Rights of Women* when I asked to join.

"It's a very serious group," Jacob told me. "I mean, I know you're serious, but Jonathan wouldn't get you. He's, like, a total egomaniac. Totally narcissistic. Totally humorless and zero fun. I'm basically the only person that can stand him."

"Hey," said Jonathan.

"The only way I'd ever kill myself is by lava," said Jacob.

"You're obsessed with lava," I returned.

"It's snowing," said Jonathan, wiping the damp from his hair. "Reminds me of that Mailer quote from *The Naked and the Dead*: 'In the night they cannot see the garbage that litters the beach, the seaweed and driftwood, the condoms that wallow sluggishly on the foam's edge, discarded on the shore like the minuscule loathsome animals of the sea.' He examined everyone. "How are you," he said more than asked.

"Did you memorize that on your way here?" I said, trying to cover my left foot with my right foot without aggravating the cuts.

"Ha Ha," he pronounced without smiling. "What have you been up to?"

"Running for president."

"But what are you running *from*?" asked Jacob. "That's what my therapist would say."

Jonathan looked around.

Jacob and Larry began laughing.

"Just sing the song," Larry said, sipping his drink and suppressing a smile.

"It's the Laaarry Vitomiiiiiiglia, It's the Larry Vitomiglia shoooow!" Jacob sang. Larry held up a pretend microphone. "Hello everybody and welcome to the show. Today's topic is parents who put their toddlers in analysis."

I applauded on cue and thought about how Larry seemed much more attractive when you imagined him on TV. He looked taller.

"A question from the audience," Larry said, bringing the imaginary microphone to my mouth.

"It's the Laaaaary Vitomiiiiiliga . . ." Jacob began again, when Jonathan cut him off with a scowl.

Larry didn't welcome anyone to the show then, but looked at me conspiratorially.

I broke the silence. "How do you feel about Gaddafi as a stage name? I mean, if I were a pop star called Gaddafi?"

"I have a bone to pick with you about Fitzgerald," Jonathan told Jacob, ignoring my remark.

"He has the best outfits," I said, still thinking about the Libyan dictator.

In the coatroom/bedroom, lit up with a blue lightbulb screwed into the bedside lamp, I found Jim and Reginald Monty III standing by the window, playing "Memories."

I walked over and looked out.

Jim: "Remember that time I put on a body stocking, straddled a cannon, and sang about heartbreak before ten thousand Marines?"

"That was Cher," said Reginald. "Remember when I was a campus activist with a substantial if shapely nose and you were blond and rowed crew, and we fell in love but it didn't work out?"

"That was Barbra Streisand," said Jim. "Remember that time we found a map in the attic that led us to the Fratellis and the pirate treasure beneath their restaurant that had the potential to save our family's house from foreclosure?

"That was *The Goonies*," said Reginald Monty III, as the girl with the gold star approached.

"We're playing Memories," Jim explained to Gold Star.

"Remember when I used to chase twisters in a van with five other intrepid meteorologists, each committed to getting the scoop?" I offered.

"That was Bill Paxton." Gold Star said. "Remember that time I slept with your husband, poured acid on your car, kidnapped your child, and boiled your bunny?"

"That was Glenn Close," I said. "Remember that time I wolfed out?"

I sat on the windowsill, lit a cigarette, and let the game go on without me.

The snow was coming down in fat far-apart flakes. It had already lined the low metal gate out front, the branches on the few trees lining the sidewalk, the flat roofs of the two-family houses across the way, and had turned a bush in the front yard into a white heap. A few hours more and all would be silhouette, a discernable detail here and there—a car antenna, a mailbox—hinting at the bulk of what I already didn't remember.

What did he say? What did I say? What did the room look like when he said that, when our friend walked in? When I laughed? Did I dance to the whole song? What color was the rug? Were there window treatments? And all the parts of the room you don't recollect? Were they even there? I don't recall the couch, but I know we sat on something.

> "If April is the cruelest month, what's February?"
> "Black History."

> "You plug in your birthdate, birth time, and birth-place and it gives you your male stripper name. Mine's 'Arnold Pheasant,'" said the guy with the mustache. "The website's already up to twenty-nine unique visitors per day. We just have to figure out how to monetize it."

> "I'm a security guard at MoMA. It's awesome. I don't have to do anything. I just stand around all day next to a puffy ice cream cone," said Mike.
> "What a privilege to devote one's life to doing nothing," said Jonathan.

"It's better than being ambitious. I am one hundred percent in the moment at all times," said Mike, shaking his glass.

"It's called *Jaws in Venice*. It's like *Death in Venice* but with a shark. There's an old man, a young boy, the canals of Venice, and a man-eating shark that symbolizes platonic beauty," I said. "Everyone dies at the end."

"I'm studying law at Fordham," said someone whose name I don't remember.

"The main character is a tuna casserole whose life is turned upside down when the revelation of a dark family secret forces her to question everything," I sighed, leaning against the refrigerator.

"*Star Trek* is better than *Star Wars*," said another, next to the potted tree.

"You wanna hit this?"

Laughter.

A joint.

Three people dancing.

"It's a novel of ideas, but with recipes," I said.

Did I leave the bedroom then? Were the walls still blue? Did I go into the kitchen to refill my glass or to the bathroom, where I had to wait my turn behind three others?

* * *

"All writers drink. There's a zillion books about it," said Jacob, as I approached the group with a full glass.

"All of a sudden, some of a sudden, little of a sudden," I said stopping next to him. "I'm drunk, are you?"

Larry went on, directing his remarks toward Jacob. "It depends on the kind of writer. Every writer has a different weakness, which results in a completely different art. Drinking makes you write like Fitzgerald; allergies, Proust; a stutter, Maugham; TB, Keats; syphilis, Nietzsche."

I took a sip and looked at my drink. "Eczema?"

"Zelda Fitzgerald."

"Clubfoot?"

"Byron."

"Epilepsy?" asked Alex.

"Byron again, plus Flaubert, Dickens, Poe, Dostoevsky, Walter Scott, Swift, and Dante."

"Dante?" repeated Jonathan?

"Dante. Also, Lewis Carroll."

"Pica?" said Jacob.

"What's pica?"

"When you can't stop eating Ping-Pong rackets and sand."

"I'll have to look into that. I'm working on a book about it," said Larry.

"About pica?"

"About the relationship of writing to infirmity. It's called *Hemingway's Orthotics*. In the intro, I discuss the myth of the writer-alcoholic, before positing that the link has been greatly exaggerated by aspiring writers who find dypsomania more appealing than Dengue fever. Through the lens of the alcoholic-writer myth, the amount you drink is proportional to your talent, making dissipation ennobling, and waste, proof of one's genius. One's lack of discipline in that light can be viewed as an act of sacrifice, a symbol of one's devotion to one's art above all."

"How far along are you?" Jacob asked.

"I'm still outlining. My thesis advisor says he'll show it to his agent when I'm ready."

"Is anyone in your MFA ill?" I asked.

"There's a girl in my fiction workshop with scoliosis who I think is really talented."

"I'm fairly certain you can't teach writing," Jonathan sniffed.

"School can make you better, but it can't make you great, I agree. You either have sinusitis or you don't," said Larry.

"And you?" asked Alex.

"I rarely get colds, so I'm focusing on nonfiction for now," answered Larry. "My dad developed a near-fatal mussel allergy in his early fifties, though, so I might be a late bloomer. God, I'd love to write a novel."

"What about Wallace Stevens?" Jonathan asked.

"What about Wallace Stevens?"

"He worked in insurance. His health was robust."

"He put himself close to malady without himself succumbing to it," Larry explained, "which accounts for why I don't love his poems. If you can't lose, in my opinion, you can't win. All my favorite writers were losers. When the revolution comes, I want to be on the losing side."

"What revolution?" asked Jacob.

"The revolution. You know."

Jacob shrugged.

"I think he was in commercial insurance," Alex said.

Alex sipped his drink, then added, "I like Ken Kesey. Psychedelics offer a more sustainable model for the writer's life. Acid expands your mind but leaves your body alone."

Jonathan sighed. "Why not expand your mind through mathematics? Any asshole can drop a tab of acid. Rare is the asshole willing to study calculus."

"I was very good in trigonometry," said Jacob. "I had a real aptitude, but I was more interested in Spanish."

"If someone told you, take this pill and you'll wake up with either a boob job, a nose job, or an appendectomy, that you might look better but you might also end up disfigured, nobody would take the pill," said Jonathan. "But when it comes to one's brain, everyone's like, 'Why not? It's a party. I'll try anything once.'"

"Are you a mathematician?" asked Alex.

"I work in the fact checking department at *Men's Health.*"

Jacob caught my eye and mouthed. "I just took ecstasy."

I leaned in.

"The girl with the gold star gave it to me," he whispered.

"I think she has a boyfriend," I whispered back.

"I don't like Joyce," said Larry. "He's either too Joycean or not Joycean enough. I think it has something to do with his being farsighted."

"I loved 'The Dead,'" I said, "but it doesn't get good until he spots the bottom of her legs at the top of the stairs near the end of the story. That party he describes is so long and boring. He would have done better to have cut the whole party scene, cut all of the dialogue, and gone straight to the moment when he sees her legs at the top of the stairs. Start with the epiphany. There's gotta be a payoff on page one or you'll lose the reader's attention, like tipping a waiter *before* you order."

"What are you, in the mob?" said Jonathan.

"The more I read, the more I realize I don't like any of the farsighted writers," said Larry.

"You should do a series of anthologies organizing writers solely according to disease," said Alex.

"That's not a bad idea."

"If you could catch any disease, which would you get?" asked Jacob.

"That's a tough question," said Larry. "There are so many interesting ones. Probably syphilis."

"That's so predictable," said Jonathan.

*   *   *

Greta was closing the refrigerator door when I walked in. "You were great in the play," I said.

"Aw, you're so sweet," she said flatly, opening a can of sparkling water. She was dressed in an Adidas tracksuit, like Madonna in paparazzi photos of her jogging.

"And you looked great," said the guy standing next to her in a tracksuit matching hers.

"This is my trainer, Dayron."

Dayron cupped her breasts and looked at me. "If you work the pectoral muscles underneath, it's like a boob job without the surgery."

"He's allowed to do that because he's gay," she said, laughing.

"Like when my father raped me," I said, laughing with them.

"What?"

"Like when my father raped me. I was cool with it because he's gay."

Silence.

"I was kidding."

"Yeah. Not funny," she said.

"That's fucked up," he added, letting go of her breasts.

I began to perspire. "So you work out?"

"I have to," she said. "It's really important that I be better looking than everyone else on account of my low self-esteem."

"Fitzgerald was promising, but minor, finally. Too caught up in social life to be truly serious," said Jonathan.

"What'd I miss?" I asked.

"You think Hemingway wasn't?" asked Jacob. "*The Sun Also Rises* is a book about people hanging out and chatting. Its original title was *Fiesta,* for god's sake."

"Maudlin macho posturing," I interjected. "The dialogue about taxidermy is pretty good, though."

"The love story is tragic," said Jonathan.

I shrugged. "Why didn't he just go down on her?"

"Oral sex is not the same as actual sex," said Jonathan.

"Look, I love cock just as much as the next guy—"

Alex nodded. "It's true. You should read her work."

"—but you overestimate the importance of the penis," I went on.

"Lesbians don't have penises and still have sex," Jacob verified.

"The real unrequited love story in *The Sun Also Rises* is between Jake Barnes and his cock," I said. "Brett's just a foil."

"He measures it in *A Moveable Feast*," said Larry.

"Not true. He measures Fitzgerald's, but doesn't give stats," said Jacob.

"I still need to read that," said Alex.

"All of Hemingway's books, including *A Moveable Feast,* are about his penis. He should have called his books, *Me and My Penis 1, Me and My Penis 2, Me and My Penis 3 . . .*" I said.

"*Me and My Penis with a Vengeance. Return to Me and My Penis,*" said Jacob.

"What are you talking about?" Jonathan sniped.

"Like, *Return to Oz,* or the *Die Hard* series. But with penises," Jacob explained.

"And that whole tip of the iceberg thing. It's so obviously a defense of his having a small cock. He's like, 'Yeah, you're only seeing the tip, but underneath! Underneath it's huge!' Hemingway is all tip," I said, pointing my drink at him.

"Hemingway did beer ads," Alex said. "He was really ahead of his time in terms of corporate sponsorship."

"In terms of illness, Fitzgerald definitely has the edge, though," said Larry.

"Hemingway shot himself! He was depressed!" said Jonathan.

"Clinically?" asked Jacob.

"Tough to say," Larry answered. "There was a family history of depression, sure. But his career only took off after his arches collapsed."

"You know his mother used to dress him as a girl. I just read a biography," said Jacob.

"Even if you don't like the books, you can't deny his influence on American Letters. His move toward minimalism was revolutionary. No one has ever said more with less," Jonathan insisted.

"I hate minimalism. Why should I admire a writer for what he hasn't written?" I said.

"It was Fitzgerald who edited his first draft, actually," Jacob said. "So if you're going to praise him for what he left out, the point is Fitzgerald's."

"Fitzgerald had a deviated septum but ended up becoming more famous for his alcoholism."

"Team Fitzgerald!" said Alex.

"It's not a competition," said Jonathan.

"When you're losing, it's not." I shook my cup. "All I'm saying is, if a book can be admired for what's *not* in it, then you should admire mine because I've not written a word. Zero words, all of them perfect. A giant iceburg fully submerged. Now give me the Nobel Prize and make me the face of Schlitz."

"You look different," Jonathan said to me, narrowing his eyes.

"I've aged," I said.

He scanned my outfit, before stopping at the bloody part below my ankles. "What's that about?"

"Trench foot."

"C. S. Lewis, Tolkien, and possibly Robert Graves," said Larry.

A punch on the other side of the room.

By the time we got a look, two guys were already restraining the guy with the mustache. Gold Star was sitting on the couch with her head in her hands. "He always does this," she said, as Jason's girlfriend's best friend stroked her hair and looked up dramatically. "He always does this!"

"Get off!" Mustache yelled, breaking free. "I'm calm!" he said, and then to Gold Star. "Let's get out of here."

Gold Star kept crying and wouldn't look up. "She's not going anywhere with you, Dan!" said Jason's girlfriend's best friend.

"Fine. I'm leaving," he said, and pulled his coat from under Gold Star. The room was quiet, but for the music: the instrumental opening of Madonna's "Like a Virgin." We watched Dan put his coat on, as Madonna started, "I made it through the wilderness..." Dan walked out, letting the door slam behind him.

Two guys hustled their bruised friend into the kitchen.

Jonathan looked at me and raised his eyebrows. "On that note," he said, and walked away.

Jacob found my eyes. "Can I tell you something?"

I nodded.

"I think that ecstasy was just a Benadryl. My nasal passages are super clear but other than that I feel nothing."

I spotted Alex across the room, standing beside the large plant again. He smiled and waved, as if he were recognizing me from across a train station platform.

"Was it a tab or was it a pill?" I asked Jacob.

"We should hook up," Jacob said. "It'll be fun."

That's the Benadryl talking."

A voice on the far side of the room: "But I love him!"

Three girls had surrounded Gold Star, still crying on the couch. Greta and her trainer were crouched at her feet. They helped her up and walked her into the bedroom.

"I'm gonna check on her," said Jacob, following them into the next room.

The living room floor, covered by a dull rug, was visible for the first time since we'd arrived. Almost everyone had retreated into the kitchen or bedroom, leaving a straight line from me to the sofa, newly empty.

Edward plopped down and let his bottle hands open at his sides. His knees fell open too, as his head fell back and he shut his eyes. The white Christmas lights above him cast his jaw, slack and slightly opened, in a romantic light. I walked over, sat next to him, and studied the empty room.

I sat pitched forward, sipping my drink as if it were medicine, and looked at my toes.

"What happened to your feet?" said the voice next to me.

I turned to find Edward's face in line with mine, his eyes trained on my feet.

"New high heels," I said.

"If they hurt, why do you wear them?"

"Penance."

"Penance," he repeated holding onto the s sound and falling back against the sofa.

I leaned back against the sofa, too, and rested my head against the cushion. "I wear high heels the way Capuchin monks wear hair shirts and spiky belts—to remind me that I'm unemployed." I studied the seam between the wall and the ceiling, then turned to him. "What do you do, Edward?"

"My name's not Edward," said Edward. "I'm a pianist."

"Why do they call you Edward then?"

Edward lifted his hands, and turned them over to show the large empty bottles attached by duct tape. "Edward Forty Hands," he said, before letting them drop to the sofa.

I curled up on my side to look at him. His gray T-shirt was worn around the collar, where a graceful neck arched out like a swan's. "You have a nice neck. Where do you play?"

"New York Philharmonic." He let out a deep breath. "I hate it. I've been playing since I was five."

"I played the alto sax in high school," I said. "I was in the marching band."

"I saw an ad in the subway for plumbing school the other day and was thinking I might try that. I'd love to work with shit," he said, turning to me. He found my eyes. "What?" he asked, half smiling.

I leaned over and paused before his lips. Then Edward wrapped his bottles around me.

* * *

"My astrologer said this would happen," said Gold Star, standing next to Alex next to the refrigerator. "Dan's a Scorpio. He can't help it. Have you ever had your chart read?"

The clock on the microwave said it was late. I began fixing myself a final drink.

"Kind of," said Alex. "But I don't know what time I was born, which is, apparently, a key component of one's celestial address. I dated this psychic when I was at clown school, and when I said I didn't know my birth time, she flipped and accused me of trying to keep my destiny a secret. I was like, 'Bonnie, relax!' So we call up my mom, right? And my mom goes, 'I don't know, it was in the afternoon, I think. Three maybe four p.m.?' So I tell Bonnie 3:30-ish, and she's like, are we talking 3:31 or 3:29? And I'm like, I don't know, does it matter? And she explodes. She's like, 'Imagine the oracle of Delphi gave Oedipus's parents their next-door neighbors' prophecy. Yes, it fucking matters.' We eventually compromised on 3:30."

"Can't you look at your birth certificate?" asked Gold Star.

"My mom says it's packed in a box somewhere at my dad's, and my dad's like 'I don't know where anything is, and I can't look now.'"

"That sucks."

"I know. So now Bonnie starts calling me 'Mr. 3:30' every time we argue, and saying how she can't trust me, that her ex-boyfriend cheated on her, and how does she know I'm not gonna cheat, too?"

"Sounds like she may have had other issues," Gold Star said.

"In her defense, she was going through a rough time. There was all this pressure on her from her family—they're all psychic and expected her to be psychic, too. She was, like, in tears when she finally admitted to me that she didn't hear voices. So I said, Bonnie, forget the circus, forget astrology. And she's like, easy for you to say, what am I gonna do instead? So I say, what about meteorology? We used to watch the Weather Channel a lot 'cause we were in Florida and it was hurricane season. She was definitely pretty enough for forecasting."

Gold Star sipped her drink, holding it with both hands.

"I'm like, it's still divination, Bonnie. It is literally foreshadowing. I mean, if the weatherman says it's going to be dark and stormy, you know you're in for some Hamlet-level shit."

Jacob joined us by the sink, as Alex went on: "Notice it's called 'The Weather Channel.' 'Channel,' as in 'channeling.' Sam Champion is to ABC what Macbeth's witches were to the Elizabethans."

"But Shakespeare's witches were ugly," said Jacob. "Weather people are always super hot."

"Except for Al Roker," said Jonathan, who'd just walked in.

"Except for Al Roker," repeated Gold Star.

"Are weather reporters actual meteorologists or are they just, like, weather spokesmodels?" asked Jacob, half to himself.

"I think they're scientists," I said.

"They're a little too good-looking to be scientists," said Gold Star.

"In the *Inferno,* Dante put fortune-tellers in the eighth circle and murderers in the seventh circle. According to Dante, trying to predict the weather was worse than murder," I added.

"Do you think Sam Champion knows he's going to hell?" asked Alex.

"Al Roker definitely knows," said Jonathan.

"Ignorance is bliss," said Larry.

"What do you mean?" asked Gold Star.

"I mean that I was perfectly happy eating at that KFC on Sixth Avenue before I saw that video with all the rats running around in it and read how they cultivate headless chickens now just for their wings. I used to eat at KFC all the time and never once got sick, so you tell me."

"Tell you what?" asked Gold Star.

"Am I better off knowing?"

The booze was out. Most of the guests had left, and the apartment was all at once large and empty.

"How do you feel about sentiment?" I overheard Jonathan say to a girl with red-rimmed glasses who was about half his size, mostly leg, and very little torso, standing near the bathroom. In the far corner Jason's girlfriend worked a hula hoop with a look of pained resignation. And on the deserted couch nearby, Jacob reviewed his vocabulary flashcards. Alex, seated across from him, had grown a beard.

"Let's go," I said, standing over Jacob.

"Prehensile!" he exclaimed, startled from the deck, and then, "Yeah, I already called a car. We should probably go outside and wait."

Jacob and Alex went out first. I went to the kitchen for a quick glass of water but couldn't find a clean glass. I'd lost track of my own. So I cupped my hands under the faucet and bent down to reach them with my mouth.

In the hall, the mountain of shoes was just a molehill. I found mine and forced my beat-up feet back into them. The pain was sobering. Music from inside the nearly empty apartment flooded the hall. "Sweet Dreams" by the Eurythmics. I was listening to it when I spotted Jacob's legs below on the first-floor landing.

Snow had covered the pavement, the parked cars, and the little metal gate we'd come through on the way in. I pushed it open and felt my hand wet with cold.

Shivering, I folded my arms over my chest and thought of that line of Voltaire's: "Candide hid in the bushes and trembled like a philosopher." Jacob stuffed his hands in his pockets, and Alex, teeth chattering, buried his hands in his beard. The temperature had dropped, despite the fact that he hadn't worn a jacket.

"What kind of bliss is this?" Alex whispered.

After a few minutes, a black car pulled up.

Wordlessly, we piled in. I sat up front with the driver while Jacob and Alex shared the back seat.

"Where to?" asked the driver.

I looked at Jacob and Alex. "I don't know where we are," I said finally.

"We're a lost generation," Jacob slurred.

I looked back and forth at the street signs, the buildings, the stoplight up ahead, all of it white, none of it familiar.

"Manhattan. Three stops," Alex said.

The cab lurched forward.

We drove in silence through a maze of streets I didn't recognize, past closed storefronts and apartment complexes, laundromats and bodegas, pizza places and supermarkets all wrapped in a wintry gauze, as if the city were an injured soldier, the whole city in a white cast. The driver turned on the radio, passed over a few channels that came in faintly over static before shutting it off again. Then he began fiddling with the heater.

"Cold?" he asked, as we began over the bridge.

I nodded.

Ahead of us, over the bridge, the twinkling lights of Manhattan came into view, and above it the sky's dark blue was already fading into dawn. I thought of that line of Fitzgerald's in *The Great Gatsby,* something about the city seen from the outside, something about hope or possibility or illusion. Something about something or other. I looked in the rearview mirror and saw Jacob and Alex asleep in the back seat, and behind them, through the back window, whatever was the night.

ethay azureway
ybay stéphane mallarmé

Ethay everlastingway Azureway'say anquiltray ironyway
Epressesday, ikelay ethay owersflay indolentlyway airfay,
Ethay owerlesspay oetpay owhay amnsday ishay uperioritysay
Acrossway away erilestay ildernessway ofway achingway Espairday.

Inway ightflay, ithway eyesway utshay astfay, Iway eelfay itway
    utinizescray
Ithway allway ethay ehemencevay ofway omesay estructiveday
    emorseray,
Ymay emptyway oulsay. Erewhay ancay Iway eeflay? Atwhay
    aggardhay ightnay
Ingflay overway, atterstay, ingflay onway ishay istressingday
    ornscay?

Ohway ogsfay, ariseway! Ourpay ouryay omentousmay ashesway
    ownday
Inway onglay-awndray agsray ofway ustday acrossway ethay
    iesskay unreelingway
Otay arklyday enchdray ethay ividlay armsway ofway
    autumnway aysday,
Andway abricatefay ofway emthay away eatgray andway ilentsay
    eilingcay!

Andway ouyay, emergeway omfray Etheanlay oolspay andway
　　athergay inway
Ilewhay isingray oughthray emthay, eightfray ofway udmay
　　andway allidpay eedsray,
Eetsway Oredombay, otay ockblay upway ithway away evernay
　　earyway andhay
Ethay eatgray ueblay oleshay ethay irdsbay aliciouslymay avehay
　　ademay . . .

Illstay oremay! Unceasingway etlay ethay ismalday
　　imneychay-uesflay
Exudeway eirthay okesmay, andway etlay ethay ootsay'say
　　omadicnay isonpray
Extinguishway inway ethay orrorhay ofway itsway ackenedblay
　　euesquay
Ethay unsay ownay adingfay ellowyay awayway onway ethay
　　orizonhay!

—Ethay Yskay isway eadday. —Otay ouyay Iway unray, Ohway
　　attermay! Estowbay
Orgetfulnessfay ofway Insay andway ofway ethay uelcray
　　Idealway
Uponway isthay artyrmay owhay omescay otay areshay ethay
　　ablestay awstray
Onway ichwhay ethay appyhay umanhay erdhay ieslay ownday
　　otay eepslay.

Orfay erethay Iway onglay, ecausebay atway astlay ymay indmay,
　　aineddray
Asway isway away ougeray-otpay yinglay onway away
　　osetclay-elfshay,
Onay ongerlay ashay ethay artway ofway eckingday earfultay
　　aintsplay,
Otay awnyay ugubriouslay owardtay away umblehay eathday . . .

Utbay ainlyvay! Ethay Azureway iumphstray andway Iway
  earhay itway ingsay
Inway ellsbay. Earday Oulsay, itway urnstay intoway away oicevay
  ethay oremay
Otay ightfray usway ybay itsway ingedway ictoryvay, andway
  ingsspray
Ueblay Angelusway, outway ofway ethay ivinglay etalmay orecay.

Itway avelstray ancientway oughthray ethay ogfay, andway
  enetratespay
Ikelay anway unerringway adeblay ouryay ativenay agonyway;
Erewhay eeflay inway ymay evoltray osay uselessway andway
  epravedday?
Orfay Iway amway auntedhay! Ethay Yskay! Ethay Yskay! Ethay
  Yskay! Ethay Yskay!

o **lost**

1 Dr. Sokoloff stood in front of the light board, staring into my X-rays as if cavities, not eyes, were the windows to the soul.

"Soft or hard?" he asked, his back still facing me.

"Hard," I answered, expecting he'd reprimand me. You're supposed to use a soft toothbrush, though a lot of people use a hard one because they believe, mistakenly, that it will more effectively clean their teeth; it only brushes away enamel. But I put Qtips in my ears, which you're also not supposed to do, and no one is going to stop me. "I put Qtips in my ears," I added for spite.

"You have a cavity," said Dr. Sokoloff, having found the source of my failings. At last he turned.

"It's the same one you filled last year and the year before," I said. "Your filling has fallen out again." I paused to tongue the declivity, then let my cheek to rest briefly against the cold of the examining chair. "The emptiness, Doctor Sokoloff, can never be filled."

I looked over to see if he was paying attention. Dr. Sokoloff was posed at the sink.

"I can patch it up right now. Won't take long. Won't even have to drill!"

"It must make you feel terrible that all of your patients wish to avoid you," I said bitterly. "That they associate you with great pain."

"Are you flossing?"

"I live to floss."

"Or floss to live?"

"Touché."

Dr. Sokoloff put his right hand on his hip and with the other parried the air before thrusting an imaginary sword into my side.

"Dr. Sokoloff, how long have I been coming here?"

"Hmm," he B-flatted. "Let me see, I've been treating you and your wife for about fifteen, twenty years, I'd say."

"We need to talk," I said. "Please sit down," I began, standing up myself. Then I raised my right hand like Marcus Aurelius, were Marcus Aurelius to raise his right hand as I had just done. "I have concerns," I proclamated.

It's true I had stopped proclamating years ago, after my wife and I had had too many arguments about it. Barbara disliked displays and said my tendency to hold forth cast me foolishly, that they, my speeches, should be minimized if not eradicated, which she sought to accomplish through strict sexual sanction. She was forever improving me this way, the implementation of her finishing touch having lasted nearly all of last year. "At least proclaim!" she'd said disgustedly over breakfast one morning.

"My appointment was an hour ago," I began. I knit my brow, another thing she'd quit him of, my knitting superfluous. "I waited an hour just to be told we must refill the same tooth we've refilled three or four times already."

"Sometimes the material doesn't bond to the tooth. In your case, there's not much tooth left for the filling to grab hold of."

"So it's my fault?"

"It's no one's fault, Professor."

"I could leave, you know. There are other dentists in the sea."

"I hope you won't."

I began to pace. "When first I came here seventeen and a half years ago, you were filled with enthusiasm. Passionate about your work! You'd ask if this or that hurt, if I wanted more Novocain. . . .

And when my mouth was filled with paste and I couldn't possibly reply, you'd ask if I was happy. Now you just bang around in there with that little mirror of yours, probably only using it to see yourself, before sending me out into the world with only ruins with which to chew, as if my mouth weren't once great, as if its deterioration or its saving weren't up to both of us. Tell me, is it so funny to see your face tiny among my teeth?"

Dr. Sokoloff looked up at me from his chair across the room. "It's true the practice has grown larger and on some days there is little time for talk. But how *is* the semester going? Your students must be preparing their final papers now, no?"

I folded my arms and leaned back against the wall. "They have submitted them."

"Ah, the life of a professor!" he shook his head. "You make me miss my student days. Sitting in cafés, excitedly debating the merits of gold versus silver—I had a semester in Paris, you know. The dentists there," he motioned with his hand, "they have a different idea about teeth." His eyes hit the ceiling, as he relaxed into the reverie.

"University life has its horrors. When I went into it I saw, like you, cafés forever." I thought back to the department meeting earlier that week; to the walls drained of color; to the faces of the faculty, listless and boiled. "But whether the life of the mind or of the teeth, you go into it chasing one thing and end up somewhere else entirely. In a lima bean room.... The world is a bean."

"Aging is a bleak system, but it has its advantages. We use porcelain now and the fillings barely show."

"So I can smile and pretend that nothing's happened. So, no one will know. But I'll know, won't I?" I looked at the floor. "Maybe I should let my mouth rot."

"I'm afraid I can't recommend that. It would hurt leaving the nerves exposed and would only lead to more decay."

"The thing that I wanted to tell you, Dr. Sokoloff, is that during my last visit, you didn't tell me I'd need to come in for a follow-up.

You wrote it on my chart and gave it to Becky, but you didn't tell *me*. I had to ask Becky what was wrong. It was Becky who told me something had gone out of it. That there is a problem, that treatment is required, that my tooth is a husk. Why didn't *you* tell me?"

Dr. Sokoloff looked not at me, but at his hands folded in his lap.

I looked at them too. Then I began proclamating again: "I want you to be the best dentist you can be! I want you to remember how you felt coming out of dental school! When you were young! Idealistic! Don't you remember? One tooth at a time, you were going to change the world!"

"Ah, youth! Did I ever tell you? In my twenties I had this idea for an extra tooth." He smiled to himself. "A purely decorative fang it would be. A sort of gazebo of the mouth."

"Yes," I frowned. "Yes, you did."

I took my eyes from him and studied the middle distance. "It's not too late," I said. Then, "Look, I don't want a new dentist. I'm with *you*, Dr. Sokoloff. But you've got to try. If we can't at least agree to try..."

Dr. Sokoloff leaned back in his chair and, resting his head against the wall behind him, let his eyes safari the room. They stopped on various artifacts: the giant card the elementary school children sent him after the field trip to his office—he had given them all candy—the certificate from dental school, the honors from the American Dental Association, an inspirational poster given him by his mentor Dr. Jonathan Calvados (a photo of a great garden over which was printed, THE ONLY [TEETH] [ARE] [TEETH] LOST. —MARCEL PROUST), the signed photograph of David Mattingly—a history. Then he looked at me.

I sat back down, rinsed out of nervousness.

Dr. Sokoloff stood up and laid a hand on my shoulder. He gave it a squeeze. "We will save the tooth, Professor."

I leaned back against the chair and closed my eyes to prevent my feelings from escaping. I nodded for Dr. Sokoloff to hit the lever then looked up at the ceiling's foam boards. As I reclined, Dr. Sokoloff stood over me, his concerned face receding from me like gums, and next to his face, the little mirror in his hand, catching in it bits of light.

I left feeling good for the first time all day. For the first time all week! In the elevator I investigated the new filling with my tongue, and it felt sound. *I* felt sound.

2 Outside it was cold again, and if I breathed with my mouth open the cold struck the nerve. I hurried over the darkening block, Central Park at my left, its trees bare, then rushed down into the subway station.

I walked a little while along the platform, looking at movie posters and advertisements for state-of-the-art egg boilers, feeling my ears tingle as they unfroze, feeling the Novocain in my cheek wear off.

A train screeched into the station.

I got off at 42nd Street and followed the crowds up the stairs and then up another set of stairs until I reached Grand Central Station and spotted a payphone.

"Barbara," I said, when she picked up.

"Hi."

"I was on my way home and figured I should call first."

"We're still moving," she said. "I know I said I'd have everything out by the time you got home, but there's more stuff than I thought. It's amazing how much crap a person can accumulate without even realizing it."

"Crap."

"You know what I mean."

"Dr. Sokoloff says you're due for a cleaning."

"That quack! He's all yours. I'm going to go to Jack's dentist. His fillings are celebrated, and he doesn't go on about Paris all the time."

"He mentioned the gazebo tooth again. Remember the gazebo tooth?"

I heard Jack's voice in the background. "Babe. What about these swizzle sticks? You want 'em?"

"Do you want the swizzle sticks?" she asked.

"Why don't you take them."

"Go ahead and throw them out," she yelled back.

"Listen," I said, and then stopped, listening instead to the wave of silence washing over me. I closed my eyes and felt the two of us being carried away by its current, felt the two of us together as before, in the beginning, when we'd pause between kisses and hear nothing but our breath.

"Are you still there?"

"Yeah, I'm here," I answered.

"I don't think we'll be more than an hour," she said.

I hung up and sat in the phone booth a while longer, looking out through the glass door at the people rushing past in both directions. A young man in a suit knelt to tie his shoelace, then took off again with a skip, waving his briefcase as if it were a lunch box.

A short balding man in a gray suit and wire-rimmed glasses leaned over and knocked on the glass, then made a phone shape with his hand. I stood up and opened the door, feeling like a middle-aged Superman who saw little point anymore in changing into the cape. I pulled at my tie to loosen it and walked over to the small crowd gathered down the hall.

A dozen or so men and women were watching an eighty-something man in a suit and tie with long gray hair thinning to the shoulders seated behind a synthesizer. There was a sign taped to the wall behind that read, GENDARME AL AND THE CONTRABAND. A little ways in front, four small electronic dolls danced in time with his music.

One doll, dressed in army fatigues, played the saxophone. Another played the trumpet in a blues-man outfit. On an over-turned plastic bucket, a little freckled boy doll in overalls moved the bow back and forth on a fiddle attached to his arm. And on the ground in front of all of this stood a blonde doll, swishing her hips in a shiny pink skirt and matching pink top. Her arms were raised above her head. She was smiling.

It was a short song. Near the end of it, Gendarme Al held one finger to the synthesizer and threw his head back and sent his eyes to the ceiling, as if to make the note ring especially. Then, instead of finishing, he transitioned to the song's beginning. The dolls continued their dance. The crowd continued their watch.

A tall woman in a scarf and overcoat stepped forward and left a dollar in the hat.

I watched and listened as the song repeated, seven, eight, or a thousand times more before I stepped away.

The music grew faint.

In the main concourse, the night sky was green and the constellations shown yellow in it, like pollen fallen on the surface of a pond.

Why did Vanderbilt commission a green sky? I read somewhere that the constellations were accidentally painted backwards. To cover over the expensive flub, Vanderbilt claimed they were not backwards, no, but had purposefully been painted that way in order to represent God's view, his looking down on the stars as we look up at them. But he was never asked about the green. "To God, the universe is a bog, and we are in it fish and frog, and the bits of bread he throws now and then when bored between stock-holder meetings." I imagined Vanderbilt stroking his beard as he proclamated. "Above me, below God, between us, a crab."

I studied the Cancer zodiac, then walked over to the departure board and looked up.

"Excuse me," said a voice at my right. "Excuse me, sir. Could you help me, please?"

Turning toward the voice, I found a frail old man with gelatinous blue eyes staring up at me. He brought his lined face close to mine, then unfolded a large leathery map, singed and broken round the edges. A pirate ship decorated an Eastern sea while a mermaid was leaping out of a Western water; Manhattan Island separated the two bodies. The man ran a shaky finger from the compass in the top right corner to the tip of an island east of this one, on which had been drawn, between two palm trees, an X. He looked up at me again. "Which way to the N train?"

"Take the S crosstown and connect on the other side." I looked about to get my bearings, then pointed him west.

He sighed. "Oh yes, yes. Thank you, young man. Much obliged, I am." Refolding his map, he started off in a labored gait, his rapier knocking gently against his left stocking.

When I looked up again the times and tracks shuffled quickly then froze as if caught.

If I took the 5:17 p.m. as I usually did, they might still be there. There would be Jack saying something beginning and ending with "babe." "Babe, you all packed, babe?" And Barbara answering. "Yeah, babe. All set, babe." I walked over to the next hall and tried to put the babes out of my mind

Bookstore, bakery, shoeshine, barber, umbrella shop, sock house, luggage, and Du Daumier's Clotheria, where a woman pulled the curtain back on the fitting room curtain just as I passed and, modeling a dress for the sales lady standing a few feet away, began twirling so that the skirt flared. The woman was still twirling as I moved past the window.

At the Biltmore News Shop, I slid round the back of a small man in short sleeves and rumpled trousers and picked up an issue of *Fatsos & Flacos*. I fanned the pages and put it back, then picked up *Car Crash Weekly*. Instead of reading, I let my eyes wander, above the stand into the next aisle, where the man in rumpled trousers was pouring over an issue of *Mechanics Pariah*. His face was scarred. One half of it looked sort of melted, like the face of one of Dalí's clocks. He looked up and caught my eye.

Quickly I looked down and opened *Car Crash Weekly*, pretending to be absorbed. I stared at a full-page illustrated ad for King Puff, featuring a handsome square jawed man in a suit and skinny tie smoking in front of an Egyptian pyramid. Behind him, just to the left, an attractive belly dancer was snaking her hips in a way that mirrored the curl of smoke coming from the man's lit cigarette. On the facing page was a photo of the I-95 pileup from last August in which seven people died on their way home from Jones Beach. A bloodied arm stuck out one of the broken windows of the overturned car. I recoiled and looked up to find the man with the scar, looking right at me, his pants unbuttoned. He shook his penis a few times, then waved it around in circles. His face was frozen in an aggressive smile, like a mask in an ancient Greek comedy that made you wonder if the figures of tragedy were actually any more pained. I refiled the magazine, then went to the counter and lay down a quarter for the *New York Mercury*.

Homeless men and women lined the wooden benches of the waiting room. A police officer roamed the aisles, twirling his nightstick like a baton, now and then flinging it high into the air before catching it to the applause of the room's ragged residents. With the paper under my arm, I continued on to the next hall and then the next, allowing myself to get lost in the station's murmur, a sound of things far away but somehow all around you, like memories.

I was standing with my hands in my pockets, counting the tiles at the end of one of the arches near the entrance to the Oyster Bar, when I heard, "You're heart is a cage," I turned toward the voice and found only the two intersecting walls. "Give me a fortune and I'll tell you your fortune," said the corner. I turned again and saw at the opposite corner, a middle-aged woman covered in scarves, her back facing me. She turned and her eyes flashed. Focusing them on mine, she repeated, "Give me a fortune and I'll tell you your fortune." Then she shook her hips and the gold coins that decorated the scarf tied round her hips jingled. "Your heart is a cage," she mouthed without sound.

I opened the door to the Oyster Bar, strode up toward the back and took a seat at the counter. The girl to my right looked up at as I did.

3 "I like the caviar sandwiches," said the girl when I'd finished speaking with the waiter. "It's like peanut butter and jelly but with caviar instead of peanut butter and caviar instead of jelly. The bread's the same." She shrugged and took a bite. She chewed and continued smiling at me with her mouth closed. She had long brown wavy hair that reminded me of the feathers on a young swan. She rested both elbows on the bar and leaned into them, letting her head sink between her shoulders, then looked in front of her at the kitchen behind the bar.

I spread my newspaper out in front of me. There was an item about Venus, about some kind of celestial event happening that evening, but I couldn't concentrate on it for overhearing the conversation of the couple to my left.

A woman was describing a dream:

> I had obtained steady work as a receptionist and had constantly to be on my guard against the men flooding the field. Showing me their diplomas, they eyed my typewriter, my desk, my chair, as if they should be the one sitting in it, as if they should be the one sleeping with the boss. Then they showed me their college pins. 'Little gold hearts,' one said, pointing to his lapel, noting his numerous decorations, 'taken from little gold

women.' He smiled—he had two bright rows of mismatched cufflinks for teeth—and offered me chewing gum from his shirt pocket.

In my dream, I kept getting lipstick on my white gloves. From blowing kisses. I had the finest posture though and kept crossing and uncrossing my legs so that the friction from my stockings made the sound of cicadas. Then the boss appeared in the doorway with an apron over his suit. It said, KISS THE CHEF. When he pressed Play on a tape recorder—the one we use for dictation—the room hummed with tiki. He swished his hips as he came toward me with his arms open. Then I woke up.

"You're a very sensitive woman, Irene," the man said. Her hands looped around the back of his neck and for a few minutes they kissed. I turned the page of my newspaper. "I have to go," was the next thing I heard. The man stood up next to his stool, and I caught a glimpse of her face. "I have to go or Lydia will be suspicious."

The woman nodded. "Of course. You're such a good husband, Frank. Lydia is very lucky," she said, her eyes glassy, her mouth straining to smile.

"She needs me," he said. He sighed. "If only she were as strong as you, then I could leave her and we could be together."

"I try to be strong, Frank, but sometimes . . ."

He leaned over and kissed her on the forehead. "You're the strongest woman I know, Irene. That's why I love you," he said and then left.

The woman stood up a moment later, brushed her skirt straight and, not seeming to see anything around her, left in the same direction as the man.

When my martini arrived, the girl to my right said, "Can I have a sip?"

I slid the drink over.

She lowered her face to the glass like a bird dipping its beak. "Stings!" she said after, scrunching her face.

"I like it."

She nodded as if I'd said something profound, then, "I'm here to see Venus." She pointed to the article in my paper. "In a few hours, visibility will be ideal. Are you interested in astronomy?" she asked.

"I don't know much about it."

"Me neither. That's why I started studying it in school. It's funny how you end up knowing more about the things you don't know than about the things you do." She shrugged. "I'm at NYU. I like it, but it's awfully expensive. The stars on the other hand are very cheap. You know you can buy them? I wouldn't buy them, but some people give them as anniversary presents. Would you excuse me a sec?" she said, before standing up and straightening her dark tie. She retucked it into the waist of her navy blue calf-length pleated skirt, then crossed the room, looking both ways first as if crossing a street.

On the other side of the street, she shook hands with a man in a gladiator costume , then handed him a large, flat envelope.

She returned and sat back down next to me.

"I've got to work full time," she said, picking up where she left off, "in order to pay for school."

"What kind of work do you do?"

She brought a finger to her lips and whispered, "I'm a smuggler."

"My. I've never met a smuggler before. What do you smuggle?"

She looked around then lowered her voice and leaned in. "Right now, certificates of authenticity and essential oils. But it changes all the time."

"Essential oils?"

"Aromatherapy," she explained.

"I didn't think that was illegal."

"I work for a specialized group of regression therapists who use scents to trigger illicit memories. You know how smell is the sense most actively associated with memory?"

"I remember Proust mentioning something about that."

"Well, if a Madeleine can open a door to childhood, imagine what sarin gas could do."

"But you're not transporting sarin, are you?"

"Well, no. Essential oils. But some scents elicit memories the US government does not want us to recall. Classified memories, if you catch my drift. Remember last year when the whole city smelled of pancakes and the mayor played dumb?"

"It was very strange."

"Came from a government lab in Gowanus."

"What was it then? What were they doing in the lab that caused the pancake smell?"

"Making pancakes," she said. Her eyes went wide. "A lot."

I nodded. "Sounds risky, your work."

"It's an education, that's for sure. You learn things about the world that you can't learn in school or above-board life. I think this: If you want to know life, really know it I mean, you need to know what's happening just underneath it. Technically I'm a criminal, sure, but I don't feel guilty. I mean John Hancock was a smuggler, so really I'm following in the footsteps of a long line of great men. It's no accident that America was founded by smugglers, tax evaders, and traitors, you know? Me, I haven't betrayed anyone yet, but I hope to. I'm a real patriot is the thing. Something you should know about me, for example—I have this recurring American dream where I can fly and also sing opera to wild animals. The point is, smuggling's a very patriotic thing to do when you think about it. And it pays my tuition."

A dapper old man in a black velvet smoking jacket sat down on my left. He touched his creamy silk cravat, then ran a hand over his neatly combed white hair and signaled to the waiter. He sighed, "Où sont les neige d'antan?"

"Have you met the professor?" the girl asked the older man.

"I haven't," said the distinguished gentleman, in an accent I could not place.

"Professor, may I present Duke Elgin Nearby?"

"My dear girl," said the duke, "considering my station, it should be the professor who is presented to me!"

"It is hard to remember these things," she said blushing. "The duke is a Foreignian exile," she said to me. "He's teaching me to be less repellent."

"She's a quick study, that one." He winked at her.

"How long have you been away?" I asked.

"Let's see, the revolution began in 1934, so how many years is that?" he rolled his eyes back to do the math, but then gave up. "I'm very fond of intellectuals. What is your field?" he asked. "You see how I did that?" he said, leaning over so he could see the girl on my other side. "How I expertly brought the conversation back to him, though I might very well have excited him with a long and fascinating story about myself? The way to win someone over, my dear, is not to impress him with your biography, but to create an opportunity for him to be impressed with his own. Show a man to himself and he will always be charmed.

"My parents insisted on charm school," he said addressing me now. "That was the way in Foreignia before the revolution. The children of the nobility all went to charm school. But not everyone continued on. Not everyone demonstrated my aptitude. I was encouraged to continue on to the doctorate level," he said, raising his chin and touching the silk knot beneath it. "Americans are so surprised when I tell them that before I came to this country I was a doctor. Here, I drive a cab. But there! Always a pleasure to meet a fellow intellectual," he said putting out his hand.

I shook it.

"In my country we don't shake hands, but grab hands and then shake our bodies. There's a bit of trivia for you!" he said, producing an ivory pipe from his breast pocket. The pipe was carved into the shape of a naked woman. Her breasts facing forward were covered by the duke's fingers. He lit it, then said, "Mind if I smoke?"

"It's a very fine pipe," I said.

"Got it in Borneo. The progenitors went to Borneo for the occasion of my birth, as was the Foreignian custom. The pipe was a birth present from Papá. I've been smoking this very one since infancy. After Mamá would finish giving me the breast, Papá would take me into the smoking room with the other gentlemen and give me the pipe. It is customary for the men to retreat from the women after dinner, my little beast," he said to the girl. "But we are all modern now, this young lady tells me, so I smoke in mixed company. What would my poor parents think of us and our modernity? They perished in Foreignia, I'm afraid. The uprising was rather bloody, and they were too old to make the journey in the wine barrels. Executed by firing squad," he said, blowing a ring.

"Oh. I'm sorry."

All three were silent as the duke raised his martini.

"To the Kingdom of Foreignia!" he said. "Mais ou sont les neige d'antan?" he repeated, then pointed to his jacket. "The family crest," he said.

I studied the four quadrants sewn into the patch. There were: a dancing bear, a man about to sit on a whoopee cushion, a woman napping as four Zs floated from her mouth, and three dogs standing atop one another.

"My first language is Foreign. But growing up, every Foreignian noble was obliged to learn French. The lower classes spoke only Esperanto. Our idea in the rarefied airs of court was not to speak a universal language but a language of exclusion and adultery. We loved the French cinema. You know the syllogism about a square being a rectangle but a rectangle not being a square? I am not a snob, but a snob is me! Or have I got that backwards?" He looked up at the ceiling to assess his remarks but then gave up.

"I come from a long line of titans of leisure, but that does not mean I was exempt from study. No, No. The training was exhausting in fact. The leisure class met for seven of the seven days, from 9:00 a.m. to 3:00 p.m., breaking only for Fig Newtons, the traditional Foreignian snack. In class we learned how to fill the hours and what kind of filling tasted best. For flaky hours, a mixture of sharp and mellow cheeses. For smooth hours, jelly. For long days and fortnights we developed our own equations, sometimes putting on theatricals. I drive the cab now, but I am by blood a man of the nap," he said with a straight back. "My passengers are always surprised by this, by my PhD and my noble blood. They say, 'But Duke Nearby, how ever did you end up in a taxi driving little me?' They don't remember the war. They don't remember the escape in the wine barrels.

"Americans remember so little really—I think it has something to do with their noses. Observe: The American nose on the whole is a rather short one. And we know how closely the sense of smell is linked to memory, do we not?"

"Proust," said the smuggler to me.

"And then the Americans are always having their noses cut, which I imagine must drastically curb what they can recall. Our girl here has got a great big bumpy nose. Thank god you never let them clip it!" he said to her. "Better off getting a lobotomy than one of those nose jobs! Though I would not recommend the former either. I cannot in good faith recommend any work on the frontal lobe—poor Aunt Harriet. But yes, the Americans have little feeling for the past. It is, on the whole, a present and future tense country. Work, work, work! Slaves to the idea of progress, you are. No, we had a very different idea in Foreignia; it was forbidden for the Foreignian nobility to work. I love America, but it was very different in my country." He took a careful sip of his martini.

"How is Gary?" said the duke.

"Down and out," the smuggler answered. Then to me, "Gary is my boyfriend. He was fired yesterday." She gave a doleful look.

"Did they give a reason?" asked the duke.

"As you know, for some time his work has been moving toward

the conceptual," she told the duke. Then to me, "Gary's a court-room artist downtown and at the conclusion of yesterday's mur-der trial, instead of drawing the witness, he presented an ash tray with a glass marble resting on a bed of pencil shavings. The judge asked to see him in chambers."

"Philistines!" said the duke, pulling his pipe from his mouth. "The poor boy." Then to me, "It's true that I myself prefer the representational, but I am old fashioned on account of my par-ents being old fashioned and their parents being old fashioned. Terrible shame about your Gary. I shall submit a note of support to The Wikipedians.

"The Wikipedians are a new organization dedicated to the cre-ation of a comprehensive encyclopedia as well as the first man-made black hole. I may be old-fashioned but I try to keep up with the new technologies never the less, though sometimes more. They've created the template for an ever-expanding encyclope-dia, written by the people and for the people, exclusively available by subscription through the mail, along with a small void located in Old Westbury. They send you a letter each day with new infor-mation and members are invited to submit articles while contem-plating the abyss. I have published 153 articles so far. When you get to five hundred, they give you a yellow cake.

"I shall submit an entry on Gary," said the duke, leaning over and nodding toward the girl.

"That's very kind of you, Duke. Gary will so appreciate it."

"In addition to my work in car and in pedia, I am a passion-ate hobbyist and am a member in good standing of a great many societies: The Emerson Society, The Fortean Society, Société des Refusés, the Club de Three Cubes, Alliance for the Preservation of Frozen Deserts, North Pole Aficionados, Ishtar Fan Club, Melville Society, Uptown Fencing Club, Poisonous Plant Fanciers, Gumdrop Enthusiast—it is also a magazine—Syndicate of Sexual Deviants, World Wide Debtors, Exact Change Anonymous, SADD (Students Against Drunk Driving), MADS (Mothers Against

Diet Soda), the Candy Collective, Sigourney's Weavers, Hair Club for Men, The Society for the Recovery of Persons Apparently Drowned, the Poe Society, the Thoreau Society, The Keith Morrison Fan Club, and The Euclid of Alexandria Fan Club, among others." He inhaled. "And though I am getting on in my years, I was and remain a practicing ufologist.

"Just recently, I am happy to report, I was initiated by the Amazonians. The Amazonians are a new organization dedicated to the sharing of books. Deep in the Amazon rainforest there is a very small hut that sends and receives mail-order requests, allowing one to buy and sell books through the post. I'm a great fan of the mail, you may have observed. They send you a monthly catalog with member reviews of each work and you are in turn encouraged to submit your own reviews. For the Wikipedians I have just completed an entry on 'Medieval Punishments,' and for the Amazonians, a review of *The Count of Monte Cristo*."

"What was your review?"

He raised his chin. "Arrived damaged."

"May I borrow it?" asked the smuggler.

"Neither a borrower nor lender be!" thundered the Duke. "I shall give it to you. Do you have any hobbies, Professor?"

I thought for a moment. "I'm fond of dentistry but rarely practice. My own dentist, who is a professional dentist—studied in Paris with Picasso's dentist—has advised me to keep it as a side passion. I did think for a while about going to dental school, but Dr. Sokoloff says it's rather different when it's your profession. Something changes when it becomes your job. I guess that's partly why I have always loved teethwork. It represents, for me, romance, freedom, the dreams of youth." I thought of the first time I saw Barbara's incisors.

"Do you think it is possible, Duke, to love a thing your whole life? To have your cake and to love it too? Or can one only love what one wants or what one has lost?"

"I love my country, that's true. But would I love her as much had I not been torn away? Nestled in the ample bosom of my homeland, perhaps I would have been smothered by the very same cleavage that now beckons me home. I don't know, Professor. Love is a great mystery, isn't it? You cannot have *and* hold, as they say, though one tries nevertheless, except for sometimes, but still a lot.

I tipped the last drop of my martini into my mouth. "Would you excuse me?" I said to the young woman and the elder duke.

I left the restaurant and found the phone booth under the arched entryway. I shut the glass door behind me and dialed.

"I love you," I said as soon as the ringing stopped. "I still love you no matter what, and I think you're a fool to leave with that jerk!"

"It's Jack. Barbara's loading the car," the voice answered.

"Hello, Jack."

"Can I give her a message?"

"I, I've thought about it, and I want the swizzle sticks after all."

"I will set them aside."

"Jack, I don't hate you. But I do despise you."

"I understand. Anything else?"

"Tell her, tell her, I might get the gazebo tooth."

"Right-o."

"And Jack. I don't hate you, but I do despise you."

"She's coming back now. Should I put her on?"

"No. No need."

"Right-o."

I heard Barbara's voice in the background. "Who's that, babe?'

I hung up and stared at the phone a while. I grabbed my chest, feeling a pain in my wishbone. It had been acting up ever since Barbara confessed about Jack.

I walked back into the Oyster Bar and ordered another drink as the duke finished his. The smuggler was saying, "It's not for me to say, 'it's not for me to say.'"

The duke nodded in answer. "On that you are right, my girl, on that you are right."

I was looking at my martini glass, wondering why it was built that way. Attractive, yes, but so nonsensical, so easy to spill, a sort of folly of the bar. Slowly, I tried to pick it up without upsetting the surface.

"Have you met?" asked the duke.

The girl tapped me on the shoulder. "Professor?"

"Hmm?" I rotated my stool to face their same direction. "Sorry then, my mind was somewhere else. What was that?"

A tall dark-haired man in a blue pin-striped suit and chrome tie clip looked down at me.

He thrust his large hand in mine. "Brimley, Jonathan Brimley," he said, before his mouth spread into a smile as wide as his face. Before I knew what was happening, I was holding his business card. BRIMLEY & FATHERS, it read in discreet gold lettering.

"Brimley," I read aloud. "The name's familiar."

"I expect you've heard of Management and Company."

"Why, of course. The Brimley Building is yours?"

"My father's. You may have read about *me* in last month's *Forbes*, however. It was I who founded the largest peanut butter and jelly sandwich firm worldwide."

I pointed up toward the famous and controversial building just north of the terminal. "You're the man behind Pan-PB&J?"

He nodded with self-contained pride.

I recalled the radio jingle citing the secret to keeping the sandwiches fresh, the famous Pan-PB&J jars, the hermetic seal.

"'*Was* the man' is more accurate. Sold the whole operation last month. At a wonderful profit, I don't mind telling you. Gotta keep moving, lest you stop moving. Objects in motion stay in motion, whereas objects at rest fall asleep—Sir Isaac Newton said that," Brimley clarified. "Marvelous businessman. His great great great great great grandnephew went to school with my cousin. Unfortunately, the elder Newton's business acumen does not run in the family. Just declared bankruptcy, Edgar did. And for the third time, the poor man. Invested all his money in this new laser pointer technology that went south. The company head turned out to be a sort of dreadful character. On the lam now. When you invest in a company, you invest in people. I told Edgar. I told him, but he insisted it was "can't lose." What more could I do? But enough about that. Now I'm onto a new venture. He made a banner with his hands. "Candy Co.," he announced excitedly. He reached inside his briefcase and pulled out a prospectus.

"Candy microcosms and candy macrocosms," he explained, handing us each our own page. "The Microcosms are gobstoppers modeled on the Earth, the layers made to scale, natch. The Macrocosm, on the other hand, is a jawbreaker modeled on the atom that is seventy-five feet in diameter and located currently in Ed McMahon's backyard in Connecticut. You can lick your way to the nucleus, or the rain can lick it for you, either way, revealing a vast hollow middle and at the center of that hollow, a tiny tiny tiny cherry-flavored core.

"Edible Voids are Milk Duds, but with dark chocolate. Void Filler is obviously a kind of marshmallow. Tobacco Cigarettes, under item five, you see," he pointed us back to the page, "are just like candy cigarettes but for adults, with the added bonus that each one takes ten minutes off your life.

"When you reach a certain age, one begins to savor the sweetness of death. So I figured, why not sell it? We also have an Existential Chewing Gum called Sisyphusichelous . . ."

"The flavor is gone after five minutes, yet one must continue to chew," I read aloud. I looked up. "What is Charcolate?"

"Charcoal that you can eat. Support the miners! Support the heartland! Support the worker, I say!"

"I work like a beast," said the duke. "Où sont le neige d'antan?"

"And what is it that you profess, Professor?" Brimley asked.

"I am also a member of the Folly Society!" interjected the duke. "Yes, yes. I forgot that one."

A man in a purple tracksuit appeared on Brimley's left. His hair was red, as was his mustache. "Hullo, Brimley," said he.

"Fred!" said the duke.

"Fred!" said the smuggler.

"Fred!" I did not say.

"Just got in from New Jersey," the man said, smiling, "and boy are my arms tired."

"Why, what have you been doing with them?" asked the Duke, raising his glass to his lips.

"A vascular issue, perhaps," Brimley said. "You should let my doctor have a look at you."

"I can look at myself, thank you very much."

"Have you met the professor?" asked the duke.

"How did you know I was a professor, by the way?"

"Your elbow patches," said the smuggler.

"But I don't have elbow patches," I said.

"Yes," said the duke, raising his chin. "Their absence has been noted."

"Fred's a chiropractor," the smuggler went on. "He doesn't care for the doctors."

I gave a shiver. "All that popping does unnerve me, I admit. Especially the popping of the neck. Don't you ever worry you might accidentally murder someone?"

"In my office every precaution is taken. All my adjustments are performed under therapeutic lamps," he said, and handed me a business card.

It read: FRED'S CHIROPRACTIC AND COFFEE PALACE along with a phone number and a Newark, New Jersey, address. "We also have a hut in the Mid-Manhattan Mall. Below the contact info was the following line: THE CRACKS ARE HOW THE LIGHT GETS IN. —HEMINGWAY.

"His writing's not the greatest," said Fred. His mustache twitched in the direction of the card. "But he knew from absorption."

"You'll never get a hand on me," said the duke. "Don't let him touch you, my girl! Keep him away from that fantastically attuned proboscis of yours. That monument to history. That great archival project!"

Fred's mustache spread into a smile, and he made as if to strangle the duke.

"It's making me nervous having the two of you standing over me," said the duke. "It is not what's done. Do take a seat."

The eyes of Brimley and Fred scattered, then settled on two chairs newly vacant next to the smuggler.

"What is it, Fred?" said Brimley once seated. "You're looking a bit down at the mouth."

"Lost my cat," Fred said, unzipping his breast pocket. He withdrew a small purple comb and ran it through his carroty mustache. "Ran off, he did."

"The only cats are cats lost," said the duke. "That's Proust," he whispered to me.

"True," answered Fred, pocketing the comb. "Though he was a cat before he was lost, too. But perhaps now in memory he is even more of a cat. Perhaps the idea of cat is more catlike than an actual cat. Hard to say. I put some milk out on the porch in case he comes back while I'm out."

"What is the name of your cat?" asked the duke.

"Alsace," said Fred.

"To the return of Alsace!" said the duke, raising his martini glass. He took a sip. "I'm sure the little feline's just out on adventure. Probably found a she-cat with a nice little bit of fluff," said the duke, casting a wink at Fred.

The duke drained his glass then motioned to the waiter for another round, "And for my companions," he added cocking his head.

"None for me," said the smuggler.

"Another round," the duke insisted. Then to the smuggler, "I will drink yours, my girl." Then to the most of us he said, "I am a man of great thirst. And with great thirst, comes great responsibility."

Solemnly, he brought his glass to his lips. He sipped, then said, "My father was thirsty as his father was thirsty as his father was thirsty. As I have no son, I must drink for him as well. Edmond!" said the duke, calling the waiter who was presumably named thus. "Bring us another round once you've finished bringing us another round!"

"Like me, father was bungey, saw the bears, kissed Black Betty, had a thump over the head with Sampson's jawbone. He was cramp'd, cherubimical, cherry merry, wample crop'd, crack'd, half way to Concord, had a cup too much, and cut his capers, if you know what I mean.

"Father's father according to father had also been too free with the creature, and having had a dark day within him, was wet in both eyes. In other words, he was fox'd, fuddled, flush'd, fettered, as dizzy as a gooseglobular, groatable and got by the glanders."

The drinks were laid before them, and the duke raised a fresh one. "To my father's father's father!" he said. "Who, like his great grandson, was jaggled, juicy, jambled, had clipped the king's English and seen the French kind, got knapt, held his kettle, was lappy, limber, seeing two moons, oiled, overset, had been too free with Sir Richard, had drunk till he gave up his half penny, and then, contending with the pharaoh, had lost his rudder. In other words, he was in the suds." The duke looked at his glass, then drained it in one swallow.

"There's a good man," said Brimley before sipping his own drink. The smuggler looked up at me and smiled.

"En garde!" said the duke, with a mouth full of olives, as he parried the air with the naked toothpick that previously held them. The duke stood up and, stepping away from the table, put one hand on his hip and began fencing. "Brimley, you swine! You coward, you cat-faced show dog. Get out here and defend your honor!"

Brimley did not turn but remained as he was, facing the kitchen.

The duke came nearer and began threatening him with his tooth-pick sword. Holding the purple cellophane side, he poked him in the back rib.

"Come on, Brimley! You sneak, you fink, you fish molester, you lover of half-priced antiques! Defend yourself!" The duke circled to the other side and as he made to thrust his sword into Brimley's waist once again, Brimley wheeled round and plucked the sword from his hand, then stuck it into his magnificent teeth.

"Good man," he said, smiling at the duke. "You have my fealty."

The duke clicked his heels together and gave a theatrical salute. "Off to the loo," he said and made for the men's room.

"Oh, dear," said the girl, looking at her watch. "I'll be late if I don't leave now."

"I shall have to leave as well," I said.

I threw down a bank note and nodded. "Thanks for the company," I said, then left the bar and found the phone booth outside.

I closed the door and dialed.

 **4** It rang.
It was ringing.
It continued to ring.

It rang some more.

The ringing continued.

Further ringing.

One ring followed by another ring.

More ringing.

Through the phone booth door, I saw Brimley, the duke, and Fred emerge from the Oyster Bar. They stood in a cluster. The woman covered in scarves left her corner and approached them.

It was still ringing.

It rang some more.

Further ringing.

One ring followed by another ring.

It kept ringing.

The ringing continued.

I hung up and imagined the ringing on the other end: the house silent but for the rattling phone.

They'd gone.

The lights would be off when I arrived home. I'd have to turn them on. And the idea of this, of my flipping the switch on the wall when I walked in, of the sound of my keys on the kitchen counter, of the quiet punctuated only by my footsteps, the friction of my clothes as I moved through the house, my breathing, made a cold feeling in my chest. I opened the phone booth door and staggered out.

"I see things," said the scarf-covered woman, stopping in front of me. "Madame Of knows you," she said, locking me in her stare. I felt drunk suddenly, but not exactly. I felt as if I were under water, like seaweed swayed by the tide while my feet rooted me to the seabed. "You are scared now, Professor, but your heart is a safe. It can be cracked by an expert criminal or by someone who's been given the combination. The thieves will smile at you to get what's inside and once they get it will take a bite to see if it's gold, before throwing it away not understanding its material." She grabbed my arm. "Captain Kidd buried his heart in Long Island. The trick is remembering where you've put it."

"Home is where the heart is," said Fred, coming up next to her. "X marks the spot." He nodded authoritatively.

"One might move," added Brimley, his face alongside the others. "Bury the thing in one place, then stay at hotels!"

I felt cold all over and reached for my wishbone. "I can't go home," I said without meaning to.

The duke squeezed my shoulder. "Terrible thing being an exile. But that is the human condition. Hobbies help. If you like, you may examine my teeth," he said sympathetically and opened wide his mouth.

"Thank you, Duke Nearby." I heard myself say, my voice sounding as if it were above the water, while I remained under it. "Maybe later."

"When I feel scared," said Brimley, "I go into a store and ask them how's business?"

"Sometimes," Fred said, "I close my eyes very tightly, but it only makes it worse. Opening them I've found works better. Light's the thing. But it's hard to remember to do that. It's very hard to be brave, but it's less hard if you are."

"Thank you," I said, still swaying in the current.

"Once," said the woman covered in scarves, catching me back in her stare, "you were a balloonist floating over the arctic. You were one of three trying to achieve the pole by air. Your balloon burst and you perished in the ice. You feel lost and tossed, because you have been lost and tossed." She took me by both shoulders. I looked up from my planted shoes and into her face; her moles suggested stars. And now, I was no longer seaweed on the ocean floor but suspended in the great darkness of the cosmos, with the closest stars and planets still very far away. Her face, the heavens, took me in.

The stars arranged themselves to speak: "Madame Of knows you," they said. She put her hand on my chest where it felt cold.

"It hurts," I heard myself say.

"Because you are alive," said Madame Of.

And with that I was returned to the room, to the hum of Grand Central, the commuters passing to my right and left, to Brimley's voice: "'The fates lead him who will. Those who won't, they drag.'" The feel of Brimley's arm round my shoulders as I looked into the open corridor. Madame Of, some feet away, speaking now to Fred and the duke. "Come on, old boy," said Brimley, as he steered me toward the main concourse, at the center of which stood a four-faced clock.

5

Under the great green sky, a few steps from the four-faced clock, stood the smuggler. Next to her, was a large white telescope with a small, rumpled man bent over the lens. The girl waved when she saw us and beckoned us over.

"This is my mentor," she said when I got within earshot. She smiled excitedly and motioned to the man bent over the lens. "Arnold. Arnold," she said again. "I'd like you to meet the professor."

The small, rumpled man withdrew his attention from the lens. He shot me a quick look out of the left side of his face, then a quick look out of the melted side. Wordlessly, he shook my hand.

"Arnold's a genius," said the smuggler.

Arnold regarded me silently, then said, "I know everything about the universe except where I am in it." He leaned over and looked back into the telescope.

The smuggler turned to me. "We are viewing Venus," she said. "New York City has too much light pollution, so we have to come here if we want to see anything. Would you like to have a look? Arnold, let the professor have a look. Arnold," she said again, tapping him on the shoulder.

Arnold straightened and stood back from the instrument.

"Come," said the smuggler. "Put your eye there." She pointed to the tiny lens.

I leaned over and tried to focus, but between the one eye on the floor and the other pinned to the lens, I couldn't see anything.

"May I?" asked the smuggler, before I felt a warm hand gently cover my right eye. At once, the heavens bloomed into focus.

I saw a galaxy spinning very fast in a sort of whirlpool. I saw Pegasus beating his wings, and the two fish from the Pisces constellation chasing each other in circles. A thin hand came into mine. "Here," said the smuggler. "If you want, you can feed them."

I withdrew my eye and looked at my hand, where in it sat a crumb of bread. I looked up at the ceiling and saw the sky, still as before, then brought my face close to the lens once more. Again the galaxies spun, the horse flew, the fish swam.

"Go ahead and throw it," she said.

I threw the crumb of bread upward and saw it ripple the green sky, before it floated in the space between the two fish, who, spotting it, swam closer for a nibble.

"Which one is Venus?" I asked, still looking.

"Look over to the eastern-most quadrant, next to the crab. It looks like a dot, but look closely and it becomes a bigger dot. Most nights you can't even see it. Visibility is very good tonight," she said. "This only happens once a year. You see Mars nearby?"

"What's that?" I heard the duke ask.

"Nothing," said the smuggler. "We're looking at Mars and Venus. They are in perfect alignment tonight."

"Extraordinary," I said, pulling away. "You can see everything!"

"The magnification on this machine is excellent," said Arnold, addressing me for the first time. "Made it myself."

"Arnold is a genius," said the smuggler.

"To look into space is to look back in time," Arnold explained. "The light from the stars is only now just reaching us, but with the proper tools you can advance a few paces and see the light of yesterday."

"Extraordinary," I told Arnold. He nodded, then bent over the lens again.

I looked around to locate the others, to tell them they must have a look, too, when, under the four-faced clock, the information booth door opened. A man in a crisp uniform decorated with golden epaulettes emerged and called, "All aboard!"

The commuters, continuing in all directions, passed by without noticing him.

"Cornelius!" said Brimley, approaching the man in long strides before giving his hand a hearty shake and depositing a folded bill within. The duke, Madame Of, and Fred walked over as Arnold began packing up the telescope. The smuggler held a notebook in which she was furiously taking notes on whatever Arnold was then whispering to her.

"Ready?" said Fred, intercepting my stare.

"Now we are," said the smuggler, pocketing her notebook. Arnold took the case and headed for the door. The smuggler followed in his wake, then turned to me.

"Come on then," she said.

Cornelius held the door ajar. One at a time the others passed over the threshold. When they'd all gone, Cornelius looked around and called out once more into the great room: "All aboard!"

Wordlessly, I stepped into the dark.

6 It was almost black inside the information booth, which contained no information so far as I could see, but just a metal spiral staircase going down. "Excelsior!" I heard the duke say, already some paces below. Footsteps echoed up, along with a tangle of voices, mostly unintelligible, though now and then a whole word or phrase escaped:

"Lard Lite is a diet soft drink made out of lard. Lard Zero and Diet Lard are similar but use different sweeteners." —the voice of Brimley.

"My first language is silence. But in Foreignia, for one of my station, a second and even third language was expected." —Duke Nearby

"I consider myself a brain worker. It's like being a sex worker, but with the brain. What do you think, Fred—is it more or less shameful to sell one's thoughts?" —Arnold

"First of all, second of all. And second of all, first of all." — Madame Of

"What I want to know is how he gets his hair to lie flat." —the voice of Fred

"No way. There'll never be a cocker spaniel in space. I'll lay money on it." —again the voice of Fred though maybe the duke

Primarily, though, it was the voice of the smuggler I heard. She was just in front of me, that is to say, below me. "You don't mind the walk, do you, Professor?"

"No, no. Thank you for asking."

I listened to my footsteps.

"Your mentor," I whispered. "I saw him at the news stand earlier."

"Yes, he goes there to read the science journals. He's a genius, you know. He's had a constellation named after him—'The Arnold Cluster.' Though he's got nothing to prove, he likes to prove things anyway. Right now he's working on a comprehensive theory of dark matter."

"What's that?"

"You know the stuff that makes up eighty-five percent of the universe's total mass, but nobody knows what it actually is? They call it dark matter. They call it 'dark' because it's only the stuff that reflects light that we can see. There is no evidence of the dark stuff except for the force it exerts on the lighted stuff. But nobody knows what it is. Some people think it's neutrinos, others think it might be axions. Arnold believes it's dead cats. I wasn't sure at first, but when you think about it, dead cats makes the most sense.

"Think of it, think of all the cats that have died in the course of history, then multiply that by nine—since each cat has nine lives, they must also have nine deaths. That's a lot of cats. And that's only the house cats and strays. Do you have any idea how many cats the ancient Egyptians mummified?

"Seven?"

"Archaeologists have found twelve million so far. Twelve million! The wish industry was even bigger then than it is now, so many got into the racket, raising cats expressly for mummification. The way it worked was you'd go to one of these cat mummy farms, see, and choose a cat to sacrifice and then mummify, and then include within its bandages a note pleading your case to whatever god that cat would be in contact with in the afterlife.

O Lost   273

When you think about it, it's obvious. Only, most don't think about it. That's why Arnold's a genius. He might get the Nobel Prize next year. If he doesn't, it'll probably go to Bob Dylan."

I looked up to see how far we'd descended but could no longer see the top of the stairs. Above me it was black. Below, black as well.

"That is certainly impressive," I said, regarding what she'd told me about Arnold. "But what I mean is . . ." I whispered. "When he saw me at the news stand. . . . Well . . . he flashed me."

"Oh, that. He just does that 'cause he's insecure about his scar. He only does it when he feels someone is staring at him. He thinks it takes the focus off his face."

"What happened to his face?"

"His wife. She threw acid on him during one of their breaks. She's a scientist too."

"The poor man! Did she go to jail?"

"For a little while. He visited her every day. They got back together while she was on the inside, and then she moved back with him after she was released. She's at home now. Stopped working last year on account of her leg. He had both her legs broken during one of their breaks, and the left one didn't heal quite right."

"My god!"

"Yeah, it's a real love story. He's totally devoted to her and pays for the best physical therapists. Fred's been a big help. They've been together forty-five years or something like that. Since they were kids. Can you imagine? That's what I want. That's what I want. I want to get married, but I'm not sure if to Gary. Don't repeat that. I mean, I love Gary, I do, but I often wonder how much love is enough."

"There is no such system of measurement," I heard myself answer. The blackness of the stairwell had loosened my tongue, and I found myself speaking with greater freedom than was typical of me. "There are no units of love. There are inches for shoes and liters for Coca-Cola, but with love it is all and everywhere or not at all. You can't bottle it, or I expect Brimley would have tried."

"Like the universe," she said.

"Like the universe," I replied, speaking with a knowledge of things I did not know I possessed. "It is impossible for a being within the universe to understand the world without. It is the same with love. When you are in love, the laws of physics break down. It is like the universe just before the big bang. It is a timeless and spaceless state, love. It is not rational," I said, imagining Barbara's face very close to mine, her eyes looking into my eyes looking into hers. "It cannot be measured," I finished.

"I like the way you proclamate," she said.

From farther below I heard Fred's voice call up, "But it'd be a little less annoying if you proclaimed, no offense."

Secure in the dark, I knitted my brow.

"I think that's what Arnold and his wife have, but I don't think I've ever felt that, that what you describe. I mean, Gary and I have a lot of great conversations, and we go to see interesting movies, and I like what he has to say about the different architectural styles, but I don't know. I've never felt timeless or spaceless with him.

"After Arnold had his wife's legs broken, they didn't speak for, like, three weeks. They both swore they were finished. But then they found their way back to each other; they always do. They renewed their vows last week. It was very beautiful. I got to go on account of my internship.

"They renew them the third Tuesday of every month, so long as they're not broken up, because Tuesdays are when you can get the best discounts. They wrote their own vows too. Hers were: 'I don't want you to die—I love you—but once you do die, I hope you're tortured in hell for all eternity for what you've done to me. Until then, though, you're my guy and I'm your girl, and I do not want to live on this planet without you.'" The smuggler sighed. "Now that's what I call love," she said. "That was after he mailed her the rattlesnake."

"Oh dear!"

"Oh, she's fine now. He immediately felt bad and came over with the anti-venom.

"Don't ask him about his face though. He claims he was attacked by Fala, the ghost of FDR's dog. She roams the station sometimes. That's what Arnold says, but I know for a fact it was from when his wife threw lye on him during one of their breaks. But he won't say a word against her. Instead, it's always 'Fala did this, and Fala did that!' He says Fala had his wife's legs broken, too. I only know the truth on account of my internship. I looked up the *New York Post* articles on microfiche at the library. It's important when you're apprenticing to learn all you can about the person you're apprenticed to. Arnold's my idol. He's not only a genius, he's also a romantic." The sound of her footsteps followed her words. "Can you imagine loving someone that much?"

"So you're getting course credit then?"

"Yes, though Arnold won't fill out any of the paperwork. I have to do everything, which is fine; it's a great privilege to study with a genius. Before me, he'd never had an intern. He can't abide most people on account of his being so much smarter than they are. And he's completely had it with institutional pencil pushing. He just wants to be left alone to do his research in peace. He left the university as soon as the first of the settlement money came in."

"He got a settlement from his wife?"

"No, no, no. He slipped and fell at a Sbarro's in Penn Station.

"'There's more money in falling than in stars,' Arnold says. But I still love the sky, even if it won't make me rich. Even if the stars are cheap. I suppose I'll be a starving theoretical physicist one day, just like my parents warned. They think I should have been an actress. I don't know. Who knows what the future holds? I might slip and fall in a Chipotle.

"The point is Arnold lives on disability now, which is great because he doesn't have to waste his time dealing with students and can focus solely on his work."

"There we are," said a voice from below.

The bottom landing was visible now. There was an opening next to it from which a great deal of light was spilling out.

From out of the opening, I saw Duke Nearby's head poke in. "Where's that nose? Where's that wonderful girl with that wonderful sniffer? Is she on her way?"

"Yes, Duke Nearby," the smuggler said in her soft soprano, "we're almost down."

After a few more steps, the smuggler arrived at the bottom and climbed through the opening. Finally I made it to the last step as well and, looking through the doorway, saw before me a bright orange room.

7 The walls were orange. The floor was orange. And the ceiling, a shiny orange reflecting all the other oranges. On the far wall, in very small orange letters, an orange sign read LOST AND FOUND. There was no obvious source of light in the room, yet it was very bright, as if the air itself were made of light particles.

An orange banquette wrapped the chamber, which was punctuated by four orange doors, each on its own wall. There were people sitting along the perimeter. I recognized one, the woman from the Oyster Bar. She wore a worried expression round the eyes and seemed not to notice me. Instead, she kept looking at her watch.

The old man who'd asked me for directions was there too. He was sitting up very straight with his hands resting flat on his legs.

Every once in a while he made as if he were about to stand but then just stayed there, looking restless.

On the facing banquette, what I had at first thought to be a couple, was a marble statue of a nude man and woman about to kiss. The woman, sitting on his lap, had her arm slung over his shoulder. His hand grasped her hip.

The smuggler opened a dark leatherbound box and from it pulled a bronze instrument with many dials.

"What's that?" I asked, while the rest watched her fiddle with the thing.

"Antikythera mechanism," she said abstractedly, turning the dials and holding it in an odd interesting way. She studied it closely, twisting the dials this way and that. At last she said, "Aha!" and lifted her head. Pointing to one of the doors, she said, "That way!" Then she put the thing back in the leatherbound box and handed it to Arnold.

The group moved toward the door and, one by one, began filing out. I was last again.

The woman from the Oyster Bar stared worriedly ahead, her vigilance blinding her to anything outside of her thoughts. The marble couple continued toward their kiss. And as I passed the old man, he looked up and caught my eye. Carefully he brought his hand to his head, then tipped his tricorn hat.

I returned his salute and stepped through the door.

8 There was no orange where I now found myself, and the sudden contrast in color and light startled me. I was standing on the platform of what appeared to be a train tunnel only, instead of tracks there were five canals, labeled numerically. According to the sign, we were on platform 357. The lights overhead, bright and fluorescent, flickered and hummed, exposing the greyness of the cement walls and reflecting off the dark water in the canals. I looked behind at the

shut door and noticed to the right of it a large bin with a variety of legs sticking out. I turned back to the company, who were now boarding a long gondola with red seats running along both sides.

I walked over and climbed in after them. Fred, at the oar, lent me a steadying hand.

"What's with the legs?" I asked Fred, once inside the boat, before taking a seat next to the smuggler, who was next to the duke and across from Arnold, Madame Of, and Brimley.

"The railroad serves a number of veterans hospitals. Because some of the veterans aren't used to their new limbs, they use their cane or crutches to get off the train, forgetting their legs. Grand Central is lousy with legs," said Fred, as he began rowing.

"It's amazing what people forget," said Madame Of. "Most everyone has forgotten the future, for example. They complain they can't remember what they had for breakfast yesterday, but have no idea how much of tomorrow they can't recall."

"The thing about forgetting," interjected the duke, "is that you forget what you forgot."

"If you can smell the future," Madame Of continued, "you can remember it. But most people don't recognize the scent, and when it reveals itself chalk it up to mold."

The duke withdrew his pipe. "Not everyone is blessed with a tuned-in schnozzola," he said, and winked at the smuggler.

"When you've tired, I'll have a crack at the oar," said Brimley, watching Fred. "I've been doing CrossFit," he announced and banged his chest proudly.

Then there was only the sound of the oar pushing the water, the sound of the oar creaking against the boat's wooden side, now and then softly knocking it. I looked out at the cement walls as we passed, seeing on them what appeared to be prehistoric cave paintings. Only, instead of figures hunting animals or performing feats of daring with bulls, there were scenes of men and women walking, in the natural, past tall buildings and each other, holding cordless phones.

O Lost

The sound of the oar was hypnotic. No one spoke but for the smuggler, who after some moments said, "It smells like jelly beans."

Silence again. The sound of the oar. And after a while, instead of hearing the sound, I began to feel I was the sound, as if the canal were not something we were floating on but were a long watery road headed somewhere within me.

We stopped.

I looked around and saw across the platform a blue, very much rusted train car, onto which, one at a time, we disembarked.

The interior, as rusted as the exterior, was bare of any seats. Without instruction, the group formed a circle and sat down on the dusty debris covered ground. I sat between the smuggler and the duke, then brushed my hand off on my trousers.

I looked at my watch and was startled to find it had lost its hands, so that it appeared to me now as just a face looking back at me, asking *me* for the time. Instinctively, I brought my own hands to my own face and tried to feel for the hour, but I could not grasp it.

Fred lit a votive candle and, laying it at the center of our circle, brought our shadows into being. They flickered against the walls of the car.

Madame Of: "We live in the space where words do not reach. Though our speech is our shelter, our walls and our doors. O lost. O lived. O crushed. O risen. O all who have loved, O liars, O lied to. O patron saint of women whose lovers never call, of men whose wives cheat, of noble fools, and of the betrayed and of their betrayers who've betrayed themselves too. O horror of the labyrinth, O bark of the dog left out at night, O wolves who lost their pack but found themselves in the hollows of dark hills. O children who will grow old and the old who will grow young. O bodies battered by time. O ocean, O stars, O days that crash into each other. O violence, O lust, O silence and the cry of the wind through guiltless trees. O tango of stars, O forever, O disco, O sleeping Ariadne, O sun. O Ariadne angry and weeping on the shore, O Theseus arching lithe oars in the abyss. O Aegeus hurtling down, O Dionysus, whose heart is full. O moment before all that, O lost, O lived!"

In a gust, the train doors closed, and the car threw us with its sudden speed. I stood up and hurried to the front window to see where we were headed but could see no further than the briefly illuminated stretch of track that was continually disappearing beneath us.

I turned to find the group's eyes on me. The duke pulled his pipe from his mouth and motioned with it for me to return.

I retook my place among the circle, feeling the floor rumble as we sped through the tunnel.

"Who are you?" I did not ask, though I was answered.

Madame Of: "We are the figures in your dreams as you are in ours. We are the people of the missing sock, the forgotten promise, and keys without locks. The mistake is our gospel and miniature golf courses, our holy place. We believe in the necessity of gazebos and worship at the feet of follies—or inside if there is a bench. We hold frivolity to be essential and the essential to be frivolous, which is thus essential as well. And though we understand, we cannot convey life's meaning, because if you have to explain it, it's not funny anymore."

Madame Of's voice deepened: "We distrust all pronouncements, including this one, and accept that reality is an emergent property of sleep, which is sleep's purpose—to create and sustain the knowable world. We recognize birds as the souls of sleepers who are flying in their dreams.

"Fred, are you taking the minutes?"

"Shit," said Fred. "I've got nothing to write with."

"Not again, Fred," said Brimley.

Fred shrugged.

"Here you go," said the smuggler. "You can borrow mine," she said, handing him her pen.

Our shadows, previously stationary, were moving now in a slow circular dance.

Madame Of: "All life is sorrowful."

"Which is why need candy," interjected Brimley. He winked at me, then made his hand into a gun before shooting me with a friendly bullet.

"We are a fellowship of the sorrowful, holy tellers of the knock knock joke, though we have long ago accepted that we will never truly know who is there. We are against abbrevs., and nonessential clothing items like thin scarves that provide no warmth but are considered from to time fashionable, or shirts that are meant to be tied round the waist but are not actual shirts—Potemkin shirts!—and dickies. We accept that only the impossible is possible."

"Hate to do this," Fred said, patting his pockets, "but can I borrow your notebook as well?" he asked the smuggler.

Madame Of rolled her eyes. The smuggler handed over the book.

"Quantum entanglement is our doctrine. Instead of 'As above, so below.'" For us, it's more, 'Here and there, and sometimes here.'"

"Hither and thither, am I right?" said Fred. He cracked his knuckles. "Get a little light in," he said half to himself.

"We believe in the uncertainty principle and are certain of only this."

"Can we fast-forward to the action," Fred interjected. "I hate the liturgy," he sighed.

"We are neo-alchemists whose primary aim is to turn gold into time. Because unlike gold, time cannot be mined."

"Not yet anyway," interjected Brimley.

"Excuse me," I said, "but what's this all about?" I was starting to worry I'd gotten caught up in some kind of time-share operation. "I'm not interested in any kind of Orlando vacation."

"Your proclamating really is annoying," said Arnold. "Sorry to say it."

"We are not a real estate group!" boomed Madame Of.

"Though I do have a good connection on a new development in the Okeechobee swamps, if you're interested," said Brimley. "We'll talk after."

"We are an offshoot of the Folly Society," Madame Of continued, now in a more congenial tone, "which was born from the ashes of the Order of the Golden Dawn, whose early influences were Mithraism and an occult branch of the Paving Stone Union, which eventually joined to form the Neo-Pythagoreans, who then joined a small group of Orphic defectors, which dissolved in short order after some internal strife, but then was reconstituted by a sect of nouveau healers who would eventually separate into the dueling camps of osteopaths and chiropractors, some of whom then broke off to form a union of phlebotomists, which has its roots in Eternalism and ties to the Free Masons, which is an offshoot of the Eschatologists, who were a lot of fun."

"And what are you called?" I asked.

"We don't know."

I raised my eyebrows.

"Wouldn't be much of a secret society if we knew all its secrets," the duke explained. "But we have our guesses."

"'Skull and Bones' has a name," I said.

"Yes, but Skull and Bones, the Illuminati . . . those are only secretive societies," explained Madame Of. "Notice, for example, you've heard of them. You've never heard of our society because not even we, its members, have. Our secrets and rites are so well concealed that even our own members do not know that they are members, though some suspect.

"Am I a member?" I asked.

"Are you?" Madame Of asked back, her dark eyes burrowing into me.

The train rumbled underneath as it turned sharply through the tunnel, jerking us this way and that. I looked around at the others, at these strangers who seemed now familiar to me, and felt I could not tell the difference anymore between what had happened and what would happen. I was gripped by the sensation that life was a book and the page I was on had come unglued and fallen out, and from outside I could suddenly see the whole thing, the pages of all that had come before and that would come after stacked atop one another, and in between them, the place where I was just then. "Have we met before?"

Now Madame Of turned to the duke: "For a time your spirit was imprisoned in the statue of a pissing boy from whose penis issued an arc of clear water into a shallow pool near the back of a neglected English estate—your punishment for having crossed a witch! Sorry. But you really were very rude."

"For a time, you were famous for having built one of England's largest Follies," she continued to Brimley, "and also the first Howard Johnson's in North America."

"For a time, you were a person called Iris," she said now to the smuggler. "You were lost, but only to yourself. Everyone else knew exactly where you were."

"You were my favorite Jacob," interjected the smuggler, addressing me.

Madame Of continued, her voice growing in power and solemnity: "For a time, I was spiritual advisor to the King of Foreignia. During the people's uprising they tried to kill me. Five times they stabbed me, but I have this protective layer of fat, you see." She squeezed a chunk from her waist.

"And you, Fred, do you recall your three fish taco face?"

"And you, Arnold, your grammar school tenure? Your time on the game show?"

"Does she mean past lives?" I whispered to the smuggler.

"Concurrent," answered Arnold. "We are there, as we are here."

"Here and there," said Madame Of.

"Hence the expression," said Fred.

"A little bit of this, and a little bit of that," proposed the duke. "Entangolamente!"

"There is no before and no after," Madame Of continued. "There is only everywhere and everything at once. Time is merely a measurement. But in measuring according to what we know, we fail to apprehend what we don't."

"Dead cats," said Arnold to the smuggler.

"Hush!" commanded Madame Of.

"Every moment exists everywhere at once," Arnold went on, speaking to me directly. "The present is only the light of consciousness shining on any given moment."

"Man is a flashlight," interjected Fred, addressing me helpfully.

"Man is the light reflecting on what it sees," said Madame Of.

"And so we cannot see what we don't see," offered Arnold.

"Everything that will happen has happened. And everything that won't happen will happen too," said Madame Of, her voice deepening, her eyes growing.

Our shadows were dancing fast now, revolving around us at a great speed so that the figures began to blur together.

I began to feel dizzy and strange, like when Sokoloff gives me the gas. I pinched my hand to see if I was dreaming.

"Ouch!" the smuggler exclaimed. Then rubbing her hand, she looked at me reproachfully.

"We are haunted by the things we cannot accept," said Madame Of, replying to a question I had not vocalized.

"Maybe that's why Fala keeps attacking Arnold and his wife," said Fred with a chuckle.

"Let's contact the bitch and have her explain herself!" Arnold said bitterly.

"Even if we did contact her," replied the duke, "you'd need a pet psychic to translate the barking, and Madame Of is not certified in that.

"Whom shall we contact then?" asked the duke. "Wouldn't

mind a chat with my parents. They were too old for the wine barrels, alas," he sighed, before bringing his pipe to his already pursed lips.

"We always have this argument," said Fred. "We waste so much time trying to decide whom to contact and then never have time to do any actual contacting," he whined.

Madame Of cut him off with a look, and as she did the train ceased. The four doors of the car opened to the sound of a ringing bell. A voice came through the air: "Transfer at Jamaica."

"See," Fred said to the group.

The company began to stand up.

Outside of each door was utter blackness. Frightened but curious, I walked over to one. I dipped a toe into the black space and when it disappeared, I quickly pulled it back in.

"Where do they lead?" I asked.

"Wormholes," said Arnold. "That one there leads to Paramus, New Jersey," he explained. "But I prefer to drive. It's only twenty minutes by car and you can play the radio.

"That one," Arnold continued, "connects to Antarctica, but you've got to transfer at Jamaica."

The duke rolled his eyes. "On the way to heaven, I am sure I will be asked to transfer at Jamaica."

"Tell me about it," said Brimley.

"Arnold built the wormholes," said the smuggler. "He's a genius," she whispered to me.

For a moment, I wondered if my cavity had been a wormhole. I imagined it remaining open, unfilled, my sticking my tongue in and the tip of it protruding into another star system, or New Jersey. Maybe that's why it hurt.

"That one there goes to the men's department at Bloomingdale's," Arnold continued, "and that one there goes to Fred's office. I made it as a favor."

Fred smiled politely. "Yes, thank you." Then, raising his eyebrows, "But I still gotta connect to the Path train to get home."

"You're always complaining," said Madame Of, "when a simple 'thank you' would suffice."

"And where are we going?" I asked, looking around at the four dark openings.

"Down," said Fred, pocketing the candle he'd just blown out. Under us, where the candle had been, was a small metal door which he now slid open, and under that, a hatch. Kneeling, he strained to turn the heavy metal wheel. The smuggler knelt next to him and pitched in. They turned and turned the wheel until it became easier and then at last came the sound of pressure being released.

10 They pulled the thing up on a hinge at the side. It was open now and beyond the hatch I saw a sunny blue sky, puffy white clouds, and birds wheeling through them. In the distance, a paper airplane was leaving a jet mark across the sky.

Brimley let down a rope ladder. The smuggler went first. Then it was Fred's turn. Then Madame Of. Then the Duke. Then Brimley.

I stuck my head through the hole to see where they were going and saw, to the right of the opening was a large basket hanging from the bottom of a great colorful balloon.

Brimley looked at me. "Come on then."

"I want to, but there's something I must do," I said, remembering something I couldn't.

"Suit your self, old boy," he said, handing me the rope ladder. "Pull it up and shut the door, if you don't mind."

I began gathering the ladder. "That's it," said Brimley. "That's it," he said, when I had nearly finished.

I stuck my head through again to see they'd already floated away some distance. The smuggler, waving, yelled, "It was nice to meet you, Professor! It always is."

The duke took his pipe from his mouth and said, "Now who's driving this thing? Not Fred again."

O Lost

"I drive very well, thank you very much," said Fred.

"Quit your bickering," said Arnold. "It gives me a headache."

"Do I need to separate you two," said Madame Of, "or are you going to behave?"

"But where are you going?" I called out, as they floated further into the bright sky below.

"Where the current takes us!" said Madame Of. "Into the great cosmic ocean! To the edges of time!"

"But let's stop off at my accountant's office," interrupted Brimley. "It'll only take a second and it's basically on the way."

"To the land of dreams!" Madame Of continued. "To sleep!"

I waved as they grew smaller, until they were only a dot in a vast blue punctuated by other little dots. When I could no longer see them, I withdrew my head and closed the heavy hatch, turning it until it could be turned no more. Then I closed the sliding door over it and looked around.

I did not want to go to Paramus, New Jersey, nor Antarctica, nor Bloomingdale's, nor Fred's office. I looked up, wondering which way to go, when I spotted an identical sliding door above. If I stood on my toes, I could just reach it with my hands. I slid the thing open and there found another hatch and another rope ladder tucked in at the side, which fell down for my use. I turned the wheel of the hatch for a few minutes and then, climbing halfway up the rope ladder, pushed the thing up and poked my head out and into the interior of what seemed to be an elevator. I climbed in and examined the buttons.

They were labeled: *You, Everyone Else,* and *Push in Case of Emergency.* I hit the button labeled *You* and heard a surge before I realized it was carrying me up or down—I could not tell.

When at last the double doors opened, I walked out and into my train.

11

The train was emptier than usual.

Usually I took the 5:17 and it was—I looked at my watch—10:21 p.m. I found a seat and looked out the window onto the platform. Gendarme Al passed with his synthesizer strapped to his back and two rolling suitcases in tow.

After a moment, he appeared in the doorway to my car and silently took the seat across from me, stowing the synthesizer on the rack above and one of the suitcases on the seat next to him. The other case he placed on the floor beside his feet.

He opened the case next to him and pulled out the banjo player, then the fiddle player in overalls, then the little soldier in army fatigues. Then he reached down to the case on the floor and pulled out the little blonde doll in her pink outfit. He closed the case next to him and arranged them so that they sat shoulder to shoulder on top of it.

They looked at me and smiled.

The train started out of the station.

Gendarme Al caught my eye and nodded. "Ca va," he said. "Ca va," he repeated.

I shut my eyes and his music flooded my ears. It was faint at first, but grew louder as I drifted into sleep.

When I opened my eyes Gendarme Al had already gone and the seat across from mine was empty. It took a moment for me to realize we'd reached my stop. The doors were open.

I stood up and walked out, feeling the crisp night air cool against my face. The platform was deserted.

I found my car in the lot and drove home. Main Street was quiet, its only life paused in the brightly lit shop windows that lined it. A mannequin in a safari-inspired suit watched me pass.

The house was dark when I reached it. I heard a few leaves crunch beneath my feet, then the sound of the wood creaking on the front steps, then the sound of the key as I let myself in.

I felt as if I were an actor in a play, that though my thoughts, my feelings, my gestures seemed new, I performed these lines and these movements nightly: I turn on the light. I lay the keys on the kitchen counter. I see the swizzle sticks in their vase.

Then I went into the basement and got the shovel from the storage room. I went out through the back door, letting it slam behind me and, under the great backward sky, trudged over the damp grass to the gazebo.

I found the spot and began digging, hoping it was still there.

acknowledgments

Special thanks to my friends at the Club de Three Cubes and the Riverhead Resort, Casino, and Divorce Lawyers. And to my adopted son, Dr. Frederic Tuten, always my first reader, whose work and person inspires and encourages me. I'd be lost without you. I'm lost *with* you, but still. Thank you to J.W. McCormack who read this in manuscript and urged me on. If you don't like the book, blame him. I am fortunate to be in cahoots with Ruth Greenstein, whose integrity and discernment is matched only by her subtlety and grace—thank you for drafting me to your team. Thank you to Russ Smith, James Sanders, the Ladies Moonlight Calisthenics Fellowship, and the folks over at Malebolge. I am grateful to linguist Dr. Meredith Landman of Columbia University, and am much indebted to Mr. Torvald Larsen at the Foreignian Ministry of Waiting Rooms. Thank you to Ari Martin Samsky, PhD, Lady Marianna Feldman Levine, and Maria Rammata. Thank you to Jacob Weber and Nick Weber. To Irene Skolnick, friend and literary agent in perpetuity—I think you would have liked this book. I miss you. Thank you to Popy Smyles, global adventurer, whoopee cushion tycoon, and my mother. With gratitude to Guild Hall of East Hampton for their continued support, and much appreciation to Vagelis Agelis and Aristea Anastasopoulo at the Naftilos Café in Kala Nera, Greece, where I wrote portions of this book. And, as always, grateful acknowledgement to the Société des Refusés, the Suffolk County Aglet Society, and the Order of the Nap, without whose patronage none of this would have been possible.

notes

For Parerga, Paralipomena, and Avleptimata, visit:
irissmyles.com/drolltales